ARLEN CLASSIC LITERATURE

AWKWARD WOMEN

for my two sisters

Mary Rose Callaghan

AWKWARD WOMEN

Foreword by Éilís Ní Dhuibhne

Afterword by the author

ARLEN
HOUSE

Awkward Women

is published in 2023 by

ARLEN HOUSE
42 Grange Abbey Road
Baldoyle
Dublin D13 A0F3
Ireland
Email: arlenhouse@gmail.com
www.arlenhouse.ie

ISBN 978–1–85132–285–5, paperback

International distribution
SYRACUSE UNIVERSITY PRESS
621 Skytop Road, Suite 110
Syracuse
New York 13244–5290
USA
Email: supress@syr.edu
www.syracuseuniversitypress.syr.edu

Typesetting by Arlen House

cover image
courtesy of Brigid O'Brien

CONTENTS

I am Duchess of Malfi still.

– John Webster, *The Duchess of Malfi*

FOREWORD

Éilís Ní Dhuibhne

Our college was like a railway station at rush hour. Day or night, people hung around, waiting. We were nicknamed 'The Tech on the Terrace' because of our situation, I suppose, and our shabbiness compared to Trinity, but we didn't feel inferior.

Mary Rose Callaghan's *Awkward Women* conveys the moods and describes the life and mores of Dubliners – especially Dublin women – at various stages between the 1960s and the 1980s more accurately and vividly than many better-known works of fiction. A world which many older people vaguely remember is brought to life in the pages of this book. I have never seen the term, 'The Tech on the Terrace', in print before, although I have heard it in the oral tradition. It sums up a lot about the snobberies of Dublin – the tuppence ha'penny looking down on tuppence mentality which characterised even the intellectual life of the city (perhaps especially the intellectual life). Capped by the gentle and subtle 'but we didn't feel inferior', which is equally telling.

Nuns who are ubiquitous and still hiding in their medieval, hijab-type habits, a university in which 'the clerics ... blacken the place like crows', shabby cafes, lounge bars with plastic seats, students discovering Simone de Beauvoir and the beckoning feminism which would not really reach Dublin until the 1970s: it's all here, described in all its colour and brightness and shamefulness with a light hand and a wry sense of humour. As a portrait of period, this work is a gem, and I cannot think of anything which surpasses it. It will delight and charm those who remember the times it describes, and enlighten those who don't. So much has changed in Ireland in fifty years.

These fictions take the form of a suite of interlinked stories, focusing on various characters who are connected in one way or another with Sally Ann Fitzpatrick, *The Awkward Girl* of the original title. Sally Ann is an interesting heroine. She is educated, thoughtful, with ambitions to be a writer or an artist and a deep interest in literature, and attractive. But she suffers from a serious lack of self esteem, and her final end seems eerily inevitable. She blunders around, unsure of herself, searching for identity, through school, college, career and marriage, over about a twenty-year period. In spite of her lack of self-confidence, her intelligence and innocence mean that she is adventurous and open to fresh experiences. The novel takes her from Dublin to France to the United States, from rebellious schoolgirlhood to living in sin and marriage. She is an unusual and unique individual, a well-developed character whose quirky decisions, and indecision, keep the wheels of the book turning. Some of the traits which seem unique may in fact symbolically reflect a typical Irish woman of her vintage: bright and open to change, but naïve and bewildered, as many were. And it is Sally Ann's less unique side, the traits which make her a woman typical of her time, which will fascinate today's readers.

The Awkward Girl was always a good book, but the passage of time has transformed it, and made it even more exciting than it originally was. It re-emerges now, 43 years after its first publication, as a stunningly vivid and insightful portrait of representative types of Irish women in the 1960s, 1970s and 1980s. History, psychology, gender and geography blend seamlessly in this story. It is not so much a snapshot as a film of a particularly interesting time in modern Irish history.

A strong sense of place pervades. The matter of fact descriptions of Dublin – commonplaces, such as the well-known Gaj's café, the picture house on Grafton Street, the convents, are all present and correct, as in much fiction about the 1960s. But it is in the more elaborate accounts of everyday life that the value of these fictions as an ethnographical document reveals itself and excels. Sally Ann's house hunting, in the 1970s, is funny, delightful and scary:

> Buying a house in Ireland is hazardous these days, especially with no money ...
> Dick was looking around stuffily. 'Is there a bedroom?'
> 'A bedroom?' The man looked puzzled.
> 'Yes. A place to sleep?'
> He opened a large cupboard door. 'You could sleep in there, I suppose.'
> Dick peered in. 'It's ah ... small. And there's no window.'

Young people of today's Ireland will find the travails of the past all too resonant. Thankfully, writers and academics have changed more than the housing market, but the witheringly satirical portrayals of artistic and academic life are all too recognizable to anyone who lived through the decades in which this book is set. This was the time when being a writer was more or less synonymous with being alcoholic. The image of academia is hardly more attractive. This was the era of pomposity, when being a professor in Ireland could endow some individuals with an extraordinary degree of self importance. It was an era of pomp and arrogance. Lecturers drank, and ignored students. Professors patronized them, ignored them or ogled them. And also drank, of course!

While all the vignettes of Irish and Irish-American life are precious, what these fictions offer above all are a wonderful insight into attitudes to gender during the twenty years they cover. It is a book about girls and women during a particularly significant period in our history:

> Ireland would make a feminist out of a stone. It's an absolute patriarchy. I'm dead serious. Take Brian de Burca: he's an older friend of Dick's and a famous historian. In college I used to be dazzled by his ilk. But I had not yet entered the groves of academe through the back door of marriage ...

Writing these stories in the 1970s and 1980s, Mary Rose Callaghan was in a good position to look back on an Ireland which was 'an absolute patriarchy', and to chart evidence of this, among much else. At the same time, partly indeed because she had one foot in an American university, where feminism was much more advanced at that time than in Ireland, she was able to recognise the evidence of patriarchy both in ordinary everyday life and in the ideologies which underpinned life in Ireland (and in some areas continue to do so to this day). Her delicate although matter of fact accounts of Sally Ann's difficulties with sex during her student years and in her twenties are brilliant, and uncommon in Irish fiction. In Irish fiction women switched from being demure, asexual madonnas who simply do not have sex at all, to being mature, experienced and quite uninhibited, somewhere during the 1970s. The bungling embarrassing uncertainty of convent girls turned feminist is blithely ignored in most fiction. But it's unlikely that the transition from a society where being sexually active was the biggest taboo, and one in which contraception was illegal until a much later date than most people remember, to a (more or less) normal healthy sexual environment, happened overnight. But those years of transition are not well-documented in Irish fiction from the female point of view. Male authors were too blind, or perhaps too sexually competitive, to admit what went on (there is the odd exception, such as McGahern's celebrated story, 'My Love, My Umbrella'). Women authors, insofar as they existed, were still too prudish, or too sexually competitive, or too embarrassed, to write anything like the truth. But Mary Rose Callaghan, almost alone of all her sex, has the frankness or courage to write about young women who had been quite naturally so terrified by the puritanical conditioning imposed on them by the society in which they developed that they are, in the words of one of Sally Ann's more unmannerly suitors, 'frigid'. Of course, frigidity is what the society these girls and women lived in encouraged and to a considerable extent enforced:

> My problem was accepting everything he said, being his mattress as well as his mistress. The holiday had changed nothing in that line. Except that I was less nervous about sex now. I'd read Edna O'Brien, so knew it was difficult for others too. Although most people implied that it was the greatest thing since sliced bread, I couldn't let go. Maybe it was being Catholic.

This is so artlessly honest that it is heartbreaking. But it's brilliant. Because when a writer dares to write the truth, in all its shamefulness, it is always a victory for that writer.

The contrast between American and Irish attitudes to divorce and abortion is also dealt with, in passages which throw light on the complete intransigence of Irish people when it came to such matters. The referendum which introduced the notorious 8th Amendment to the Constitution, thereby preventing abortion in Ireland under all circumstances until another referendum repeals that outrageous clause, receives attention:

She skipped to the leading articles: one on the Middle East, another on the coming Abortion Amendment Referendum. Judging by the letters to the editor, readers were getting hysterical ... One suggested that a 'No' victory would open the door to divorce – signed by a man, naturally. What if one of them became pregnant? Church teaching might shift then. They might stop ranting about sex and concentrate on the gospel of Christ ... She read another letter. It suggested that a pluralist society would be the death of Catholic Ireland. What rubbish. Pluralism was the only hope for such a benighted land. Divorce would eventually come. The Church would have to accept the inevitable, something it had never been good at.

Mary Rose Callaghan was one of the first of the wave of 'women writers' to be published by the revolutionary Arlen House with her novel *Mothers*, which came out in 1982. Steadily producing novels, non fiction and memoir over the past forty years, she has recorded, in her lightly humorous, disarmingly frank voice, the changes which Ireland has undergone from the 1950s until now.

The foreground of her novels has provided for strong stories of strong or weak or vulnerable characters. The background, the setting, is the Ireland of that period, and she captures its tone, its mood, its attitudes, its irritating and endearing qualities, better than many much more celebrated writers.

These stories are wonderful. They have aged well and are probably more interesting now than when they first came out – which has happened often before with good fiction. That Arlen House has had the good sense to reissue these short stories is a cause for celebration. An inspired decision.

AWKWARD WOMEN

Postmen like doctors go from house to house
– Philip Larkin, 'Aubade'

I

RITA

'Hello,' Rita snapped into the phone. 'This is the Superior.'

'Are you the Reverend Mother?' a man's voice asked.

Parents, she sighed. 'I am, yes.'

'Ah! Alan Murray here, manager of the Dublin Roches. Ah ... lookit, I'm afraid there's someone here dressed up as one of your nuns.'

'If this is some sort of joke –'

'It's no joke,' he said, laughing. 'She claims to be Sister Margaret Mary O'Connor.'

'Sister is one of our nuns!'

'You'd better come in, so.'

She kept her voice level. 'Just tell me the problem. I'm far too busy ...'

'The problem,' he mimicked icily, 'is that Sister was apprehended leaving this shop with items of underwear she didn't pay for. And if you don't come in, I'll be forced to call the guards.'

Rita's face felt on fire. 'I'll be right in. Give me an hour.'

'Good, I'll wait.'

'Eh – it might take longer. The traffic ...' She cleared her throat and continued firmly. 'It must be some mistake. The convent will, of course, pay for anything Sister bought.'

Click. The phone went dead.

Rita replaced the receiver and paused by the hall windowsill. Maggy May? The infirmarian. The little ones doted on the flabby old lay sister, trailed after her everywhere. Only this morning when that spindly-legged child fainted at Mass, she was first over and carried her out, whispering wheezily, 'That's my pet, my girl.' The convent buzzed at the faintest hint of gossip. Good thing she came to the phone herself. The less said ... and no recriminations. Maggy May would see a psychiatrist. But underwear? It was a case of senility.

Car keys were needed now. Chequebook. Outside it was rainy and already almost dark. After ten years in the States, she'd never again get used to the twilight of Irish winters. Only a few hours of daylight. Lapland with those wintry trees. No time to go to her cell to change. Or get a coat. Luckily she had her suit on. She'd promised Mother General to wear the habit in public, but no matter. Heavens, it was nearly 1967. In Florida she'd gone around in shorts. But no one wore civvies here. At first they'd gaped at her jumpers and skirts, but now she was accepted as an oddity. No doubt because of her stint in America.

As she turned abruptly, the green baize screen clattered onto the floor. Obscurantist, but the old nuns insisted on privacy. She lifted it, suddenly queasy from the smell of floor wax. It permeated the house, along with incense, chalk and cabbagy dinners. The odious smells of an institution, she thought, seeing a child lurking at the far corner of the big hall.

Sally Ann Fitzpatrick, the troublemaker from 6B. What had she heard?

Rita crossed the flagged floor, noting the girl's too short uniform skirt, torn tights, unruly dark hair. 'Why aren't you in class?'

'I've a terrible headache, Mother.' The girl was pale, her eyes red from crying. A bit of Sellotape held on one wing of her glasses. 'Sister Margaret Mary's out, so I've to ask your permission to go to bed.'

'Go to bed with a headache?' Rita mocked, searching the unhappy young face. 'We're getting very soft!'

'But it's a bad headache, Mother.'

'Have you taken aspirin?'

'After breakfast. And lunch. I've had it all day.'

'Have you been wearing your glasses?'

Sally Ann nodded, pushing the broken frames up on her nose.

Rita glanced irritably at her watch: 3.10. Surely a seventeen-year-old could take better care of her glasses? The girl was neurotic, an attention seeker, probably avoiding a test. 'If it's not better by study time, go to bed then. Back to class now!'

'Please ...'

'Back to class this minute!'

The girl went away, sniffling. When she rounded the corner, the noise changed into loud sobbing. Rita hesitated. It sounded heartbreaking, but there was no way she could give in to that. As she hurried through the mossy gloom to the bursar's office, the noise faded. There was always some problem with Sally Ann. A bit of a misfit. Lately she had affected a tragic pose – Hamlette. It was infuriating. She was always sulking. In the wrong place at the wrong time. You only had to tell her to do something and she'd do the opposite. And last week she'd almost knocked out Jane

McMahon with a tennis racket. Rita had had to drive the child into St Vincent's emergency, but thank God she was all right. It was an accident, but she'd given Sally Ann a stern lecture. It wouldn't have happened if she hadn't been disobedient. The courts were meant for netball now. It was typical of her to be playing tennis in December. Then there was that silly fuss about her hair. She did art as an extra and was always clashing with Clement, the teacher. The older nun insisted she should have it cut. It was in her eyes and she was 'wearing it out' by pulling at it. Rita had listened, but refused to make her cut it so long as she pinned it back tidily. She always tried to be fair to the children. Not one of the fascist dictators she had known in the novitiate. But the very next week there'd been another ridiculous row with Miss Murphy, the Irish teacher. The woman had brought Sally Ann to her, complaining that she'd given cheek. Apparently, they'd had words about her choice of hobby for discussion at the Irish Oral exam. Sally Ann had chosen fishing – *iascaireacht* – for which she'd learnt all the vocabulary.

'But what's wrong with it?' the girl had pleaded.

Rita had silenced her, although secretly wondering the same.

'Women fish,' Sally Ann had argued.

'Do you?' Rita snapped.

'No, but ...'

'Then it's not really your hobby, is it?'

In the end Rita had ordered the girl to choose a more suitable topic – something more feminine, like knitting or sewing. Even stamp collecting might do. It was ridiculously petty, she knew, and unfair. But she had to back up the staff. After all, she'd recently taken the girl's side about the hair.

Mother Clement, who doubled as a bursar, was dwarfed by a big oak desk. She was dressed in the order's brown habit. 'Is anything wrong?'

'No!' Rita met her watery gaze. 'I want the car keys. Anyone out?'

'Only Margaret Mary.' The older nun reached behind her for the keys. 'She went into town on the bus for her glasses.'

'I'll be back in an hour. Give me the chequebook. Or do you have any cash? About fifty pounds would be fine.' Better too much than too little.

The older nun looked consumed with curiosity. 'Wouldn't a cheque do?'

'Have you no cash?'

'Yes, but I've made out the lodgement slip.'

'A cheque might be difficult. Give me cash as you've got it.'

Clement's bloodless lips curved downward as she pulled out the desk drawer. As she rooted grumpily, Rita fiddled nervously with the brown ornamental puppy on her desk. Ridiculous, having to consult the bursar about every halfpenny. In the States she'd dealt with all finances, picket lines, construction unions. The Irish religious orders were still in the dark ages. Pope Pius XII glared suspiciously from his portrait on the wall. Surely it was time for a successor? There'd been two popes since – John and now Paul – yet fifties attitudes prevailed. You'd think there'd never been a Vatican II. It would have had no effect here, if Archbishop McQuaid got his way. He sat out in Killiney with his head in the clouds, unaware that his world was collapsing. It was rumoured that the Jansenistic idiot had recommended lacrosse instead of hockey for girls, as being more ladylike. And he didn't approve of Tampax because it might enflame illicit passions.

'Mr Felice paid Maria's fees this morning. In five pound notes!' Mother Clement laughed cattily, counting out the money. 'Bet it's counterfeit. Italians look sinister, if you ask me.'

No one is asking you, Rita thought. Idly she picked up the ornamental puppy. Yellow tears splashed down his cherubic brown face onto his chubby paws, I MISS YOU in large red letters on the base. 'Whose is this?'

Clement smiled slowly, her face transforming. 'It's Margaret Mary's Gary. God bless him!'

Rita frowned. 'Gary?' Goodness. Not a statue of that stupid little yapper she'd insisted be put down? Perhaps she'd been too harsh. Was the pettiness of the convent getting to her? Making her inflexible? She could still hear Sally Ann's sobbing in her head. It wouldn't have hurt to be kinder to the child.

The older nun pushed ten fivers across the desk. 'Margaret Mary dropped him. But I have a good glue.'

Rita put the ornament down.

'Is it for a bill?'

Rita wasn't going to be drawn. She pocketed the money, letting the question float over her. There was an atmosphere of fear and mistrust in the convent. It needed fresh air, new ideas to blow out the cobwebs. But it was impossible to change others. You could only do something about yourself. Perhaps she should ask Clement to see to Sally Ann. 'You might go over to 6B.'

'Yes?' The older woman looked up, hoping for a clue.

'Never mind!' Rita glanced at her watch. With the girl in that mood, there might be another row. Clement wouldn't handle her properly. She'd dash over to the school herself and call Sally Ann out of class.

As Rita entered the classroom, the girls of 6B rose noisily to their feet. The Irish teacher turned from writing on the blackboard, flustered. 'Yes, Mother?'

Rita signalled the class to be seated. 'Miss Murphy, would you mind excusing Sally Ann Fitzpatrick?'

'Not at all.' The teacher looked to the back of the classroom. 'Sally Ann!'

Sally Ann got up sulkily. She was still pale and sick-looking.

Rita waited outside the door. 'How's the headache?' she asked cheerfully when the girl appeared.

Sally Ann wore her martyr's expression. 'Terrible.'

'It might help to lie down?'

'That won't do any good. It's probably a brain tumour.'

Rita kept herself from smiling. 'Well, go to bed. I'll have your supper sent up.'

The girl turned back to the classroom door. 'No, thanks.'

God, she was infuriating. 'If it's that bad, you should rest.'

'I'd prefer to suffer.' And she pulled open the door.

Rita was suddenly short of breath. 'Come back here!'

Sally Ann closed the door, staring sulkily at her feet.

'Go to bed, this minute!'

But she stayed rooted to the ground. Rita felt like laying hands on her. She wanted to drag her upstairs to bed. She struggled to control herself. 'Sally Ann, did you hear me?'

The girl nodded.

Rita kept her voice low. 'Then why won't you obey me?'

Sally Ann looked at her defiantly. 'You jeered me.'

'I didn't jeer you.'

'Yes, you did! In the front hall.'

Rita looked at her watch. She hadn't time for this nonsense. Clenching her fists behind her back, she said in a deadly quiet voice. 'You have one second to get yourself up that stairs.'

Sally Ann stood there.

'One second!'

The girl turned abruptly to the stairs and went up them.

Rita took several calming breaths. Stop getting angry. Stop it!

Speeding down the drive, she waved to the gardener hoeing by the massive gates. Hard to imagine that he had chauffeured them everywhere in the novitiate. They were forbidden to go out by themselves. Still, happy days then, a gaggle of girls flapping round the grounds after tea, with rambling blackberries everywhere and angry swans attacking anything in trousers. Now the swans were gone: the male was eaten by a fox and the female had pined away. And the novices were dwindling to two a year. The choir had given up singing the *Benedictus* in chapel, and sickly rows of new houses were sprouting on the lower hockey field.

After the village she accelerated for the long stretch before the shopping centre. Friday evening's mad rush would delay her coming back. Tonight she must phone her father about his arthritis. It was worse recently, but he never complained. On her last visit home he had brushed off her concern. 'Ah, don't worry about me, child. Amn't I almost with herself?'

Rita had looked away. The hypocrite! After the life he had given their mother. He wasn't just a drunk, but a mean drunk.

Later that evening he had said gently. 'Child, would ye not wear the veil?'

She couldn't answer.

Why did he still upset her? He didn't drink now. And her brother said he boasted that she was Superior of the Irish mother house at thirty six. Had rebuilt the convent in Florida. And had taught the professors in Florida State, getting a Ph.D. Her brains were something to boast of. Hmm ... no matter. She would never forgive him her childhood. She could see him now, red-faced and eyes bulging.

'The bitch is gone! Gone! Left me with six brats! And I didn't want one of ye! Not one of ye!' He swerved drunkenly, children and dogs scattering.

Poor Mama, married to that.

Then hungover breakfasts when he had to be up to teach, the children eating in strained silence with him shakily sipping tea. But someone would always be picked on before the day was out.

'Look at this room! What, cheek me? Get me the strap!' Then screams followed by the swish and smack of leather.

Once he had caught her chatting to a college boy and had dragged her home through the town, crying 'Hussy! Is this what the nuns teach you? Is this what they do with my money? My eldest daughter going to the bad! Over my dead body! My dead body!'

Rita braked for traffic lights. Going to the bad? Honestly. If he'd been drunk she could forgive that beating. But he was on the dry for Lent. He always gave it up then and gave them a life of hell. He had no control, that's all, picking all Mama's tulips after her funeral and strewing them on the ground.

'Twenty nine! Thirty! Thirty one! Only ...' He fell on the earth, clawing it.

White-faced, Rita had gathered the wilting heads. 'Mama's tulips! Mama's ...'

'What? Here! Give me those!' He grabbed the flowers, scrunching them into the earth. 'Look! Take a good look! That's where your mother is!'

When Rita said she was entering, he had muttered, 'One less to feed!' And didn't look up from his newspaper.

'But who'll make the porridge?' her little sister had whined. Later she found her brother crying in the garden.

'I'm not going far. Now stop! Please stop! There'll be holidays. And you can visit.'

A giant Christmas tree floodlit the pillars of the Bank of Ireland. Childhood. Christmas lights. Funny how it all came back. The square in Ballaghdereen, cluttered country shops. As children they had made the most of their presents. Unlike today's young. The big event was midnight mass, then walking home through the inky night. *Come follow me and I will be thy God.*

She felt nothing in the chapel now. Nothing moved her, not even the books she read. Nothing. Still, she worked on her Wallace Stevens book, joined a women's political group, humoured the old nuns. And she slogged for the honours Leaving class, helped them understand poetry. No one had bothered over her. Her father had once slammed-shut her copy of *The Waste Land*, shouting, 'Poetry? Ha! It doesn't even rhyme!'

So much for a country schoolmaster. What did he recite in his cups? '*Alas for the rarity, of Christian charity ...*' How did the rest go? He always finished with a flourishing, '*Under the green sod lies!*'

At O'Connell Bridge she waited for the guard's signal to move on. It was nearly an hour since the man had phoned and she didn't want to be late. Being Superior was exhausting. She was always running, seeing to this and that. Adjudicating quarrels between the nuns. It drove her crazy. And why should she be pestered about Sally Ann's headache? Why couldn't Patrick cope with it? She was Mistress of the Upper School. Rita sighed. Now she felt guilty for getting angry with the girl. Hmm. Adolescents and their moods. But had she been wrong about Gary? Was Maggy May having some sort of breakdown because of her harshness? The old woman had loved the stupid mutt but he yapped at everyone else's ankles. One bite meant trouble. And who had to face the parents? Who? An amiable dog that would stay outside might've been different. She was running a boarding school after all, not a menagerie.

Then the reprieve.

In the bus on the way to the dog's home, Maggy May had met Mrs Farrell who had agreed to take him. Now they phoned each other daily. Or if Mrs Farrell was on holidays, the convent was flooded with telegrams:

NEW DOG FOOD SUITS

HAS FOUND LITTLE FRIEND

IS ENJOYING SEA AIR

Once she had met Maggy May at the phone in the hall. 'Ah, Mother, the Lord punishes those He loves,' the old woman muttered. 'Poor Gary ...'

Rita had nodded dismissively and picked up the receiver.

But the old nun had grabbed her arm. 'They left him alone all day yesterday. God help him! I knew he'd be desperate, so I waited outside.'

'In this weather?' Rita kept a straight face.

The old woman shook her head, going on her way. 'But didn't he see me? And bark through the window! Ah, the Lord punishes!'

Town was crowded. Christmas lights winked magically on the trees lining the centre of O'Connell Street. Clery's looked like something out of fairy land with a Santa in the window. Why didn't Maggy May get her underwear there on account? The old nuns weren't used to modern self-service shops, still wore the habit, couldn't adapt to being ordinary people. And couldn't even have the pleasures of ordinary people.

She'd been wrong about Gary.

And she was in the wrong with Sally Ann – infuriating though she was. The girl looked ill and was probably unhappy about something. She was motherless with a neglected look. She'd been the victim of last year's fashionable illness – appendicitis. At least five girls had come down with it. Odd, the way symptoms ran through a school. Mass hysteria. One sheep over the fence, all sheep over, Rita had thought at the time. But Sally Ann's case had been genuine. The father had muttered something about an infection, possible complications later on.

He was a doctor with a busy Dún Laoghaire practice. And the vaguest man. His wife had died young, leaving him with two children to bring up. Sally Ann had come to the school in first year and, according to the other nuns, had always been a problem. Obviously she was suffering from the loss of her mother. You didn't get over things like that. There was a younger brother in school somewhere in the country. He and Sally Ann ran wild during the holidays, she had heard. No supervision. Sally Ann seemed to do all the cooking and minding. It wasn't fair to weigh her down with responsibilities at such a young age. Why couldn't the father employ a housekeeper? You never saw a poor doctor in Ireland. He should at least replace Sally Ann's glasses. Rita had written to him, but received a reply she couldn't read. Perhaps she'd ring him. No, it might bring his wrath down on the daughter. Last year he'd been summoned to the school about her report. It had taken several phone calls and messages through Sally Ann to get him there. Rita was only trying to involve him in his daughter in a friendly way. She'd tactfully tried to point out that Sally Ann had trouble concentrating and that perhaps this was a psychological problem. But he wasn't interested in this theory. In his grumpy way he seemed fond enough of his daughter, referring to her as 'Cordelia.' He hadn't a good word to say about the son. Rita was about to ask if he were the bastard, Edgar, but had lost courage. He'd gone on and on. How he'd thought he could depend on Sally Ann, but she'd been such a grave disappointment because of her poor results in Latin. How would she now be able to study medicine? Rita had asked politely if the girl wanted to study medicine. But he hadn't heard this, he was too busy complaining at length about 'the tedious generation.' Children didn't survive that.

No wonder the girl looked unhappy, didn't work. Associated with that clique of troublemakers in 6B. She was easily an A student, but lazy and inconsistent. She needed someone to sit on her, more than anything, someone to take an interest. Tonight I'll talk to her about moving up to 6A, for English at least. That way I can keep an eye on her.

She parked behind Roches Stores and weaved her way through the crowds to the Henry Street entrance. 'Oh, come all ye faithful ...' a group carolled in the distance. 'Oh, come ye, oh, come ye to Be-e-the-le-hem.' Mothers with wailing children pushed parcels in prams. Girls linked happily. Street traders shouted and waved balloons. Everyone hurried. Rita had her nieces and nephews to shop for, but was this getting and spending all it meant? And what was the store manager's name? He had sounded so sure of himself. Rita suddenly felt sick with nerves. The children, even the parents, were in awe of her. But a store manager? Who insisted Maggy May had stolen?

A sales assistant pointed her to a door marked 'Manager.' She knocked and almost immediately a burly young man came out, looking enquiringly at her smart tweed suit.

'I'm Mother Rita Hynes,' she said, walking in. Maggy May sat in a corner, bent over a hanky. Briefly their eyes met.

'I was expecting a nun!' He laughed, offering his hand.

'I am a nun.' Rita shook hands limply, taking in the several pairs of frothy panties on the green formica-topped desk. A skimpy bra cascaded down one side.

He pulled out a chair. 'Sister, a seat! Ha! You can't tell who anyone is these days.'

'Thank you, I'd rather stand.' Rita opened her handbag. 'How much do these come to? We have to get back.'

He waved away the uniformed figure appearing in the doorway. As the door shut, he pointed again to a chair. 'A seat, Sister!'

Rita remained standing, eyeing him obstinately. He smiled back with his mouth. She put two five pound notes on the desk. 'This should cover it.'

'Ah, I'm afraid it's not so simple.' He held up a pair of panties. 'Sister was apprehended leaving the shop with these items.'

Rita felt herself reddening. 'I'm sure she meant to pay for them.'

He dropped the incriminating garment onto the table. 'Hmm! ... Well, I'm not so sure. She didn't have the money. And she could hardly wear them.'

Rita ignored his fat smirk.

He planted his palms heavily on the desk and leant towards her. 'Look it ... in this shop we fight a constant war against shoplifters. I prefer the word *thieves*. And when we catch them, we make it hot. Hot!' He gestured towards the old nun. 'Sister here is a nun! She should know the difference between right and wrong!'

Maggy May began to sob. Rita looked over helplessly. 'It's surely not just a case of right and wrong,' she said after a second.

His eyes were an incredulous blue. 'But if nuns do it!'

'She's not different because she wears a uniform.'

'Ah! So you admit she's not different from other people.'

'Yes – yes, I do!'

'Well then!' He folded his arms triumphantly. 'Why should she be treated different?'

'I- eh-'

'Take yourself now. You don't want to be treated different.'

'Why do you say that?'

'Well – your clothes.' He glanced appraisingly at her suit.

Rita looked away, flustered. 'Can't you see she's an old woman?' she said after a second.

'Hmm! We have them all ages. All ages!'

Rita groped for the chair and sank into it. He sat down too and, folding his arms, stared at her quizically. Maggy May wheezed noisily. A newspaper lay folded on the desk. Headlines flashed into Rita's mind's eye.

NUN CAUGHT SHOPLIFTING! JUDGE CAUTIONS CONVENT!

Mutely she fingered the money. It'd be awful. There'd be courtrooms, clamouring parents, the Bishop. Oh God, she must think of something. Say something! Quickly she caught the manager's cold blue gaze. What was keeping him? Why not call the guards and be done with it? Why was he dragging it out?

He picked up the phone. She braced herself, looking supportively at Maggy May. I'm behind you, she wanted to say. You're not alone. There was an awful silence.

'Send in a bag and a receipt for four pounds, ten shillings,' he said at last. He replaced the receiver, sternly eyeing Rita. 'You'll take charge of Sister? You'll guarantee this won't happen again?'

She put five pounds on the table. 'Yes! Of course!'

When the uniformed guard came in with the bag, he told him to bring back the change. Then slowly, carefully, he folded the garments and put them one by one in the bag. 'I wanted you to realise the seriousness of the situation.'

'Yes!' Rita snapped. 'Yes!'

'I know she's a nun, but next time ...'

'Yes!' Hastily she pulled Maggy May up and steered her out to the white light of the shop. It was closing time, and a cluster of sales assistants stared as they made for the door.

'Sister! Sister, your change!' The guard caught them in the street outside.

Numbly Rita pocketed the money. They walked on, but suddenly the older nun stopped. 'Mother ...'

Rita pushed her gently onwards. 'You don't have to say anything.'

'I – I couldn't stop thinking of him ...'

Rita sighed guiltily. 'Yes, Gary, I know.'

The old woman smiled sweetly. 'Ah, no, Mother. Not Gary. A boy I knew. Long, long ago.'

'A boy you knew?'

'Ah yes, Mother ...' The old eyes hazed over. 'We'd go up the fields together ... and once ...'

'What are you saying?'

Maggy May shook her head. 'It was a terrible sin.'

'What?'

'We did it.'

Rita felt hysteria bubbling inside her. In a minute she'd lose control. 'What are you saying?'

'He went to England afterwards.' Maggy May smiled dreamily. 'There was a big family.'

'Stop it! Do you hear me? Stop it!' Rita shook the old woman's arm. 'You'll never go out alone again! Do you hear me? Do you hear?'

Rita plunged frantically into the crowd with the old nun tottering after. She had to get home. It seemed miles to the parking lot. At the car she fumbled shakily for her keys and, glancing over the top, saw Maggy May pale and hunched in the rain. Dear God, what was the point of being in a convent? Of slogging for other people's children if she made an old woman cry?

'What was his name?' she asked when they had joined the snake of traffic sliding homewards through the dark.

II

PAUL AND COLM

I think of Paul whenever I'm in Earlsfort Terrace now. Sometimes I imagine him still standing in the Main Hall, homespun and slightly balding, his big red hands deep in his pockets. As always, he's apart from the other males who cluster by the noticeboards, smoking or eyeing the talent – any female, bar nuns, crossing to the Annexe for coffee. Our college was like a railway station at rush hour. Day or night, people hung around, waiting. We were nicknamed 'The Tech on the Terrace', because of our situation, I suppose, and our shabbiness compared to Trinity, but we didn't feel inferior. Cherry blossoms cheered us up in spring, and we had year-round ducks in nearby Stephen's Green. We were the alma mater of Joyce. Hopkins had taught in our mausoleum and we could boast of being founded by Newman, who had a house called after him. In first year English, we read his dull prose, learning that he intended our university for the Catholics of Dublin. There's evidence of this in the clerics who blackened the place like crows.

They flocked in daily from the seminaries, disappearing into the cloakrooms in the bowels of the building.

The university was to move to the suburbs the next year. But four of us students were in a certain place at a certain time, Earslsfort Terrace in the late sixties. We didn't realise it at the time, but something happened which affected our whole lives. Imagine a drab tutorial room at the top of the building. It was an afternoon in October 1968, and the second History tutorial of my second year. Paul was late that day. Colm, Tom, the clerical swot and myself waited for Professor O'Dea to discuss the problems of the fourteenth century church. Colm had been my big crush since first year, but although he had asked me out a few times, it hadn't gone anywhere.

At last, the professor popped his head around the door. 'Second Arts, general?'

We nodded and he swept in, carrying a briefcase. He was a typical academic, Irish variety, and wore a shabby elbow-patched sports jacket with baggy cords. Unusually short in stature with floppy grey hair and a red, whiskey-veined face, his penetrating blue eyes perused you through steel-rimmed spectacles.

He sat in front of us, rooting impatiently in his briefcase. 'Eh – Mr Connolly?'

Colm put up his hand.

'This is an excellent essay, Mr Connolly. I want you to read it to us later.'

Colm shambled up for his paper, brushing his unruly hair with a mixture of pride and embarrassment. He was lithe, dark and handsome with the rumpled look of either a busy or a sloppy person. He was brainy but spent most of his time on the barricades for this cause or that, and then sailed effortlessly through exams. I'd often seen him reading in the library without taking a single note, while I always ended up with reams. He was a founder member of SDA –

that's Students for Democratic Action, the group that organised the so-called 'Gentle Revolution'. He'd been on the front page of *The Irish Times*, being dragged off by a policeman on a civil rights march in the North. The odd thing was him being in our group. 'General', I should explain, is the polite word for 'pass'. We were considered the pits by all departments. It was their policy to fail as many as possible – the place, after all, was crowded.

The other odd thing was us having MacDarragh O'Dea. A world-renowned scholar usually had an honours group. He'd written a book about the Irish monks at the court of Charlemagne – I forget the exact title. We Irish, by the way, had kept the flame of knowledge alight in the Dark Ages. I learnt later that we were to have had a doctoral student as our tutor, but he'd had some sort of crackup.

As the professor shuffled through his papers, I waited nervously. My essay had to be next. My father, a widowed doctor, had urged me to study medicine but I had refused. He was an amateur historian and couldn't understand why I had to do a degree in something he did for a hobby. But knowledge was an ocean in which to immerse myself. I soon discovered that, like the ocean, my ignorance was boundless.

Tom Mansfield got his essay back and I waited my turn. Lately I'd lost all confidence in myself. In school Mother Rita read out my English essays, but everyone in college was miles more intelligent. I had actually mispronounced John Donne's name at an English tutorial and said he was the epi*tome* of something. Everyone gaped, so I never went back. I got through the year without writing a word, except at the exams. I was obsessed with all things French, but at registration a lecturer had babbled uncomprehendingly at me, so I did Latin. You didn't have to speak a dead language. Philosophy, my third subject, was ok, but history was a jumble. For one thing, I had no historical background.

My father had said that, to understand the present, you had to know about the past, but I understood neither; I was clogged with facts. They absolutely froze my brain, so I daydreamed at lectures, and on hearing the word 'watershed' imagined a shed with buckets of water. It had occurred to me that this was a weird metaphor, but I didn't look up the word. It's a 'line separating two river basins, a divide'. But I know now that, as there are turning points in history, things happen in life by which we are changed.

'Miss Fitzpatrick?' Dr O'Dea was peering at the corner of my paper.

Nervously I raised my hand.

'Yes ... indeed ...' He cleared his throat. 'We can all learn from Mr Connolly's essay. Especially you, Miss Fitzpatrick!'

I felt myself shaking. I'd spent hours on the essay. Could it be that bad? Reclaiming it, I noticed a red line drawn through the first page, the second, and the third.

'I couldn't give you a mark, Miss Fitzpatrick.'

I was in total shock.

'Why, do you think?' His thin voice had a trace of his Cork origins.

'Eh ... I ...' I turned to the last page, hoping for some sort of a clue. There was only a scribbled UGH! I wanted to die.

'Why no mark, Miss Fitzpatrick?' His blue eyes were merciless. 'Read us the title of your essay!'

I was aware of Colm's heavy breathing beside me. Everything else had turned the vile green of the walls.

'What's the title of your essay, Miss Fitzpatrick?'

I could barely see. 'Eh "The Most Important Movement in the Fourteenth Century Church".'

'Good. Now read us your first paragraph.'

I kept my voice steady. 'All history is a nexus,' I began, 'especially that of the fourteenth century church. There were many events in that time which were interdependent. At first glance, it would seem that the residence of the papacy at Avignon instead of at Rome for over seventy years would be the most important movement. But was it so important? Was it an unmitigated disaster to the church? I think not ...' Somehow I went on. 'In the fourteenth century, there was a new element of thought among the laity. Dante was the first lay critic of ecclesiastic affairs. The seeds of revolt which was to follow in two hundred years were sown. This was a very important movement, if not the most important movement.'

'That's the first paragraph,' I said.

The professor was looking out the window. 'Quite a plausible one. A bit unsophisticated here and there in your use of the first person, but decent enough.' He stared at his nails. 'Now, what would that paragraph lead a person of ordinary intelligence to expect?'

'Well ...' My mind refused to work.

'What thesis have you set up, Miss Fitzpatrick?'

As the professor sighed impatiently, I studied the first paragraph again. Then Colm whispered behind me. 'The new element of thought among the laity.'

'I didn't ask you, Mr Connolly.'

'The new element of thought among the laity,' I repeated.

'What are your next six pages about?'

'The Avignon Papacy.'

'Yes! You set up an argument which you completely ignore. You go off on a tangent. Presumably you knew more about that subject?'

I nodded weakly.

'You could've used your information intelligently.'

I prayed for him to stop.

'How, Miss Fitzpatrick?' It was like some sort of inquisition. 'We're waiting, Miss Fitzpatrick.'

'She could argue that the Avignon Papacy was the most important movement.' Colm broke the silence at last.

The professor glared at him coldly. 'Thank you Mr Connolly. Now, Miss Fitzpatrick. Tell us how you'd make the case for the Avignon Papacy being a movement?'

I searched my essay for a clue.

He went on relentlessly. 'Did the Avignon popes bring about any changes?'

'Well ... the abbeys began paying the popes.'

'Good!' He spoke slowly, as if explaining something to a child. 'By about 1363, every major benefice, that is every bishopric and abbey, became a source of papal income. So we could argue it was a time of papal consolidation?'

I nodded.

'And could this be described as a movement?'

I nodded again.

'Good!' He pushed his spectacles up on his nose. 'So we have our argument! The Avignon Papacy was a time of movement towards centralisation. What else contributed to this?'

I cleared my throat. 'Well ... they were good popes. They ordered the friars back to the monasteries. Wandering friars were a problem.'

He nodded encouragingly. 'They were indeed. Did the popes initiate any other reforms?'

'Eh ... they favoured the Inquisition.'

He raised one eyebrow. 'Is that a recommendation?'

Everybody burst out laughing. Then the door opened and Paul came in. We had been on several dates – to a Synge play and some French films. He was keen on me, I knew, but, such is life, I had no interest in him. Colm was my obsession. Mostly I hid behind a book in the Ladies Reading Room and even crossed the Main Hall by going up one stairs and down another. I was terrified of people, I think.

There was even a student revolution that I hardly noticed. My only concern was passing the exam which I did, barely. As I've said, Paul was from Wicklow and had an agricultural air about him. His forehead was high from losing his hair and he was spotty and sleepy-looking from being up all night – he worked as a night telephonist to pay his way through college. He was a mature student of about thirty, years older than Colm or me.

As he went to the back of the room that day, the professor snapped, 'You there! What's your name?'

Paul turned, startled. 'Brady, Paul A.'

'Why are you late?'

Paul shrugged. He had a way of holding one shoulder higher than the other. 'Couldn't get a bus, professor.'

'What bus?'

'The 8 from Dún Laoghaire.'

I knew he had probably overslept. The professor thumbed irritably through his papers. 'Did I get your essay?'

Paul shifted uneasily. 'I gave it to the secretary. Your box had been emptied.'

'When did you go to my box?'

'Eh – I think it was last Friday.'

'If you'd gone to my box on Friday, you'd have found it full.'

'It might've been Saturday.'

'It was full then too. And on Monday, and Tuesday. I suggest you didn't go to my box at all. I suggest you're lying, Mr Brady!'

Paul could hardly breathe. 'Actually, I – eh – gave it straight to the secretary.'

'Let's go and collect it then.' The professor pushed his chair back and stood up.

We all gaped at each other. Paul looked as if he was going to cry. 'Dr O'Dea, you see ...'

'We'll collect it now, Mr Brady!'

The professor strode purposefully to the door, pulled it open and waited for Paul to follow him. Then he marched him out. We heard their footsteps all the way down the corridor to the department office.

Colm broke our stunned silence. 'Phew, what a Nazi!'

Even Tom Mansfield looked upset.

'It's like school,' I whispered at last. 'He told me he hadn't time to finish it.'

Colm put his head in his hands, moaning, 'Stupid, Brady.'

Tom Mansfield tidied his notebooks primly. 'He shouldn't have lied.'

'Ah, shut up, fuckface!' Colm growled. 'You try staying up all night!'

Then we heard the footsteps coming back. Professor O'Dea came in first, followed by Paul, who slunk to the back of the room. The professor fiddled irritably with his glasses. Then he fumbled madly through his papers. 'Read us your essay, Mr Connolly.'

Colm began in a deep gravelly voice. 'The most important movement in the fourteenth century church was the revolution of John Wycliffe. This Englishman was a teacher at Oxford when ...'

He stopped. Loud sobs came from behind us. I had never heard a man cry.

Paul never came back to the tutorial, and we didn't think anything of it. The place, as I've explained, was a railway station where people came and went. Anyway, I was still infatuated with Colm, and had no time to think of Paul. After all, I didn't owe him anything. Ok, he'd brought me to the pictures, but so what? I saw him once in the Main Hall dawdling the way the men did. By then I'd shed my fear of crossing it, and had dyed my Afro style hair red. He shifted nervously as I approached. He looked spottier than ever and in need of a shave.

'What've ye done to yerself, Sally?' He ogled my new hairstyle.

I ran my fingers self-consciously through it. 'Do you like it?'

'You're gorgeous anyway, Sally. Too gorgeous to be cooped up here. Come out to the hills.'

There was drink on his breath. 'I've to finish an essay.'

'For O'Dea?'

I could've said something consoling about his débacle, but didn't. 'We're lucky to have him.'

He loosened his grimy white collar. 'Yes, indeed.'

'He has an international reputation.' I echoed Colm.

'Come out to the hills with an old tramp, Pegeen.' This was a joke between us. He came from Wicklow like Synge, whom he adored, so he often called me Pegeen Mike, and himself an old tramp.

'I can't – my essay.'

He picked at a pimple. 'Well, come for a coffee. I'll buy you a cream bun.'

'I really can't.'

'You're turning me down, then?'

'I – I don't believe in personal relationships.' I was echoing Colm who had lectured me on love being a bourgeois invention. Paul looked as if he'd been slapped. I felt sorry. 'Look, I'll go some other time.' So we made a date for the pictures next week. I didn't turn up. A few days later I received an anonymous verse in the post.

When by thy scorn, O murderess, I am dead
And thou think'st thee free

It was from Paul. We had first met at the back of an English lecture on John Donne. He'd asked my name and I'd said it. Then he'd said his usual, 'Brady, Paul A.' Then I'd laughed, and we got talking about Donne, his favourite poet. Although I knew hardly anything about him, I said he was mine too. You'd never think it, but Paul was a wizard on poetry and literature, as well as on films.

I've no excuse for my behaviour. I should've said no first thing, or else gone. I liked him ok, but couldn't imagine anything else. I had vowed to conquer my fear of sex for Colm – the only problem was he never asked me to the pictures or 'tried' anything, because we were never alone. I suppose it was too bourgeois, and, in a way, I was relieved. Although I had become a Maoist for him, I couldn't shed my hangups. Luckily we did everything in a group. I saw history now not as something to guide me through life but as class struggle, something which had never struck me before. I had just accepted my family and friends as middle-class, but now everything was different. My friends were the masses, and my enemies all those in league with imperialism – 'the warlords and bureaucrats, the comprador class, the big landlord class and the reactionary section of the intelligentsia attached to them.' Colm had given me a copy of Mao's *Quotations*. He'd also invited me to meetings and helped me with the next essay for Professor O'Dea. 'You'll have no trouble if you think clearly, Sally,' he said, handing it back.

I realised that up to now I'd been afraid to think. I'd worked ok, but in the wrong way. I'd spent hours in the library, hours copying out chunks of books and stringing them together for an essay. I now tried to arrange my thoughts into a coherent argument. And then another misfortune turned to my advantage. Thanks to my awful

Latin results, I was forced to continue with philosophy. At first I believed myself condemned to a limbo of clerics, because nearly everyone else in the class was in religious black. But when we read Plato's *Republic*, I realised philosophy was the poetry of life. All art was decadent. Ideas would reclaim our fallen nature, and politics were ideas in action. Aristotle said that happiness was the final end of man, and Mao that happiness could only be brought about by the triumph of the proletariat. How had I lived so long and remained so ignorant? Colm said it was my upbringing, and he was right. As well as Mao, he was for Trotsky, Jesus Christ and Che Guevara, and against everything else, from the university curriculum, to Vietnam, to the Archbishop of Dublin. Sometimes he'd collect me from the library to occupy the Pro-Cathedral or else for a sit-down outside Mountjoy. At the first hint of a famine in Africa, we'd be fasting on O'Connell Bridge to collect money for hunger. A new age was dawning, and we were bringing it about. In Rome, Vatican II had radicalised the church and, a few years back, women students had done their bit by liberating the college library so that women could wear trousers – we all wore them in one day, so what could the authorities do? Even degrees were part of a decadent system. Colm was doing one to please his mother but he wouldn't stoop to honours. He was the son of a wealthy solicitor who disapproved of his radicalism. So he lived in a commune and supported himself by working for the Labour Party.

Housing was one of the issues of our day. While thousands went homeless, speculators bought up old houses around the city and neglected them until they had to be condemned. Then they were bulldozed, and offices or flats built on the grounds – flats for the rich, I need hardly say. It was a crying shame: a Georgian city was tumbling around us. The derelict mansions were usually guarded by patrol dogs to prevent squatters, but people still broke in.

One man was thrown into Mountjoy and his wife and children put on the side of the road. So the Dublin Housing Action Committee – a pressure group – organised a march to Mountjoy in his support. 'We should support whatever the enemy opposes and oppose whatever the enemy supports' was one of Mao's maxims. The enemy was capitalism. I had relations all over the city with houses full of empty rooms. My father had an empty garage. Why couldn't he convert it into a flat for some homeless person? I had become a zealot for change. There was no way I'd miss the march to Mountjoy. Our rallying cry was:

We will fight and we will win,
Ho, ho, Ho Chi Min.

There was to be an all-night vigil outside the prison, so I brought my sleeping bag. We met at the Dáil and marched through the darkening city over O'Connell Bridge to the north side. Colm was unperturbed, but I felt shy at first. In the streets people hurrying home stopped to read our placards: RELEASE DENNIS DENNEHY! and FAIR HOUSING and ONE FAMILY, ONE HOME. As well as students, there were workers with families and children – all arm-in-arm. The feeling of comradeship made me forget myself. All my life I'd been blind to injustice, but now I saw.

At the prison gates, men made speeches from the back of a lorry. They condemned our uncaring government which had betrayed the ideals of Connolly. Capitalism was the cause of all ills, and socialism the cure. Colm was making a speech, and as he clambered up on the lorry the crowd cheered. He wore his red anorak which contrasted with his olive skin. When he held up his hands for silence, the crowd cheered.

'Comrades!' They cheered louder. At last he got a word in. 'Comrades ... comrades, we meet tonight to protest against the unlawful and unjust imprisonment of a member of our committee ...' There was another raucous shout. 'Dennis Dennehy ... along with his wife and children ...'

Then there was an altercation at the back of the crowd. I turned to see the guards roughly dispersing students and workers. They resisted, and soon everyone was linking arms and singing, 'We shall overcome ... We shall overcome ...'

I sang too, but nervously. As more people were hauled off into a big black van, others sat on the pavement.

'Sit down, Sally Ann!' Colm called to me as he jumped from the lorry. At that moment two burly guards grabbed him and hauled him off.

My legs turned to jelly. Suddenly I had a mental image of my father's tired face. He was old before his time, paying for my younger brother in boarding school, and my college fees. I saw myself behind bars and him bailing me out. So I picked up my bed and walked.

Colm was beaten up by the guards. I told myself his family were wealthy and could pay his fines, while my father was always short of money because he never sent out bills. What would happen to my part-time job? I earned a pound a night over the weekend at a Dún Laoghaire restaurant for pocket money. If my name got into the paper, I'd lose it. Then how could I go to college? I told myself all this, but it was no use. Like St Peter in the garden, I had denied my beliefs at the first test.

But Colm didn't blame me. As always, his father paid up, and there was the usual family row, which ran off him. Things like that didn't worry him. I think he sort of gloried in strife. One evening about a week later, he walked me to the train and showed me his bruised stomach. 'I can't be caught again.'

Gently I touched his blackened ribcage. I had never seen such bruises and was amazed at the brutality of the police.

He closed his eyes. 'Phew!'

'Sorry!'

'No, do it again! Touch me.'

I did and he pulled me to him, kissing me. 'Give, Sally! Give!'

I tried to. But we were outside Westland Row station and had to stop.

'Come back to my place! I've got a hard-on.'

I glanced nervously at his crotch. The thought of anything sexual gave me butterflies. I could manage kissing boys in the pictures, because they paid and expected it. 'Eh, my father wants me home early,' I lied.

The truth was he wouldn't notice if I disappeared.

'Come for the weekend?'

I nodded and ran blindly into the station. I got onto the train in a daze.

As it pulled out, he appeared on the platform, shouting, 'Do you know where the house is?'

'Yes!' I mouthed from behind the carriage window.

'I'll be home by teatime. Come then!' And he waved me out of sight.

I told my father that a school friend had invited me for a weekend and packed a rugsack. Colm and some other Maoists were occupying a house in Sandymount. They hoped to found a commune, and had squatters' rights while the case was being tried in court. The house was halfway down Serpentine Avenue in its own grounds. A sign on the gate said BEWARE OF DOG. I pushed it open and crept cautiously up the spooky tree-lined avenue. There was no sign of life, but triffid-like branches clawed my face. The house stood forlorn in a jungle of weeds at the end. The plaster facade had once been pink, but now was diseased with brown patches of damp. Missing slates left large holes in the roof. Gutters sagged limply, and a down-pipe dangled like a broken limb. The downstairs windows were bricked in, and the hall door was padlocked.

Could Colm really live here? I knocked, but no one came. Was it the right place? I tried again. Finally I walked around the house, past a weedy tennis court to the kitchen door. I knocked again, and this time heard footsteps.

'Who is it?' an Englishy voice asked suspiciously.

'Sally Ann Fitzpatrick.'

The door inched open, and a pale skinny boy peered out. He had thick blond page boy hair and wore a beret like Castro. 'I'm Tom. Who sent you?'

'I'm a friend of Colm Connolly. He's expecting me.'

He jerked his head, indicating I was to enter. We passed through a dank and dilapidated kitchen to the hall. There was rubble everywhere, and wallpaper hung in strips from the walls to the ceiling. The smell of must was terrible. Floorboards were ripped up, and only odd rails remained of the bannisters. I followed him up the rickety stairs.

'Is Colm here?'

'Not yet!' He pointed to missing floorboards. 'Mind yourself there!'

I followed. One false step and I was finished. 'When are you expecting him?'

He shrugged. 'You never know with Colm.'

'Are you at Trinity?' I asked on the first landing.

'I was.'

'You got your degree then?'

'I left. It's an imperialist institution.'

I had to admire his courage. Although I'd opened my mind to other things besides exams, I was still hooked on getting a degree. I longed to be an intellectual like Simone de Beauvoir. I even had fantasies of going on to do an MA. It was so silly when I couldn't even write an essay.

We went up another flight, coming at last to a large, cluttered room which seemed to be the field of occupation. There was a worse smell here: a mixture of cooking, dirty socks and rank bedclothes. In the murky light, I could make out a table with a basinful of dirty dishes. Coffee cups and beer bottles littered the room. In one corner there were stained mattresses and, by the blackened grate, a lumpy couch.

He pointed to it. 'Take a pew. Colm should be back soon. I'm typesetting the paper.'

I looked at the squalid table. 'Will I wash up while I'm waiting?'

'Whatever you like!' he called from the hall. 'There's water in the kitchen. You'll have to heat it on the fire.'

The fire was almost out. So I threw on some coal from the bucket and carried the kettle back down the stairs. I knew squatters couldn't be choosers, but why didn't they wash up in the kitchen? It had a sink big enough to bathe in.

As I ran the water, something moved in the corner. A mouse? I couldn't see anything, so I threw a piece of wood in the direction of the noise. To my relief, a tiny lapdog ran out the door.

'Here!' I called, as I like dogs. But it was gone, so I carried the filled kettle back up the stairs.

Tom was still typing in the other room. While the kettle boiled, I waited, saying, 'There was a dog downstairs.'

He stopped typing. 'A dog?'

'Yes, in the kitchen. I was wondering what breed it was.'

He roared laughing. 'That was probably a rat. The place is infested. That's why we stay up here.'

I was speechless, rats horrify me, at least the idea of them. I don't think I'd ever actually seen one before. I'd done the dishes when another squatter came in. She was a tall, burly girl dressed shabbily in jeans and a man's raincoat. I said hello, and she nodded curtly in recognition, then took some groceries out of her pocket: a tin of baked beans, a packet of sausages, and rashers.

She looked at me coldly. 'Who are you?'

I felt in the way. 'Colm – eh – invited me.'

She said nothing.

'We're in the same history tutorial.'

Grumpily she put the pan on the fire. 'Pity he didn't let us know. There's not enough food.'

'I'm not very hungry.'

Then Tom came in the door with a manuscript. 'Take a look at this, Rosemary.'

While she read it, he ignored me. Then there were noises downstairs and the sound of someone coming up. I fervently hoped it was Colm. It was.

'Sally! You made it!' He came in the door, wearing his rumpled suit. Then, forcing a smile at the others, gave a Nazi salute. 'Heil, comrades!' They didn't look up from the manuscript. 'This is Sally Ann Fitzpatrick. Eh – Sally, this is Tom and Rosemary.'

'We've met,' I said cheerfully. They nodded curtly in my direction.

He rubbed his tummy hungrily. 'Sally's staying the weekend. What's for tea?'

They were both glaring at him. He took off his tie and stuffed it in his pocket. 'Well, there's enough for her, isn't there?'

Tom broke the silence. 'I suppose we can all have less.' I was definitely *persona non grata*.

Somehow we got through the meal. Colm talked to me, while they munched silently. Afterwards he brought me for a pint in Horse Show House, his favourite haunt.

'They're pissed, 'cos I didn't ask permission for you to stay. They have all these Nazi rules,' he explained. 'I ignore them.'

I sipped on my Guinness. To me it tasted like rusty water. I didn't really like it, but everyone else did, and I feared being different. I feared everything: Rosemary and Tom, the rat, but mainly sex. It loomed ahead like some ordeal. How would I manage? And would it hurt? I'd never even used a Tampax. I couldn't get it in, so I was sure I hadn't a proper opening down there.

'Colm, I think I'll go home.'

'What're you scared of?'

'I dunno ... pregnancy!'

He took a condom from the hanky pocket of his suit. 'I've taken care of that.'

I was falling into an abyss. We sat in the pub till closing time and then went back to the house. There was no one around, and we went straight up to Colm's room on the top floor. It was a little less squalid than the rest of the house. On one wall was a large poster of Fidel Castro and on the other a photo of James Larkin with his arms upheld to support the socialist cause. I now recognised Colm's stance on the truck as imitating the Irish Labour leader. In one corner there was a mattress with a cheerful duvet quilt.

'Sit down.' Colm put on a record of Bob Dylan, and as it whined out a song, 'It ain't me, babe ...' he pulled me down on the mattress and began kissing me passionately. I kissed back. After a while he opened my blouse and put his hand inside my bra.

'Take it off, Sally.'

I obeyed, and he kissed my breasts. My nipples actually became pronounced. He seemed to be in a trance. Then he pulled off his trousers and underpants. I had never seen an erection, and the sight of it, dangling like another limb panicked me completely. I jumped up and pulled on my clothes.

'What is it?' Colm put his arms around me.

'I've got to go home!'

He was trembling. '*Please* don't go, Sally.'

'But I can't.' I frantically pulled on the rest of my clothes. I was acting like some terrible teaser of men, but couldn't help it.

Resignedly he put on a towel dressing gown. 'You've missed the last bus.'

'I'll walk.'

'To Monkstown?'

I pulled on my coat.

'Stay, Sally! If you want, I'll sleep on the floor.'

I began crying. 'I'm sorry.'

'I shouldn't have pounced on you.'

'Do you think I'm peculiar?'

He sighed, putting an arm around me. 'No, you're not ready for it.'

Then we heard a noise on the stairs, and someone knocked on the door. 'Are you still up Colm?' It was Rosemary.

'I've been up for some time,' he said.

'But are you up *now*?'

'Sort of. Why?'

Her voice was insistent. 'I wanted you to look at something.'

We were both in stitches.

'Can it wait?' he asked in a level voice. 'I'm not up anymore.'

I put a pillow over my mouth.

'I don't know what's so funny!' Her anger seemed to burn a hole in the door.

We slept that night like brother and sister. I awoke first and lay staring at Colm's handsome, sleeping face. He had very dark skin for an Irish person and looked almost Italian. I wanted more than anything to be *engage* with him. To rid myself of my terrible virginity, but I couldn't. And I don't know why to this very day. How did everyone else in the world enjoy sex?

We had tea and toast for breakfast. Colm brought it up to his room and then went into his job at the Labour Party. I said I'd go home, but he persuaded me to stay for the weekend as arranged. I had my café job that evening, so he said we'd go for a walk on Sandymount Strand in the afternoon.

At about ten o'clock I went downstairs for a cup of tea. Rosemary and Tom were checking sheets of typing at the table. They didn't look up as I came in. The dishes were strewn around the room again, and again I offered to wash up.

'Will you see about the evening meal?' Rosemary looked up wearily. 'We take it in turns to shop and cook.'

I nodded cheerfully. 'I've only a pound till tonight. I get paid on a Saturday.'

'You won't need money!' She laughed sarcastically.

Tom looked up. 'We usually liberate it.'

'You mean shoplift?'

He nodded.

'But that's theft!' I was horrified.

'So is all property,' he quipped.

I was Oliver fallen among thieves. If I were caught, my father would disown me.

Rosemary stood up and reached for a book on the shelf. 'Our new member doesn't know the rules. She seems to be full of bourgeois shit.'

'I'm not. I just can't steal.'

Tom leafed through the book – *Quotations of Mao* – saying, 'We're in a disorganised state now. But we operate on strict Maoist principles. I'll read you what he says on discipline. "One: The individual is subordinate to the organisation. Two: The minority is subordinate to the majority. Three: The lower level is subordinate to the higher level." He looked up. 'All three apply to you. But if you don't want to stay ...'

'I'll do it!'

They smirked at each other. I wanted to stay with Colm, even if I didn't really believe in the Utopia he talked of. I was no longer middle-class: all property was probably theft. I had once read in a magazine article that people shoplifted by hiding a bag under a coat. So I shortened the strap of my shoulder bag and concealed it under my anorak. Then I walked casually to the big supermarket in Sandymount Green. My chances would be better in a big shop like that. I picked up a basket going in. I had a pound so I could buy a few cheap items to allay suspicion. I decided on dishwashing liquid and a bag of potatoes. Next I lingered by the meat counter, fingering the packets of steak. A sign warned SHOPLIFTERS WILL BE PROSECUTED, but I ignored it. Checking that no one was looking, I slipped two big sirloin steaks into my bag. No one had seen me.

I dawdled to the cheese counter. 'How much is the Danish Blue?'

'10/6 a pound,' a white-coated boy said.

'It's a bit expensive.'

'I can cut you a few ounces.'

'No thanks.'

I went casually to the checkout. There was only one woman in the queue ahead of me. Trying to ignore my thumping heart, I put my basket on the counter. The woman moved on, and the checker emptied my basket, ringing up the prices.

'18/11, please.'

I paid and put the items in a plastic bag.

I was at the door when a voice called, 'Miss! Miss!'

I stopped, frozen with fear. A future of imprisonment flashed before me. My father's tired face. Should I try and outrun them? Then a hand tapped my shoulder.

I turned, as the shop manager held up a brown woollen glove. 'Did you drop this, Miss?'

It was mine. I took it.

My heart racing, I walked numbly out of the shop and around the corner. Once out of sight I ran all the way back to the house. It had been so easy. And I felt a strange exhilaration. I now understood the thrill of the criminal life.

That afternoon on Sandymount Strand with Colm, I mentioned that I'd got steak for tea. To my surprise he offered to reimburse me for what I'd spent. So I told him of the morning's conversation with Tom and Rosemary and my adventures in the supermarket.

He gaped at me. 'What? They told you we stole everything? Well, that's not our arrangement! We have a kitty. We all put in money. I've put in some extra for you!'

He was absolutely fuming. I was speechless. Colm suspected they'd told me to shoplift as a way of making me leave in disgust. This made Colm more determined for me to stay. So I did. I'm vague about exactly how long.

My father says one of my mother's maxims was 'Know when you're happy'. According to her, this was the secret of life, and, although I couldn't talk to her, I knew I was happy. My relationship with my father was ok. I suppose it was like any girl's with her father. I mean, he gave me money when I needed it, but I think he probably didn't even notice I was living away from home. Now everything was different. I had Colm to talk to on walks and at demonstrations, and often till the small hours in his little room.

To avoid Rosemary and Tom, we often ate out in Gaj's Restaurant in Baggot Street. I loved the cheerful kitcheny look of its pine tables and gingham tablecloths. We met other students there and often writers and intellectuals. And when the restaurant closed, we would sometimes go to a flat for late night coffee. As Colm's girlfriend, everyone deferred to me in a way that was new. I now had status. I existed because someone loved me. Or so I thought.

One evening along with some others we were in Gaj's, discussing plans for a fast on O'Connell Bridge to aid the victims of some war in Africa – I forget where – when Paul came in. He looked really bad: pale, unshaven and downright dirty. I saw him queue for food, but said nothing to Colm who was deep in argument with someone.

'Sally and I'll take the shift from eight till noon. Then you two. Mansfield's actually volunteered.'

I watched Paul sit at a corner table. I was glad there was no room at ours. What would I say to him? But I felt very badly about my behaviour, and something made me nudge Colm. 'Paul's come in. Will we ask him to join us?'

Colm looked round quickly. 'He's got funny lately.'

'What do you mean?'

Colm tapped the side of his head. 'He's gone nuts!'

I sat with my back to Paul, while the others argued loudly. There was no way Paul could avoid hearing or seeing me. Then Colm went to phone someone, and I decided to go and talk to Paul. Ignoring a friend was too much, even an ex-friend. But when I turned round, he was gone. His food was untouched so I felt sure he was in the loo. But he never came back. He must have seen us and fled.

After our first débâcle, Colm hadn't tried to make love again. Living with him helped conquer my fears. So on the night of our second Sunday together, we were kissing each other goodnight, when I suddenly said, 'Let's try it again.'

He hesitated. 'Are you sure, Sally?'

I nodded, feeling the panic of someone taking a high dive. It hurt a bit when he penetrated me, but I felt no desire. I didn't seem to have a hymen either, because there was no blood. As he moved up and down inside me I felt only discomfort. In a few minutes he was finished.

'Sally,' he sighed.

Nothing had happened for me. What did people make such a fuss about? Then as he pulled out of me, I felt wavy sensations.

'Wait!' I whispered.

There were more sensations inside me. And the next thing I was a woman. I giggled with relief. He started laughing too. At that exact moment, there were loud voices in the garden, and the sound of crashing.

Colm pulled out of me. 'Christ, what was that?'

The noise got louder, and someone spoke through a megaphone. 'This is the Gardaí! The house is being demolished! All trespassers must vacate the premises immediately!'

Colm jumped out of bed. 'Get dressed! They're pulling a fast one and demolishing the house!'

We scrambled into our clothes and ran down the stairs to the kitchen door. Luckily the fuss was at the front of the house, and we escaped through the back garden.

'It's jail if I'm caught, Sally. Hurry!'

I tripped, twisting my ankle painfully.

'Come on!' He pulled me up.

'I can't. You go ahead!'

At that moment a vicious police dog pounced on me. I screamed as Colm ran in terror through the trees. A burly guard pulled the dog off me, grabbing my arm.

They found marijuana in the house. All the others had got away, so I was charged with possession of drugs and trespassing. I spent the night in Sir Patrick Dun's Hospital, flanked by a woman garda. Also I lost my contact lenses.

People sympathised with my father over his wild daughter, but he stuck by me. He hired a solicitor and a barrister to speak for me, and I got off with the Probation Act for a first offence. For months I hobbled around on a broken ankle. But the pain was nothing to the pain inside me. Colm wrote that it would harm me to be associated with him and that we shouldn't see each other for the moment. He never even comforted me. I saw him once in college with another girl and ducked into a classroom. Later I heard they got engaged. I was afraid to go back to Professor O'Dea's tutorial where I'd meet him for certain. I retreated back into my shell and the Ladies' Reading Room, avoiding the Main Hall and Annexe. I wanted to leave college completely, but my father wouldn't hear of it. I was abandoned and betrayed, Christ weeping in the garden, an outcast whom nobody loved.

Now I realised how badly I'd treated Paul. If only I had another chance. If only he'd ask me again to do a strong line. Or go out to the hills. Or even for a cup of coffee and cream buns in the Annexe. I looked for him in all the usual college haunts, but to no avail. I knew he'd forgive me, if I could only ask him.

So I stalked the Annexe and Gaj's Restaurant, knowing he sometimes ate in those places. But I never saw him. I called at his digs, but his landlady said he'd left Dublin. He'd always been secretive about his sister in Wicklow, so I couldn't find out anything for sure from her. I didn't even know who she was. Finally I rang the operator in the

Tinnahealy exchange, and someone there said he'd left for England.

But he hadn't.

Soon after the Christmas holidays, I was slinking through the Main Hall when someone called 'Sally Ann!'

It was Colm. He was standing talking to the college chaplain, Fr O'Connor, a tall young redhead. Fear suddenly choked me, and I pushed my way blindly through the crowded hall. If only I was nearer to the safety of the Ladies' Reading Room.

But halfway down the corridor, Colm caught me. 'Sally! Wait!'

People were looking, so I had no choice but to face him.

'Did you hear the news?' He looked ashen-faced, and before I could answer blurted, 'Brady's committed suicide!'

'What?'

'He was pulled out of Lough Dan this morning.'

I was stunned, saying at last, 'Maybe he fell in?'

Colm shook his head. 'There were stones in his pockets.'

I felt I was going to faint. 'I was unkind to him.'

Colm looked upset too. 'We all were. Remember O'Dea's tutorial? We should've walked out, but we sat there!'

The memory of the tutorial will wound me forever, as much as my not turning up for that date. I don't flatter myself that Paul drowned himself out of unrequited love or anything like that. He had problems, and I didn't help him. None of us did, and he was to suffer even more indignities.

Father O'Connor drove Colm and me down to the funeral the next morning. We had to go over a bleak mountain in the rain, and it was nearly ten o'clock when we arrived at the mean little church on the outskirts of a Wicklow village. Surprisingly there was only one other car, and men were already carrying the coffin up the steep hill to the graveyard. We hurried after them.

'I thought there was to be a Mass,' Fr O'Connor said breathlessly to the men at the graveside.

They looked at each other, and went ahead lowering the body with ropes into the open grave.

'Who's performing the burial rights?' Father persisted, puzzled.

As one of the men started shovelling in clay, the other muttered grumpily, 'The parish priest is afraid of scandal, Father. He's a manifest sinner, Father.'

'A what?' Colm said.

'It's a term from Canon Law,' Fr O'Connor said.

Now the men were both shovelling, I stared into the deep grave. One day I would lie in one, but in the meantime was I worthy of life?

'Stop!' Fr O'Connor shouted. 'I'm ringing your parish priest.'

They did, leaning lazily on their shovels. The priest ran down the hill to the church. In a while he came back, his young face set in anger.

'He quoted Canon Law at me,' he said to Colm and me.

'What about Vatican II?' I said. 'Hasn't it changed everything?'

'Christian burial can still be denied at the discretion of the individual PP,' Fr O'Connor explained. 'We'll say the Our Father.'

As the men filled in the grave, we said those ancient words, begging forgiveness of God as we forgave others. I was sorry I couldn't remember John Donne's poem about death being not proud. But death was proud and won in the end. Here was the final end of man, despite Aristotle, Marx, Mao, the lot. What did anything matter? Paul had needed us and we failed him. Our college days were the best of times, and the worst of times. We were meant to be the 'gentle' generation, the harbingers of change, of the Brave New World. We would support any foreign cause, but had stood by when one of our own was humiliated.

III

DEIRDRE

'Do you want to wait on?' the barman called across the great counter.

Deirdre looked up from her evening paper. 'Huh?'

'Do you want to wait on, or do you want to order something?' He wiped the counter top deftly.

'I'll wait ... uh ... if that's ... uh,' she bit the inside of her lower lip.

'Righto,' he said, giving her a curious look.

Deirdre studied the paper sightlessly. She hated sitting on her own in a pub, and there was nothing left to read except the small ads and the death notices. Surely he didn't object to her sitting there, not drinking? She'd read that some Dublin pubs didn't like women. But, sure, there were women's voices coming from the other bar. Why couldn't Sally Ann, if she was going to be this late, have agreed to meet in a cafe?

She folded the paper neatly and placed it on the table before her. Her hands lay moistly in her lap, the fingers red and stubby, but looking better now that she'd finally given up biting her nails. Well, except when she met new people. That had been her big dread about coming to Dublin. But, on her second lunch hour from the Grafton Street branch, who should she meet but Sally Ann? She was dressed completely in black. The hair was different, frizzed out, sort of Afro. And no glasses. But it was Sally Ann all right. The same old Fitzer, her best friend, ambling down the other side of the street, wrapped round a tall boy with dark, crinkly hair. Deirdre remembered his hair and the curved slouch of his back as he waited with his hands in his pockets.

But half past eight. Where was she? What if she wasn't coming? The nerve! Fussily, Deirdre flicked a piece of fluff off her new skirt. No, Sally Ann would turn up. She wouldn't do a thing like not come. Going home now would mean waiting in the cold for a bus. And she was beginning to like the warmth of the pub. But she was hungry. Missing her usual chop from the shop near her bedsit, she'd had a skimpy omelette in a place on Grafton Street. Not that she liked omelettes, they were just cheap. A pity she couldn't afford one of those delicious Rum Babas on the desert tray. Say, a bite of the Mars bar in her handbag would keep her going. But she could hardly eat it here. Unless she slipped out to the ladies? No, she might miss Sally Ann.

After her meal she had used up her free time window shopping. Now the whole evening was wasted. Still, she'd only be sitting in at home. Even if Sally Ann came now, they mightn't get into the pictures. Or they'd have to join a queue with all the other pairs of girls you saw in Dublin. Maybe it was just as well. If she went home now the takeaway would still be open, and the landlady might invite her in to watch

Kojak and offer her tea with that delicious homemade ginger cake.

The door flashed open, and a man left. Deirdre shivered as a blast from the December night penetrated her tights. She'd give Sally Ann another few minutes, then make a dash for the takeaway. Have a nice ...

'There you are! Hiding away in the corner!' Sally Ann plonked her basket on a chair and, beaming through her smudgy mascara, leaned to kiss Deirdre. 'How are you, chérie?'

'Uh ... I didn't see you coming in,' Deirdre started. What if someone saw them kissing? People at the bank never did that.

'There's another door. Fabulous in here, isn't it? So genuine.' Sally Ann threw off a raggy fur coat and squinted rapturously.

'Genuine?' Deirdre turned her head. Genuine what?

'That ceiling. I could sit in here for hours, gazing at that.' Sally Ann giggled happily and flopped into the chair opposite.

Deirdre contemplated the clusters of plaster fruit on the ceiling. Nice, sort of old-fashioned, but genuine? Sally Ann lolled facing her. She wore dirty skin-tight jeans rolled at the ankles to reveal thick red socks and shiny black high heels. What a get up. Like a little girl in her mother's shoes.

Deirdre broke the silence. 'Don't you still have to wear glasses?'

'Contacts! I had a hell of a job getting the old man to fork out. He's an awful miser.' Sally Ann flicked out her curls and stretched her legs under the table, taking up all the room. 'What are you drinking? Nothing. Never mind. They'll be over.'

'Well, I ... eh.'

'You'll love Dublin, chérie. Devastating place.'

Devastatingly lonely, Deirdre thought. She'd die if she couldn't go down home at weekends. Every Friday found her in a bus queue for the country.

'This pub, for instance, reeks, I mean absolutely reeks of atmosphere. I wanted to come in here last night. But Colm! Do you think he would? It was Horse Show House again.'

'Was that Colm I saw you with?' Deirdre managed to interrupt.

'Saw me with? When?' Sally Ann blinked her blackened lashes.

'Last week. When we met.'

'Oh ... Then.' Sally Ann tapped her chin with a badly nicotine stained index finger. 'Now, let me see, who was I with that day? Hmm, confusing sometimes, keeping track. Yes, that probably was Colm.' She smiled quickly. 'Did you like him?'

'Well, yes, I ...'

'We're living together.'

'What?'

'Co-habitating.'

Deirdre felt herself go hot.

'I'm never getting married. It's a bourgeois invention. I don't believe in the nuclear family.'

'Weren't your parents happy?'

Sally Ann looked at her quickly. 'My mother died, remember?'

'I forgot, sorry.' Her mother's death was years ago, and Sally Ann never referred to her. It must have run off her like water off a duck's back. 'Do you miss her?'

Sally Ann hesitated, before changing the subject. 'Of course Colm's brilliant, but a philistine about art. Walks round with his head in the air. Totally, I mean totally intellectual.' Sally Ann sank suddenly into deep thought.

'Well ...' Seeing the far-away look in her eyes, Deirdre broke off. If he was her boyfriend what was he doing then with that other girl? Last week on her half-day, after looking round the boutiques, she'd cut through the Green and seen him dawdling with another girl. She'd followed, a few paces behind, to make sure it was him, then passed them out as they dangled arm in arm over the bridge. It was him, she remembered his hair and dark good looks.

'Always joking about me being a film snob,' Sally Ann said abruptly.

'What?'

'But I'm a good influence on him. Yes, I am. Do you know, I refuse, absolutely refuse, to go to Clint Eastwood.'

'Oh,' Deirdre said. Clint Eastwood? She'd seen him in a cowboy film.

'Yes, I'll only go to French films. I think ...' Sally Ann's eyes focused impatiently on the bar. 'I'll go and get us a drink. What're you having?'

'Pineapple juice,' Deirdre said, taking in the multi-coloured scarf Sally Ann wore round her red polo-necked jumper.

'Try something stronger,' Sally Ann coaxed.

'No, I don't drink at all,' Deirdre said quickly.

'Just as well, chérie. You might get addicted.' Amusement flickered in Sally Ann's eyes as she walked jauntily off to the bar.

Addicted indeed! Chérie? How affected. And those jeans were too tight. Still, they suited her in a way. Even in a school uniform, Sally Ann managed to look ... what was the word? Distinctive, maybe. Certainly unusual. But she seemed changed. The red jumper was too tight for her. With her blackened eyes, she resembled a circus clown.

'Here we are!' Sally Ann's high heels clicked as she came back with a pineapple juice and a pint of Guinness. 'I'm training myself to like this stuff. Wine of the country, and all that.'

'You should let me pay. After all ...'

'Oh, fooh! As I was saying, it's crazy to drink anything else when there's a natural drink available. Given to nursing mothers and all that. I used to take nothing but double crème de menthe with ice. But that's a little affected, *n'est-ce pas*?'

'Er,' said Deirdre.

Sally Ann suddenly clutched her side.

'What is it? Are you all right?'

'I've just ovulated.'

'Have you?' said Deirdre. There was an awkward silence. 'Do you ever see anyone from school?'

'That place was a jail!'

'The other day I thought I saw Mother Rita on a bus.'

'Jesus, I'd forgotten her. She was a bitch.'

'I don't know,' said Deirdre slowly.

'I do,' Sally Ann rolled her eyes upward. 'The cow confiscated my art books. Not enough fig leaves in the pictures I suppose.'

'Well, she was strict all right, but she liked you, everyone did.'

'Do you think so?' Sally Ann looked pleased, then said slowly. 'I wasn't very popular with the nuns. They hated me.'

'Oh, I don't think so.'

Sally Ann picked up her pint and looked at it distastefully. 'Rita made my life hell in sixth year. God, I had to report to her every night. She was demoted you know.'

'That must've been after I left. I left after the Inter, remember?'

'I'd forgotten.' Sally Ann grimaced as she sipped her Guinness. 'I'm bracing myself to throw this back.'

'I wish you'd have let me pay. You're not working yet.'

'I get the occasional few bob for my writing efforts.'

Gosh, Sally Ann a writer.

'Do people,' said Deirdre slowly, 'actually pay you for writing?'

Sally Ann shrugged. 'I report for a student paper – *The Irish Student*. I'm a Maoist.'

'I'd like to read your articles.'

Sally Ann frowned, and then fished a paperback out of her basket. 'Have you read duh Beaver's memoirs?'

'The whose?'

Sally Ann passed the book over. 'Duh Beaver.'

It was the second volume of the memoirs of Simone de Beauvoir. Had Sally Ann forgotten all her French? See moan de Bowvwar, surely?

'Satyr and she would ...'

'Who?'

'Satyr. Well, Sartre then.'

How silly, Deirdre thought.

'Sartre and she would go round the bistros in Paris, and all that. It must have been too ...'

Bistros, weren't they places for soup? And too? Too what?

'When they visited the different parts of France, such as the provinces, they'd taste all the local wines. But they liked the working-class places best. Do you ever go down to the quays here? You should. I mean to. It's an education in itself. But Colm ... of course, it's always the plastic lounges of the petit bourgeois for him. Funny, when he's a Maoist. I'm one too, by the way.' She flicked through the tattered paperback reflectively. 'As well as politics, I'm into all things French. Wine, sex, snails, everything. Will I lend you the book?'

Deirdre shook her head, so she put the book back in her basket. 'Well, what film are we going to?'

'There's a Peter Sellers at the Savoy.'

'Peter Sellers? Wouldn't that be a comedy? I never think the subject is serious enough in comedy.' She held out a small casket with brown powder in it. 'Like to try some?'

'Is that ... dope or something?'

'No,' said Sally Ann darkly. 'That's snuff.' She shook a little powder onto the side of her hand and sniffed. 'Try some. Don't be afraid.'

'I'm not afraid,' said Deirdre hastily. 'I'm off everything like that – since Lent.'

'Pity, it's marvellously relaxing.' Sally Ann sniffed again, then her nose began to twitch. 'Oh, dear! Ah-ah-ah-tishoo!'

'Are you all right?'

'Of course, I'm ... ah-ah-ah-tishoo!'

'Do you want a ...?'

'Ah-ah-ah-tishoo!' Sally Ann shook her head and brushed the tears from her eyes with the sleeve of her jumper.

'Are you sure you're ...?'

'Of course, it always affects you like that. You have to get used to it. A politics lecturer gave it to me. Well! I think we should go to the Truefoot film at the Astor. He's fantastic on triangles – he made *Jules and Jim*. You'll really like him. Give us a look at the paper.' Sally Ann snatched the paper, and rustled through for the cinema ads.

'I think we're a bit late,' said Deirdre. 'Truefoot? An Indian?'

'Yes, the last show is nine-twenty. We'll make that. What time is it anyway?'

'Nine!' Didn't she realise she was late?

'Good, that's settled then. You'll love Truefoot. His stuff is always about *ménage à trois,* and all that.'

'Oh,' said Deirdre. 'I've heard of him.'

'I assure you it's an education in itself.' Sally Ann sipped her drink slowly. 'Colm refused point blank to go with me. Says he wants value when he goes to the pictures. Plenty of blood and guts.' She paused reflectively. 'And his latest kick is to go round quacking when I say anything even slightly uplifting.'

'Quacking? Like in ... quack-quack?'

'Yes.' Sally Ann leaned forward confidentially. 'Unfortunately I told him that Satyr's party piece in the thirties was an imitation of Donald Duck. And last night in the pub he really embarrassed me. I tried to tell him about this novel I've read, *Le Grand Meaulnes.* I'll lend it to you – it's marvellous. Well, anyway, last night I started to tell him about it and he went "Oooogh, oooogh!" And I said, "What are you doing?" And he said, "That's your novel – *The Great Moan."* And I said, "Well, Sartre liked it." And that's when he got up and began flapping his elbows and hopping round the pub on his haunches, and going "quack quack-quack-quack." Then of course all his intellectual friends burst out laughing ...'

'That must've been embarrassing,' said Deirdre. Then when Sally Ann didn't answer, she said, 'Do you remember the time we nearly won the netball cup?'

Sally Ann looked vague. 'When was that?'

'We were on the same 3D team.'

'Were we?'

'It was a near thing, wasn't it?'

'The 3D netball team?' Sally Ann said slowly, bewilderment somewhere in her hazy eyes. Then jerking upright, she said quickly, 'Yes, it was a near thing. Though, mind you, I'm not always so easily embarrassed. But later when we were walking home, I said, "What about joining the Film Society, Colm?" You know, casually, and he began quacking again in the street. Of course, the people with us howled, like the idiots they are. Big joke! Well, enough of that.' She looked quickly at Deirdre. 'Do you know, I discovered a marvellous cure for constipation!'

'What?' said Deirdre, startled.

'Anal sex. It really works.'

Deirdre's face set stonily. God, was that what they expected of you in Dublin? Violently red in the face, she stretched for her pineapple juice and sipped it in silence.

Sally Ann was the first to speak. 'Do you have a boyfriend?'

'What?' Deirdre looked at her nervously.

'Are you going with anyone?'

'Yes,' Deirdre lied. 'A boy at home.'

'Best place for him. Frankly, men bore me. All wet from their mother's milk. But still if you wanted to get fixed up, the people in our house are giving a party, and you might enjoy it. That's if you want to come?'

'I would! I'd really like that.' Deirdre's eagerness suddenly faded. 'I wouldn't have to do anything, would I?'

Sally Ann waved a hand. 'Of course not!'

Deirdre sighed with relief. Now she was sounding like the old Sally Ann. 'Are there many living there?'

'Yes, it's a commune. They're all bores really. Except Colm! But it might be nice to meet someone while you're in Dublin, for weekdays. Duh Beaver and Satyr were separated for long periods. They never got married at all. Did you know that?'

'Eh, no.'

'Yes, and once they even had a triangular affair. Satyr wanted to be free. Let me see ... maybe I can find the bit.' She retrieved the book and leafed through it. 'Yes, he wanted to be free to "experience life and give it expression". Good way of putting it, isn't it?'

'I suppose so,' said Deirdre. 'Give what expression?'

'Well,' Sally Ann shrugged, 'life, of course. Reality and all that. But the affair with Olga led to complications.'

'Is that what Colm and you are doing?' Deirdre said suddenly.

'Finally they decided it wouldn't work. There were blistering scenes, wrenching for everyone concerned.' She looked up suddenly. 'Sorry, what did you say about Colm?'

'Nothing,' said Deirdre.

'Doing what?'

'You know, experimenting with other people, managing au trois. Like Jean Paul Sort.'

'Not yet. I wouldn't say we'd get to that stage for a while yet. Still ...' Sally Ann regarded Deirdre pensively. 'It'd be perfect. You could be Olga.'

'Olga?'

'Why not? You and I have a relationship, and the three of us ... why not? I'm not talking about now, but sometime. As I said I'm against marriage, the nuclear family and all that.'

'I don't think so,' said Deirdre, feeling uncomfortable. 'It'd be an occasion of sin.'

'No, it'd be perfect. We could try. You never know till you try.' Suddenly the eagerness drained out of Sally Ann's voice. 'You said something about Colm?'

The three of them? What was Sally Ann saying? Had she gone mad? 'Yes. I saw him last Saturday morning with another girl, in Stephen's Green.'

'That must've been someone else,' Sally Ann said flatly.

'Yes,' said Deirdre innocently, 'it definitely wasn't you.'

'Well,' said Sally Ann finally, 'it was probably his sister.' Nervously she pushed back the cuticles on her nails.

'No, it couldn't have been his sister.'

'Brothers and sisters don't always look alike.'

'That wasn't what I meant. No,' Deirdre insisted stubbornly, 'it couldn't have been his sister.'

Sally Ann bit her nails worriedly. 'What time is it now?'

'Ten past.'

'Ten past what?'

'Nine!' Didn't she realise they were going to the pictures in a minute.

'Have to go to the loo.' Sally Ann stood up abruptly, fumbling for her purse. 'Back in a tick, chérie.'

Deirdre watched Sally Ann swagger to the back of the bar. Had she been tactless? No. A thing like that wouldn't take a feather out of Sally Ann. Not the way she went on, about sex and all. But why was she so changed? Wasn't there more to talk about besides films and things in books ... and a Maoist? What was that, anyway? When they first met, they were two daffodils in the school play. It was nice then. They were both eleven, and every day after tea they'd play behind the tennis courts. Deirdre would be *Black Beauty*, Sally Ann steering her through various adventures. Sometimes they'd imagine another book, but mostly it was *Black Beauty*. For four years they'd been best friends. Then Deirdre's father had died and she'd had to go to a commercial college in Galway. It was the summer after the Inter. When Sally Ann heard, she came for a visit. They'd cycled all over Mayo. Sally Ann ahead, clutching her wide straw hat, swerving from side to side.

'We'll write! We'll always keep in touch!' Sally Ann waved frantically from halfway out the carriage window.

Bereft, Deirdre had stood awhile on the empty platform. After that she hated stations, and she hated the commercial college in Galway. School had been so much nicer. After lunch on Saturday washing your hair. Learning useful things like recipes for lentil soup, or notes on the character of *Hamlet*. Even Latin, even geometry theorems hadn't been that bad.

Deirdre drained the last of her pineapple juice. She had hardly seen Sally Ann after that summer. In spite of the pledges they'd made. Once Deirdre had visited school and someone had jeered her about doing the commercial course – 'ticky tack'. There'd been an outburst of giggles. But Sally Ann glared, and everyone was quiet. No bitter bread of charity for Sally Ann. Her father was a wealthy doctor. She'd gone to UCD and was now in her second term.

A boy snatched Deirdre's empty glass. Then he stooped towards Sally Ann's unfinished, not even half-finished Guinness. 'She's coming back!' Deirdre's eyes snapped up to the clock, high up on the wall, near the plaster fruit. Sally Ann had been gone almost ten minutes. Was she sick? Fainted in the ladies? Drowning in the lavatory? Slipped and broken her back? Jesus, Mary and Joseph, why had she been so mean to Sally Ann? Grabbing her handbag, Deirdre dashed towards the back of the pub.

The sign, 'Ladies', arrowed down the stairs. Deirdre bustled down them two at a time, and then stopped dead. Who was crying? Spinning round, she gaped up. At the top of the stairs, Sally Ann was hunched and shaking over the phone. Was she all right? Those noises? Was she on drugs? Was it the snuff?

'Quack, quack, quack,' Sally Ann's voice quavered into the phone. 'Quack, quack ...'

She replaced the receiver, and taking out a rumpled hanky, savagely wiped her eyes, messing her mascara. Then, she walked blindly back to the bar.

'Sally Ann,' Deirdre whispered, stumbling up the stairs after her, 'Sally Ann!'

IV

JIM

The birds awakened Jim.

'Nora,' he whispered to his sleeping wife. 'Nora, wake up!'

She groaned, rolling to her side of the bed.

He plumped his pillow and sat up. Outside the birds chattered away. There was the occasional cough of a distant car engine, then the clink of milk bottles. Normally he was up by now, gone by 6am. But that was before he was laid off from his temporary job at the post office. There was a chance he'd eventually be taken on permanently, but in the meantime this was the life. He squinted at the alarm clock. 7.10. By this time he was usually halfway up the Glenageary Road, stuffing the usual bundle of bills into the flats at 122. A peculiar place that, tenants always on the go. Letters handed back, marked 'Not Known Here' or 'Please Forward'. Well for them. Wonder what those flats rented for? Too much.

The purple and gold-starred wallpaper of his mother-in-law's spare bedroom glimmered in the half-light. Horrible. Yet, she'd done it up especially for them. But those colours made the room even pokier. What with their bed and the baby's cot, you couldn't swing a cat. But even this bed wasn't big enough for some people. He curled round his wife, fondling her behind gently.

She flung his hand off. He blew into her freckled face. She wrinkled her nose and turned away. He reached inside her nightgown. 'Jim!' She pushed his hand away again. 'I'm jaded tired.'

'Ah, come on! You can sleep later!'

'You know I can't! And stop it! You'll wake the baby!'

But the baby was breathing steadily, his little back rising then falling.

He pulled off his pyjamas. 'Come on, Nora!'

'Not now!' She was suddenly wide awake.

'What's wrong with now?' He kissed her eagerly.

She pushed him off her, whispering at the wall. 'Mammy!'

'Ah, to hell with Mammy! Nora! Please!'

'Ssssh, will you?'

'Mammy!' he shouted through the paper-thin wall. 'Mammy! Can you hear us?'

The baby started crying. 'Now, look what you've done!' As she got out of bed, the crying got louder.

He covered his head with the pillow as it rose to a crescendo. God, there was no peace! He was going deaf. He grabbed the blanket and slammed out to the bathroom. He stood naked over the toilet, drowning the floor with urine. The Mammy would scream when she saw that, but he didn't care. She could clean it. Or else Nora could. Serve her right. She took her mother's side in everything, and she'd gone off him since that purple frog was born. The kid took up all her time. She was always tired and didn't seem to do anything but breastfeed, day and night, night and day. It drove him mad with jealousy to watch the kid sucking her breast. What about him? They had no communication anymore. There was nothing to talk about since she wouldn't read. He tried giving her novels. But the Dennis Wheatley was lying half-read on her bedside table and she'd never even opened the Conrad. Now she wouldn't even have sex.

On the hall landing, they passed without speaking. 'There now,' she soothed, carrying the baby downstairs.

He slammed the bedroom door shut and threw himself back onto the bed. Kids were awful. Christ, why had no one ever told him?

He grabbed the pillow again, muffling the crying. He'd been led a dance. Marry me, Jim! I love you, Jim! And now Mammy before breakfast! Well, he'd show them! Tonight he was getting plastered with the boys. He'd drink twenty pints, like Kevin once did. Kevin, who liked to be the last man standing, would get him home. He had avoided the pitfalls. 'Play it cool', was his motto. Had all the women he wanted. Last week he'd sauntered up to that blonde mot at the bar. And the next thing, she was buying him drinks.

There was a low muttering coming from downstairs. Then his mother-in-law's voice pierced the ceiling like a saw. 'What was all that shoutin'?'

The baby drowned his wife's reply. He pictured her rocking him back and forth, her red hair on her shoulders. He shouldn't have frightened the poor little bastard. Well, not quite a bastard. He stared dismally around him, then pulled the eiderdown over his head. He was a prisoner for life. When he'd met Nora, he'd been doing the Leaving at Killester Tech at night. He wanted to go to university. Get some kind of degree. Then get out of Ireland. Travel to some remote place. Have the life of adventure he'd always read about in Conrad and Dennis Wheatley. He'd be like Conrad's Marlow. It had all started with reading Captain Marryat's *Mr Midshipman Easy*. What a book. Maybe he could write a novel, charting his own adventures like Dennis Wheatley. Or maybe the definitive work on Livingstone. Yes, that sounded ok. But for that he'd have to do research in Africa. That was a dream now. He'd never write anything. Nora had seen to that.

Through the jungle darkness, he crawled on his belly like Alan Quartermain. Light peeped in the distance. Yes, he'd pitch camp there. Pick up some natives for the journey. Read his piled-up post. Fling back Nora's letters with a scrawled 'Not Known Here'. Of course, she'd probably follow him to the bush with the baby. 'Sorry, Mees, we no see Bwana Jim two year now,' a black boy would tell her. She'd cry, of course. Then the baby would start up. 'Go that way!' the black boy would say, pointing toward the Nile, the heart of darkness in the centre of the bed.

Someone prodded his back. Nora was sorry. Well, she should be. He threw off the eiderdown to see his mother-in-law standing over him with a mug of tea.

'You?' He covered himself quickly.

Her bulging eyes didn't even blink. 'Take this!'

He did, spilling some of the tea. But instead of going, she stayed at the end of the bed. Her platinum hair was in plastic rollers and her chin jutted like Woody Woodpecker. A gaudy pink dressing gown covered her scrawny body.

'The gas is comin' today,' she snapped. 'Make sure you get back early with yer dole money. I'm not forkin' out again!'

He sipped his tea. Thank God, Nora wasn't skinny. And didn't wear rollers. The woman was made of plastic. She put plastic on the cushions, plastic strips on the carpet, plastic flowers in the sitting room. They ate out of plastic dishes and had to look at a dish of plastic fruit.

'Did you hear me?' she screeched.

He nodded.

'I'm not forkin' out again.'

When he didn't answer she flounced out of the room. He fixed her back with his index finger and fired. Bang. Mercy killing. Jesus, she was like something out of a play. You could laugh at mother-in-law jokes. But it was another thing when you found yourself landed with one. Maybe they should rent a flat, not wait for the corporation house. Get away immediately. No, they couldn't afford it. They could hardly afford to breathe.

He lay there feeling depressed, then looked at his watch. Come on, Jim! He finished his tea and hauled himself out of bed. Then washed, dressed and hurried from the house.

Halfway to the dole he began to feel better. Poor Nora. She hadn't wanted to live with her mother. Christ, she'd married him to get away from her. Now she was landed right back under the thumb. Never mind, they'd leave as soon as he got a job. In the distance, the sea was a brilliant blue. Summer was coming. He'd teach the baby to swim. You threw them in, he'd read, and they swam to Wales, like little fish.

The Dún Laoghaire Labour Exchange was conveniently beside the pawn shop in George's Street. Already a line of men stretched raggedly to the corner. His friend Kevin was near the top. He was an unemployed mechanic with the wiry dark good looks women went for.

Jim slipped in beside him. 'You're up early for a change.'

'I'm off to Greystones for the day. There's a practice rugby match there. Old Belvedere are playing. Why don't you come?'

'Thanks, but I've to get back. And there's a bus strike, remember?'

'Ah, come on! We'll hitch down. It'll be gas.'

The door opened and the line moved slowly. While Kevin joked with another man, Jim remained silent. He'd never been to a rugby match, only football. Kevin was interested in all sorts of sports. It'd be fun all right, but there was no way he could go. It wouldn't be fair to Nora. She'd only think he was still annoyed about this morning.

'What's the use, if you can't enjoy life?' Kevin said when they stopped again.

Jim said nothing. Kevin didn't understand marriage. You weren't free anymore. At the hatch he handed in his card. The girl counted out his money: thirty pounds, forty pence.

Jim took it, frowning. 'There's meant to be extra. The wife's had a baby.'

The girl studied his file. 'There's nothing about a baby here. We have a note of your marriage two months ago.'

'He's proved himself!' Kevin butted in from behind. 'I'll testify to that.'

There was a giggle along the line. The girl coughed. 'You'll have to see the supervisor.'

'But I did. Last week.'

The girl went away. In a few minutes she was back. 'We'll have it for you next week, Mr Nolan.'

Kevin got his money without a hitch. Outside he said, 'Come on, Nolan! The mot'll live without you for a day.'

Jim shook his head. 'Sorry!'

'Put yer foot down from the beginning!'

'I ... can't.'

'God, she has ye henpecked!'

Jim turned away. Did Kevin really think that?

'Henpecked!'

'Ok. I'll go!'

They headed for the Bray Road. After all, Nora hadn't even bothered to say goodbye when he was leaving the house. She probably sent her mother up to taunt him about the gas money. That old hag never stopped reminding him how much she was doing for them. She talked nonstop about money. And Nora didn't stand up to her. Allowed herself to be bullied to avoid rows. Yes, it'd do her good to worry. Do them both good. Maybe they'd appreciate him better then.

The first lift was from a taciturn truck driver who left them at the Wexford turning. They waited for an hour there before deciding to walk on through the town of Bray. It bustled with shoppers and activity. At the other side they stopped at a garage. Except for another girl hitchhiker it was deserted and had signs hanging from the pumps: NO PETROL.

'That's a bit of all right!' Kevin eyed the girl professionally.

Jim glanced over. She had black curly hair and gold granny glasses. She wore a yellow anorak and black jeans. And a red bandanna around her head. Probably some sort of hippy. He'd definitely seen her round Dún Laoghaire. She had a nice little arse on her, but Kevin would grab anything going.

'How are you, love?' Kevin called.

She waved, but didn't come over.

'That's a stuck up piece!' Kevin joked. 'I'd like to get her down on her back.'

Jim ignored his crudeness. Kevin went over to the petrol pumps. 'Arabs holdin' the fuckin' world to fuckin' ransom.'

Jim smiled to himself. Kevin's language got choice when he started philosophising. 'What about CIE?'

'What about them?'

'The bus strike's holding us to ransom,' Jim argued.

'That's a fuckin' just cause.'

Jim said nothing. He was looking at the girl. She was much slimmer than Nora. Nora had a nice arse when they first met, but she'd put on weight with the baby. Now she could only think of things like gas to dry his clothes. But how would she dry them without any gas?

'Did ya hear me, Nolan? CIE's a fuckin' just cause.'

Jim nodded. So was Nora's gas. He should never have come. He'd been mad to give in to Kevin's taunting, and he didn't even like rugby.

'It's about time you fuckin' wised up, Nolan.'

'What do you mean?'

'To the fuckin' cause of the workin' man. Did you read that life of Connolly I fuckin' lent you?'

Jim nodded. 'It was good.'

Kevin sat on the curb. 'It was fuckin' marvellous. You're wrapped up in your own fuckin' problems. You've got to think globally.'

'What do you mean?'

'I mean the fuckin' world situation! It makes our fuckin' problems fuckin' pifflin'.' Kevin leaned back, his head supported by his hands. 'Nothin' seems fuckin' worth doing. I'll never understand how people can have fuckin' kids!'

'It happens ... you meet the right person.' Jim looked regretfully at the girl. Would he have any chance of getting off with her?

'Not me!' Kevin shook his head. 'Not with the holocaust comin'.'

A truck roared up. The three of them thumbed frantically but it passed. 'Waitin' long, love?' Kevin shouted.

The girl joined them. She was carrying a sketch pad in a basket and seemed oblivious to the coming holocaust. 'About half-an-hour. I'm trying to get to Wicklow.'

Jim thought her accent posh.

Kevin went into action. 'For a dirty weekend?'

The girl looked alarmed.

'He's only messing,' Jim said.

Kevin smirked. 'Any crack down there?'

She shrugged. 'Dunno. I'm only going for the day.'

Kevin winked at her. 'To see a fella?'

'Yes, in a way. I'm visiting his grave.'

The boys looked at each other.

'He committed suicide,' the girl went on, 'in college.'

Kevin snorted. 'Fuckin' eejit! Are you in college yerself?' He glanced at the sketchpad. 'Art college?'

'I did a BA. Now I'm unemployed.'

'That makes three of us!' Kevin sidled up to her, putting an arm around her shoulder. 'Listen love. I'm Kevin and this is my pal Jimbo ...'

'I'm Sally Ann Fitzpatrick.'

'Why don't we hitch to Greystones together? Have a drink there?'

'Three's hard for lifts,' she said. 'You two'd be better sticking together.'

'The two of yous go on,' Jim said. 'I should get back.'

Kevin glared him into silence, turning to the girl. 'Three's fine. You thumb. Jim and I'll hide by the wall. When someone stops, we'll run out.'

Sally Ann shrugged. 'Ok.'

Then a red sports car screeched to a halt beside them. A girl with long blonde hair pushed open the passenger door. 'I'm going to the Burnaby.'

Her voice sounded rich and she wore riding clothes. The rich looked so healthy, Jim thought. Their skin kind of glowed. Must be the right vitamins or something.

Kevin leaned over the car. 'That's great.'

She took a riding hat off the front seat. 'I can take two.'

Jim stood back. 'Sally was here first.'

But she stepped to the back of the pavement. 'That's ok. Go ahead!'

Kevin winked meaningfully. 'In you get, Jimbo.'

The blonde driver relented. 'Look, we're not going far. The three of you can squeeze in.'

Kevin now switched his attentions to the driver. He chatted her up as the car jerked forward and roared up the hill to Greystones. Jim found himself curled into the back with Sally Ann. He couldn't believe his luck. Several times their thighs touched, causing him interesting sensations. He'd try inviting her for a drink when they stopped. Then who knows what might happen. Nora would never know. How could she?

She held onto her bandanna. 'It's windy.'

Jim put an arm around her. 'It's great!'

He could hear almost nothing of Kevin's conversation. Just as well. Jesus, this was the life! He'd never been in a sports car before. Fields flashed past. At the top of the hill, the driver ground the gears for the descent. He could see the harbour through a hedge. The sea was a blue band. Christ, he was happy, he never wanted to stop.

But they came to the Harbour Bar.

Kevin got out, turning to the driver. 'How about a drink?'

To Jim's amazement she agreed. She hopped out of the car with the litheness of a greyhound. Kevin ogled her clinging white jodhpurs. He was almost drooling.

Sally Ann climbed out, lingering hesitantly. Jim smiled at her. 'What about you, love?'

She shrugged. 'Why not!'

Jim swallowed. Jesus, he'd have to pay for her. Inside the pub, he said, 'Sit down there, love.'

Then the two men took orders. Miss Jodhpurs wanted a gin and tonic. Sally Ann ordered a glass of Smithwicks.

'Have a pint,' Jim urged.

She shook her head. 'A glass is fine.'

The two men gave the order at the bar, adding two pints of Guinness for themselves. When the barman turned his back, Kevin whispered to Jim. 'Let me handle this.' It was Kevin's boast that he never paid for a drink. As the barman served them, he said, 'Put that on the slate, pal. We'll be back for more.'

The women were chatting at the table. 'So you have your own horse,' Sally Ann was saying.

The glamorous one flicked back her hair. 'Yes. I stable it at a riding school – the Bel Air Hotel. It's in Ashford.'

Kevin sat beside her. 'Could we go there for a dirty weekend? Get that into you!' She giggled sexily and he sat with an arm poised on the back of the seat. They immediately started up a flirtatious, jokey conversation.

Jim took out his tobacco and rolled a cigarette. He offered it to Sally Ann. 'Smoke?'

'No thanks.'

Then he offered it to the other girl. She declined, waving her manicured hand.

'So you have an arts degree?' Jim said to Sally Ann. 'I always wanted to study that.'

'You still could.'

'I have commitments.' He couldn't tell her he was married. 'Old parents.'

'Oh! ... but people manage. The person whose grave I'm visiting was a telephone operator at night.'

'If he's dead, that isn't a recommendation!'

She sipped slowly. 'You could do a night degree.'

He changed the subject. 'Have you ever heard of Conrad?'

'Everyone's heard of Conrad.'

Jim swallowed. Not where he came from. Nora thought he was talking about some friend. 'He's my favourite writer.'

'I like *Youth*.'

He hadn't got around to that yet. '*The Nigger of Narcissus* is great. Or *Lord Jim*. I mean what a story!'

'Have you read "The Secret Sharer"?'

'I don't know that one.'

She laughed. 'You haven't read everything by your favourite author?'

Jim felt annoyed with himself. 'I have, mostly.'

'It's a novella, where he introduced the doppelgänger?'

'The what?'

'The doppelgänger! That's a double. The alter ego.'

Jim had never heard of the term.

'In literature, that means a double who experiences things for you. In the story the fugitive does the growing up for the young captain.'

Jim took a gulp of his drink. He'd never met anyone who could talk about Conrad.

'You've good taste. My father's a Conrad fan too,' the girl went on.

This cheered him up. 'Do you like Dennis Wheatley?'

'Who's he?'

'Ah, you must've heard of *The Prisoner in the Mask*. Or *The Second Seal*?'

She stared into her glass. 'He sounds like some low-brow bestseller type.'

Jim felt himself getting angry. What did she mean lowbrow? Only last week he'd found an article on Dennis Wheatley in the Dún Laoghaire library. As well as being a bestselling author, he was on Churchill's staff during the war. 'He's a great writer, renowned for historical accuracy. You've heard of *The Satanist*?'

She shook her head. 'Sorry.'

He tried again. 'Well, what about Captain Marryat?'

'A poor man's Conrad. But pretty good, I'll admit. I read him when I had the measles.'

Jim stared at her. A poor man's Conrad! Did she think he was poor or what? An inferior?

'Kafka's the greatest,' she said heedlessly.

Jim had never read him.

'Pre-existentialist.'

He knew this term, but he didn't want to make a fool of himself again. So he fell into a grumpy silence. At least Nora didn't think him an inferior. Sally Ann gave him an odd look. 'You know, "angst" and all that.'

He didn't answer.

'You should read the bug story "Metamorphosis".'

Sulkily Jim tuned in to Kevin's chat. He had all the luck. He always had all the luck.

'How about a drive down to Glendalough,' he was saying. 'A toss in St Kevin's Bed. Finish up with a nice meal in the Delgany Inn.'

Miss Jodpurs raised an eyebrow in amusement. Jim kept a straight face. Who was paying for that? It sounded much more interesting than the other one's blasted existentialism. Kevin was the man to pick them. He'd succeeded in getting his arm around the mot. It was a treat to see him in action. She was lapping it up, every so often letting out a peal of laughter, a rich musical laugh. But then he whispered something Jim couldn't hear. She shook the ice in her glass, suddenly downed her drink and got up. 'Sorry, must dash!'

Kevin was flummoxed. 'You're going?'

She looked at her watch. 'Have to. Sorry!'

'Ah, have another!'

'Sorry.' She flashed a diamond-ringed finger. 'I'm engaged.'

Kevin ran after her. 'I didn't know anyone did that anymore! Anyway, that's half the fun!'

But she wouldn't wait. Jim sipped his drink. Kevin had backed the wrong horse this time. It was consoling in a way that he didn't always win.

'I'd better be off too,' Sally Ann said.

'Ah, wait. Have another.'

Kevin came back, looking as if he was going to cry with disappointment and went straight to the gents. When he came out he looked sharply at Sally Ann. 'Will you have another, love?'

'She will!' Jim laid claim to her. 'We're going to a rugby match. Like to come?'

She shook her head. 'No, but it's really nice of you.'

What did she mean? It was really nice of him. Did she think she was too good for him?

The two men went again to the bar. 'I was hoping to stick Miss La-de-da for the drinks,' Kevin snarled.

'Well, you didn't succeed!' Jim whispered. 'And we can't do it to her.'

Kevin laughed. 'Why not?'

'It wouldn't be fair.'

'What's fair? You'll never get a ride out of her. She was comin' on the intellectual. No good in a woman!'

The word 'intellectual' mortified Jim. She had shown him up as an ignoramus.

'You know my motto,' Kevin taunted. 'Love them and leave them!'

Jim reached into his back pocket for his wallet. But it was gone. Where was it? Frantically he tried his other pockets. 'Jesus, I've lost my wallet!'

'You search the bar! I'll try and stop the car!' Kevin ran out the door.

Jim combed the area where they had been sitting. But it wasn't there either.

'Was there much in it?' Sally Ann was crawling around the floor.

'My dole money. I have a wife and child.'

'Gosh, I'm sorry.'

He ran through the bar out to the road. The sports car was nowhere in sight. Kevin stood on the other side of the road, looking into the distance. 'Did you see the number?' Jim called.

'No! But you might have dropped it on the road. Or in the lorry. Come on! Let's get away from here.'

Jim walked over. 'What about Sally?'

'What about her?'

'The drinks?'

'You know my motto.'

'But ...'

Kevin thumbed down a car. Jim hesitated, looking back to the bar where Sally Ann was standing in the doorway. He should go back, but hadn't she ridiculed him? Maybe Kevin was right and she needed a lesson. With that posh accent, she must have money. The car stopped and they got in. Jim sat in the back with his head in his hands. Jesus. Now what'd they do for the week's money? Nora would cry, and her mother would scream. He'd have to go to the pawn shop with his good suit. Then he might never be able to get it out. What if he was called for an interview?

The rugby club was outside the town. It consisted of a clubhouse and a field beside a road. Buses were parked nearby and a straggle of supporters lined the edge. The match was about to start, but Jim had no interest in it. He could only stare miserably in front of him. Nora always called the day before the dole her 'waiting day'. It was the day they had to go easy, sometimes eating nothing but porridge. Now she'd had two 'waiting days'.

'What'll Nora say?' he muttered miserably.

'Here,' Kevin took out his wallet. 'Take a tenner!'

'You can't spare it!'

'Take it, and stop worrying!'

After about ten minutes, Jim said, 'I'm off.'

'Don't be mad! You've come all this way.' Then Kevin let out a cheer as a goal was scored. 'Christ, did you see that!' The rest of the watchers roared in appreciation. Jim watched without enjoyment. A sense of dread sat on his stomach like lead. How would he face his mother-in-law with no money? He'd never live it down.

During halftime, people spilled carelessly out onto the road. There was a sudden screech of brakes. Then a thud and screams of alarm. People ran over to the scene of a crash, and Jim followed them. In trying to avoid one of the spectators, a motor bike had hit a wall. A crowd gathered around a young man who lay on his back with his eyes closed.

'He went right down on his head!' someone said. 'It's what comes of not wearing a helmet.'

Jim saw he was a boy of about sixteen. He had lank blond hair and a school scarf. Blood trickled from his mouth, but otherwise he looked as if he were sleeping. The bike was a tangled mess. A medical student came over and declared him dead. Nevertheless, someone covered him with a coat. It'd been so simple, a thud. He'd never even opened his eyes.

People stood about on the road, waiting for the ambulance. It came finally, and the body was loaded gently onto a stretcher. A garda car screamed up and took names and addresses. Jim avoided talking to them. He wasn't in the mood; anyway he hadn't seen anything. The match went on, as if nothing had happened. Jim stood there, watching it mechanically. He seemed to have lost all willpower. He felt stunned by the accident. 'He's dead meat,' was all Kevin could say.

Kevin wanted to go drinking afterwards, but Jim didn't stay. He started walking out of Greystones towards Dublin. After a while he got a lift, then another outside Bray. All the way home he felt terrible. It had been the worst day of his life. The poor fucker's death had depressed him terribly. In a way it made all his worries seem pointless: unemployment, losing the money, his mother-in-law. Christ, death was so near to everyone. Yet you never thought of it. What was that poem he'd read in the Protestant church? Last Sunday Nora and he'd been out walking the baby – walking was the only entertainment they could afford. They'd come across this church with the door open. Nora hadn't wanted to go in, thinking she'd be excommunicated or something stupid like that. But he'd persuaded her it was ok. All that was changed now. There was a new spirit of ecumenism in the air and you weren't damned forever. Still, she'd been reluctant. Inside it was sort of musty and full of memorials to the dead of both wars. Then they'd come across a plaque on the wall.

> Remember me, as you pass by
> As you are now, so once was I
> As I am now, so shalt thou be
> Remember man, eternity.

Normally he hated poetry. He couldn't see anything in it. But that was the most touching thing he'd ever read. He'd learnt it by heart and copied it into his notebook as soon as he got home. He kept a notebook for interesting passages from books. Who could have written it on that plaque? Some poor fucker from another age. Yet he'd felt connected to this person. 'Remember me ...'

You forgot, that was the trouble. You forgot and most of the time acted like a shit. It was shitty to leave that girl to pay for their drinks. He should have gone back, said he'd lost his wallet, offered to wash the dishes or something. And it was shitty bullying Nora about sex, being jealous of a tiny baby. Nora and the baby were the only things that mattered. What if you died before you realised something like that? Like that poor motorcyclist.

The two women waited in the speckless kitchen. Jim knew they'd been fighting. Nora eyed him mutely. Her hair was newly washed, her eyes red from crying.

'You took your time!' the older one snapped, her hair still in curlers. 'Where's my gas money?'

Jim put his tenner on the table. 'That's all I have.'

She looked triumphant. 'If ye've been drinkin' ...'

'I haven't. I lost it.'

She started to dance with rage. 'Yer a liar! A liar! He's been drinkin' Nora!'

Jim looked at his wife. 'Can I've something to eat?'

Nora went nervously to the fridge and took out rashers and eggs.

'Don't you dare cook them!'

She took the frying pan from the rack and put it on the stove.

'Well! You connivin' bitch! Put them back!'

Nora ignored her, putting rashers on the pan.

'Put them back!' Her mother's face turned an ugly red as she struggled to control herself. 'I paid for that food! Yer not givin' him my eggs!' When she got no reaction, she grabbed the box of eggs and threw them on the ground, then slammed out of the room.

They looked at each other, then at the oozing egg carton. 'Good riddance!' Nora snapped tearfully.

Jim took her in his arms, burying his face in her hair. He loved the smell of shampoo. 'I'm sorry!'

'I was so worried.'

'I know ... How's the baby?'

V

Doc

People always think doctors make wonderful parents, so I don't disillusion them. It's their aura, or their place in society and all that rubbish. Anyway, it isn't true. Our father, for one, feels a complete flop – not that he is entirely. He puts this down to his vast age of sixty-something and the generation gap. But the reasons are otherwise: mainly his refusal to talk to my brother and me.

He talked *at* us ok, but not *to* us.

There's a difference, I usually tell people. And while he always ignored our physical health to the point of death, he blindly dosed us with culture – novels, poetry, music, paintings *et al*. As children he even made us learn a poem a week which we had to recite on a Sunday evening in the drawing room. It was absolutely Victorian. Unfortunately nothing took. Not permanently. I could hold my own in any conversation about books, and I liked Simone de Beauvoir and Virginia Woolf. But I now considered literature obsolete compared to film and was lately only interested in modern art, while my younger brother Tim is obsessed with cartoons and pop music. In both cases it's the natural result of force feeding.

But my father doesn't see it like that. He complains nonstop about his loutish children, warning all who will listen about the evils of a late marriage. He was forty four when he married my much younger mother. And they had ten delirious years until one Christmas Eve long ago she died from cancer. It left a terrible gap. I mean, it was all wrong. My father had expected to die first. But for her sake he tried to make us happy. And we tried to be happy. And basically we were, considering. But despite your man Tolstoy's generalisations about all happy families being the same, we were unhappy in our own peculiar way.

Christmas was our time of trial. I always ended up not talking to Tim, and my father wanted to murder us both – more than usual. He always said that two weeks of dressing gowns, Christmas trees and chocolates got on his nerves. But although he never mentioned her, the real reason was my mother. Take last year. One morning in the aftermath of the festivities, my father arose from the breakfast table, glaring at my brother. 'The windows are filthy!'

Tim was still in pyjamas, harmlessly chewing muesli. Although only seventeen, he was taller than a man, with long black hair like a Rolling Stone, and as usual insulated by a Walkman. The Hoover was at his feet – this was his dog. We called him that because he ate everything in sight: curtains, cushions, shoes, even golf balls and calculators. Once he had irritated the neighbours so much he'd been put on tranquillisers. They say dogs reflect the psyches of their owners. Ours was quite mad, but Tim loved him.

'An absolute disgrace!' snapped my father.

This brought a puzzled growl from the Hoover. He was a golden labrador with worried brown eyes and now rested with his head on his paws. I was in my dressing gown and deep in *The Irish Times*. I looked up, resenting this dawn raid on my sleepiness. It was hard enough to be cheerful in the morning. My father rubbed the window pane with his hanky. He was dark too with a look of the greying Robert Donat. And, as usual, he was fully dressed in his one three-piece striped suit and puffing angrily on his pipe – it's odd to see a doctor smoking, I know, a sort of paradox. Breakfast was a meal he always insisted on, which meant I had to get up to cook a big, greasy fryup – another oddity for a doctor. But, like all men, my father's peculiar about his stomach.

'Filthy!' he fumed.

He's peculiar about a lot of things. Normally he keeps to his study reading, but, as I mentioned, Christmas, the season of goodwill, brings out his maniac streak. It was then that he always fussed about crazy things like cleaning the insides of presses. So I thought that this was just his yearly tantrum.

He waved the hanky at Tim, who was still oblivious to all sound. 'Well? ... Well, young man?'

This brought more growls from the dog.

'He can't hear you,' I suggested tactfully.

My father coughed on some smoke. 'He'd better!'

I nudged Tim, who removed his earplugs. The Hoover's ears cocked too, ready to spring to his defence.

My father waved the hanky. 'Look at this dirt!'

'Hmm ... Probably tobacco smoke,' Tim muttered in his gravelly voice. Then he replaced his earplugs. The dog settled back to snooze, but Tim had incensed my father, as did any reference to the evils of tobacco. He had taken up battle position with his back to the stove and was angrily emitting large mushrooms. 'Take those mufflers out of your ears!'

This made the dog growl more, so I nudged Tim again to take out the plugs. He obeyed, giving me a look which meant the old man had finally 'flipped' – gone senile, which was his greatest fear for my father. My brother spoke a sort of lingua franca: things are cool, brill, brillo, neat, ok, a-ok, ace, wow, or fab.

My father pointed his pipe stem at him. 'I'm addressing you, sir!' The Hoover was now all ears.

Tim shovelled in more muesli. 'Me?'

'Don't speak with your mouth full!'

Tim chewed on.

'Well?' ranted my father. 'Well.'

The Hoover echoed him with barks.

'Well, what?'

Another yelp, as the Hoover got more excited. My father was now breathing heavily. 'Enough of that puppery!'

Tim was an angry red now, but he reassured the Hoover, grabbing him by his collar. 'It's ok! Quiet now! Look, what's up Doc?' He always called our father this.

'The windows are filthy!'

'So what if they're filthy?'

'So when are you going to clean them?' My father's voice was low and menacing.

Tim shrugged. 'I had plans for the day, but I can scrap them.'

'Good! Clean the bedroom windows too! Get the ladder out.'

'Dad, we could hire a window cleaner,' I suggested.

Then my father turned on me. 'You're willing to pay for one?'

I went back to my paper. 'He might fall off a ladder.'

My father's eyes narrowed into angry slits. 'Stop interfering, Sally Ann!'

'I wasn't!'

'Don't answer back!'

This renewed shouting brought more dog growls. I was sick of being treated like some sort of kid. 'I have a right to speak.'

'Go to your room!'

I looked at the ceiling. Tim calmed his dog.

'Go to your room!' screamed my father.

When I ignored him, he stepped towards me. At this my brother jumped up, towering threateningly over my father. For a second they were eyeball to eyeball. Then my aged parent raised his hand. I jumped between them, receiving the blow intended for my brother. The dog started his din again.

Clenching his fists, Tim started shadowboxing. 'Step right up and fall right down!' This was a saying of Poopdeck Pappy, the Pride of the Pacific – Popeye's father. I pushed him away. 'I can take him, Sally! Step right up and fall ...!'

'Go away!' I shouted.

'Say the word, Sal!' The dog yapped on hysterically.

'Just go!'

'Ok.'

'And take the Hoover!'

'Ok! Ok!' He grabbed the barking dog, dragging it from the room. 'Cool it, Doc. Ok?'

At least it was quieter, but my father's breathing sounded dangerous. 'The pup! ... the pup!'

I was in tears. 'Dad, he's not a pup.'

'No! He's a cur!'

'I'll clean the windows. Tim wouldn't be safe on a ladder. Remember the time he fixed the tap?'

'A lazy cur.'

'The house took weeks to dry out. I've to go to work now, but I'll do the kitchen windows this evening. We'll get someone for upstairs.'

My father said nothing. He sat down and moodily tried to get his pipe going, so I went to get dressed for work. I was on the dole, but had a part-time job in an art gallery.

'Come back!'

'I'll be late for work.'

He laughed shortly. 'You wouldn't know the meaning of the word! Neither of you would!'

I kept cool. 'That's hardly fair.'

'You're the most highly-qualified waitress in Dublin.'

'I'm a gallery assistant now.'

'You're no better than a servant. Why can't you use your degree? I've brought up a couple of layabouts! Freaks!'

'Freaks?'

'Look at your brother's hair.'

I sighed inwardly.

'I've made an appointment with his Dean of Studies. He can make him cut it! Or he's going back to Rockwell.' This was a religious jail my brother had run away from. He was now a day boy in Blackrock.

'Dad, Tim's ok.'

He pointed his pipe stem at me. 'That dog's going ... Is he on drugs?' My father perused my face.

'No!'

'What does he do in his room all day?'

'He draws cartoons.'

My father laughed. 'He's insane! It's both inherited and induced. You realise your great uncle died in an asylum?' This was our father's comment on any aberrant behaviour. He seemed to expect us both to explode with madness.

'Dad, Tim's very talented.'

He bit his pipe stem. 'Hmm, cartoons will take you a long way!'

'He could be a millionaire ...'

'Good! Then it won't be my task to feed him.'

'You shouldn't hit him.'

'I should've done it years ago!'

'Well, it's too late now.'

Of course, it was ok to hit a woman. But without a word of apology, my usually mild-mannered father pocketed his pipe and slammed out of the kitchen to the surgery at the front of our large and shabby house. I thought once Christmas was over he'd lapse back into his usual indifference. The windows were forgotten about, but now he quarrelled at the least opportunity. He gave away my brand new guitar for a jumble sale, saying he thought it was junk. He nagged Tim nonstop and kept threatening to have the Hoover put down. He even put an ad in the paper offering to give him away. Some people came, but luckily the dog got hysterics and they fled in horror. It was crazy – having ignored us all his life, our father was coming the heavy.

I'd always been a referee between Tim and him. I felt responsible for my brother, because I had almost brought him up. In school, when he was little, I'd always be sent for, to help him find his football boots. He could never find anything. But the other boys would be coming back in by the time he was ready. Maybe I was too impatient. Once I hit him – it was something I've always regretted. If he had problems it was probably my fault. He did spend all his time in his room now, but who would blame him for wanting to avoid my father? Luckily he had school to save him. And my gallery job had come in time for our father's personality change. But I was driven crazy with his nagging, about me being 'little better than a servant' when he'd paid out 'good money' for a degree. Blah, blah, blah.

Since college, I'd worked in a succession of restaurants. For heaven's sake, there were no jobs. And my father had all these middle-class notions about his daughter 'serving' people. But didn't a doctor serve people too? Look down throats, into ears, or worse. To avoid rows, I refrained from pointing this out. But there was no pleasing him. I had become his butt. He had the decency not to mention my criminal record for being caught in Colm's house. I have to admit he was good about that, bailing me out with the line he'd quoted to me in all the griefs of childhood, 'I am Duchess of Malfi still'. Then he'd insisted I stay in college. But now, for no reason, I was a bad example to my brother. Did he deserve a child like me? Hadn't he worked like a slave to bring us up alone? Was his surgery ever empty?

True, even if he forgot to send out bills, my father worked hard. He was known all over Dublin as a soft touch. Every malingerer in search of a cert ended up in our waiting room. He did house calls every morning and often on Saturday and Sunday. He got up at night for people. In his spare time he'd even written a history of Dún Laoghaire. So we were probably a great disappointment to him. But neither of us were scientific: Tim was an artist who wouldn't get into medicine, and I'd faint at the sight of blood.

My father's latest kick was nursing. We were both to train for free in one of the big English hospitals. Then we'd be able to get pensionable jobs, and, unlike him, be able to retire. I was to pave the way for Tim, who could follow after his Leaving and be a psychiatric nurse. Maybe some day he could manage a hospital for the disturbed. It was daft, considering I was a terrible hypochondriac. I'd only to talk to a patient on the phone, or read one of the medical journals which avalanched through the letter box to imagine symptoms. Last year alone I'd had rheumatoid arthritis, mitral valve prolapse, cancer of the shin bone and the latest – gum cancer. I got a gum boil at which the dentist had shaken his head; he wouldn't give me a diagnosis. When I'd asked my father if it was cancer, he'd yelled, reminding me of our mad great uncle. That's another oddity about doctors: they're kind to the whole world, but impatient with their own. When I said that now they were discovering many illnesses were psychological, he had retorted, 'They've always known that! Physician means healer of the soul.' He told me then that many of his patients had nothing wrong with them, that time cured most things. I couldn't agree with this. I mean, he was a case in point.

So the fear about my gum took root. On top of this, things were going badly with my job. It was only temporary, a fill-in for my American friend, Kathy, who had gone home for six months. But it got me out of the house and I was earning twenty pounds a week on top of the dole. I'd never been richer in my life. Although the gallery owner, Kingsley Kelly, was difficult, and had reluctantly agreed to me, it was great to be working. I took the bus from Dún Laoghaire and walked up O'Connell Street to the gallery in North Great George's Street. It occupied the ground floor of one of the big Georgian houses in that seedy street. The high ceilings and tall windows were wonderful for light, and there were dividing doors between the huge front rooms. Belvedere College was at the top of the street, which had a faded charm, an old world elegance that was part of our history. Mahaffy, the famous Trinity College preservationist, had once lived there, as had John Dillon, the patriot and friend of Parnell. The street had now fallen on hard times, but there was a fight by the Georgian Society to save it, in which my employer Kingsley Kelly was involved. He had completely done up his house, treating it for damp and all.

Kingsley was an Irish art critic who had been to school in England. He was theatrical with a pale floppy face and mournful, doggy, blue eyes. He was also puffy and bald with two wings of greying hair. His girlfriend, Anabel, who lived with him in the upstairs flat, was darkly glamorous and complemented Kingsley's velvet evening jackets, the gallery's thick pile carpets and hushed air of money. Their aim was to make Dublin, through the gallery, the mecca of the western avant-garde art world and a rival to Edinburgh. (We'd even shown a woman who painted in menstrual blood). My job was generally to assist: make coffee, vacuum, send out invitations, and, in between, sit there looking interested.

One morning soon after the row with my father, I was late. I think I missed a bus or something, but, as it was a first, I didn't worry, but said good morning cheerfully. Kingsley had opened up the gallery himself and was frowning at the bundle of half-done invitations on my desk. He was in day wear, a striped grandfather shirt and white button-on collar and tie. He didn't return my greeting.

I sat down. 'Sorry I'm late.'

He still frowned, wrinkling his bald patch. He held up one invitation, raising his eyebrows at me. 'Could you possibly write more legibly, Sally Ann?'

I felt awful. 'Eh – yes. Can't you read it?'

He pursed his lips. 'It's legible all right. But it doesn't have any tone.'

'Tone?'

He looked mournful. 'Kathy had a beautiful Italic script.'

I was completely thrown. 'She had a special italic pen – an Osmiroid. I could get one in Easons.'

He flung down the invitation. 'Do that! And address the envelopes again. Remember, these are very important people. Very important people.'

'Will I get the pen now?'

He glided to the door. 'Yes! Take it out of petty cash.' Then he paused, turning to stare at my legs. 'And Sally Ann ...'

'Yes?' I was walking towards him.

'Could you wear something longer?'

I looked down. 'I – I have a midi skirt.'

He raised his eyebrows again. 'That sounds lovely. Remember, the gallery has a tone.'

I hid my embarrassment as he forced a smile. 'Do you need anything else?'

He shook his head and I escaped to O'Connell Street for the pen. I was fed up: at twenty three I felt about ten. I'd thought my green suede mini, black top and tights were 'it'. God, it was the mid 1970s. His girlfriend Anabel wore short skirts, so why did he pick on me? When my friend Kathy had worked in the gallery, she always wore denim jeans and a man's tweed jacket. Where was the 'tone' in that?

I did the invitations again. Later I studied the VIP list, which included a number of politicians and business people. I suppose they were important, and we had to make an impression, but it was extra work. The opening was in three weeks, so they had to be sent out quickly – that night, in fact. The gallery had recently had a coup: Jan Wessell, the internationally famous Dutch conceptual artist, had agreed to a show.

His weren't the usual statues, but post object – it was the idea more than anything. Jan Wessell had made his reputation in New York by exhibiting a battered old van with a wild dog inside, to represent the two poles of civilisation. Another time he'd lain in a coffin with candles around him. I suppose this was to make people think of death, but I was glad we weren't doing anything like that. Our exhibition was to be inanimate – a collection of stones which the artist had gathered around Wicklow. The man was a genius. He had suffered appallingly in the war from the Germans, and recently he'd come to live here to avail of Haughey's tax deal for artists. The show would be great for the gallery, and the artist himself was to open it.

The preparations were endless: wine, food, more invitations for the press, radio and TV, but the day came at last. I wore a new blouse with my midi. I invited my father –

so he'd see I wasn't a servant and to impress him with my job. He accepted, hiring a locum and buying a new white shirt and striped tie. He arrived early, so I hung up his worn camel overcoat, got him a glass of wine from the flitting waiter, then showed him into the gallery.

He looked at the bare walls, and at a line of stones down the centre of the room. 'I thought it was a sculpture exhibition, Sally Ann.'

'It is,' I whispered.

'But they're stones!' he shouted.

I nudged him. 'Shh!'

He sipped his drink. 'Why didn't you tell me? I could've brought some.'

'It wouldn't be the same.'

He sipped more wine. 'Why not?'

'They wouldn't be Wessell's concept.'

'No, they'd be stones.'

'Please, Dad!'

He smiled, the first time since Christmas. 'I promise not to say another word.' He drifted off into the crowd, stopping at another pile.

I went to the door to give out programmes, as the gallery was filling up. The VIPs were a motley crew. Despite Kingsley's decorum about clothes, only one or two were in evening dress, the rest wore jeans and ordinary clothes. All made a dive for the drinks table at one end of the gallery. Jan Wessell came in with a harem of women. He was a bronzed, weasely man dressed in artistic denim jeans and bomber jacket over a white Aran sweater. He also wore an Aran tam o'shanter – he had a thing about oiled wool – and instead of a scarf, he wore a snake. I had heard he did this, but didn't expect it now. I recoiled in horror, and it brought a gasp from the crowd. People backed away from him, as Kingsley and Anabel hurried over. He wore his black velvet jacket and red cummerbund, while she looked ravishing in strapless black.

She blinked her furry lashes. 'Sally Ann, take Mr Wessell's things?' She had a shrill English accent.

'His things?'

Kingsley whispered, 'Offer to take the – eh – snake, Sally Ann.'

Then Jan Wessell unwrapped his scarf. I gaped at the slimy thing, its tongue darting viciously, but luckily he rescued me. 'A chair, my cheeld. A chair vor Cocoa.'

'A chair? Of course!' I got one from behind my desk.

'Ye can leave it dere. Goot!' The snake poured itself revoltingly into the chair and he patted it. 'Cocoa, stay dere!'

'What an original statement a snake makes,' Anabel fawned over the famous artist.

'Ah, no. Cocoa ees chusst a pet,' Jan Wessell smiled benignly.

'Wine for Mr Wessell!' Kingsley snapped at me.

'Red or white?' I asked.

He wanted red, and I got a glass from the waiter. Then, as Kingsley and Anabel chatted him up, I went to see if my father was all right for wine.

'I'll coast on my pipe, my dear.' He looked in the direction of Jan Wessell, chuckling. 'Is that your famous artist?'

I shuddered. 'Did you see the snake?'

This transported my father into more chuckles, and, at that moment I had one of those epiphanies Joyce was always writing about. I realised my father was giddy with happiness because I'd asked him here. Had Tim and I both shut him out, thinking he wouldn't be interested in our lives? If he didn't talk to us, we didn't talk to him. A relationship takes two, but how do you change things?

Kingsley glided over and I introduced them. 'Ah, good evening Dr Fitzpatrick. I'm delighted you could come.' Then turning to me, 'Jan requested a blackboard. Where is it?'

It was the first I'd heard. I had been asked to set out rows of chairs in front of a podium because the artist was to give a talk.

'Why didn't you get it?'

'Oh – sorry!'

Kingsley had an angry red blotch on his pale cheeks. 'I pay you to see to these things!'

'You can't trust *stawff*!' Anabel shrieked. 'How many times have I told you?'

I looked at her nervously. Jan Wessell had never requested a blackboard, and I don't know why I didn't say it. Instead, I stood there, apologising. Then I hit on a brilliant idea. 'I can borrow one.'

Kingsley raised his eyebrows. 'At this time of night?'

'There's a school next door.'

'Well, try them!' And he stalked off to greet the head of the Arts Council.

A flustered young nun opened the huge convent door. She agreed to lend us a blackboard so long as I guaranteed to have it back before the morning. Together we went down to the basement for it. Then, as it had an easel, she helped me carry it out to the street and next door to our gallery, where I set it up at one end of the double room in front of the chairs on which people were already sitting. I asked the nun to stay for a glass of wine, but she wouldn't.

Then Kingsley gave a short introduction and Jan Wessell began his lecture.

He looked even smaller now, swamped by his Aran sweater and still wearing his tam. 'People always ax mee to expleen my work. Yell, in dis exheebition of de stones, I breeng de nature into de gallery. Und by breenging nature into de gallery, to breeng it to you. De nature dat ees all around you in dees country ees var more beauteous dan anyting you veel ever see in de gallery. Und so, de nature ov my work ees vot I call de social sculpture.'

My father, standing with me at the back of the crowd, gave me a knowing look. But everyone else listened politely as the artist took a piece of chalk and turned to the blackboard. He drew two circles, one large and one small. 'Now in dis small circle we 'ave de eenspiration.' He drew arrows to the large circle. 'Und in dis beeg circle we 'ave de people.' Then he drew another arrow from the people circle to the inspiration circle. 'Art ees de flow from one to de oder.' Then he drew a lot of wavy lines between the two arrows. 'See de flow from one to de oder. Und so, vat am I saying?' He looked expectantly at the crowd. 'Vat am I saying here?'

No one said anything. 'Pleese, vat am I saying?'

I looked at my father. He clenched his pipe between his teeth, staring in the direction of the empty chair. The snake was slithering across the floor. 'God,' I muttered, frozen. My father pursed his lips in amusement. Kingsley, from across the room, looked at Jan Wessell with a kind of rapture. No one else had noticed.

'Vat am I saying here now?' Jan Wessell tried to get a reaction from his audience, but no one spoke.

Then Kingsley raised his hand. 'You're suggesting that art is a democratic activity.'

'Anyone can become an artist?' Anabel added.

'Ah yes!' Jan Wessell's face lit up, and he held up his arms like the Pope. 'Dat ees it! You are all de arteests! An arteest cannot hog de inspiration, zo do zay.'

The snake had now disappeared under the chairs. I signalled desperately to Kingsley, but he was still gazing adoringly at Jan Wessell. Then a woman screamed. There was a mad rush and scraping of chairs. I just stood there.

Kingsley ran over to me. 'What is it?'

'The snake's escaped!'

He put his hands to his head in desperation. 'Well, do something!'

I looked under the chairs.

Then Jan Wessell's voice came over the crowd. 'Now vat ees all dis fuss? Pleese keep de seats. Cocoa veel harm no one.'

By now everyone was in the front room and the snake had coiled calmly in one of the vacated chairs. 'Do something, Sally Ann!' Kingsley hissed.

'Eh – Mr Wessell,' I shouted over, 'Can we put Cocoa in the loo?'

He came to my rescue. 'Cocoa in de loo? Vat are you saying? Cocoa veel be vith mee.' And he came over, picked up the wriggling monster and threw it around his neck. 'Eet's all right now. Gome back, now! Gome back!' He made signals like a traffic guard and the people dribbled back onto the rows of chairs.

He finished his lecture. Afterwards Kingsley tried to get the audience to ask questions, but they were too thoroughly dampened by the sight of the snake – although the party livened up when drink was served again. It was meant to be over by seven, but at eight was still in full swing. Finally Kingsley ordered the waiters to collect the glasses and serve no more drink. This worked, and people began to go in dribs and drabs. Then, as arranged, Kingsley and Anabel took Jan Wessell and his party to dinner at the Lord Edward, leaving me to tidy up.

'See, you're a servant!' my father grumped. He had put on his coat and scarf and was helping me gather the remaining glasses and ash trays. In his worn camel coat, he looked like a giant teddy bear. 'And as for that snake charmer!'

I tipped ashtrays into a black plastic bag. 'Dad, he's world famous!'

'Who says so? Here, let me help.' And he held open the bag. 'Just tell me who says he's an artist?'

'Qualified people.'

'Kingsley Kelly, I suppose?' My father laughed shortly. 'He's really qualified.'

'He's a Renaissance man. An art critic for the Sunday papers.'

'He's a charlatan. Everyone's an artist, what rubbish! It's typical of your generation to expect fame without work.'

'Dad, please!'

'Why didn't he bring you to dinner?'

'I'm ...'

'A servant!'

'An employee! You don't have to bring your employees to dinner.' I was now running the carpet sweeper over the thick carpets, and getting more irritated with my father. What had persuaded me to invite him here when he never did anything but grumble?

He waited for me in the hall. 'I'll take you to dinner.'

'It's not necessary.'

'Get your coat! We'll go to the Lord Edward.'

He stood there, smiling at his brilliant idea, and my irritation went. He was right about the way Kingsley treated me, but I wouldn't admit it. 'Well, ok ... but we're not going there.'

'Do as you're told!'

'Somewhere else, Dad!'

He thought for a minute. 'The Gresham then!'

'I have to give back the blackboard.'

I rubbed off Jan Wessell's scribbles, ignoring my father's accompanying mutterings of 'Nonsense ... Utter nonsense.'

Then we hauled it together next door where the same young nun allowed us to leave it in the hall. The pupils would bring it back to the classroom in the morning.

Then we walked down to the Gresham, where we got a table without any trouble. My father has a great sense of occasion. I suppose it's his aura, or something to do with being a doctor, but waiters always flock to him. He would've made a good courtier in olden times, because he was so deferential to women. He even held my chair. As we studied the menu, I watched him across the table. He'd had his only suit pressed and with the new shirt and tie looked distinguished. Why hadn't he ever married again? Surely Dublin was full of single women and widows. Life must've been lonely for him, especially as he had no relationship with us. Why was that? He had no trouble talking to the rest of the world.

He put down his menu. 'What're you having?'

I studied the pastas. 'Spaghetti.'

'Have a steak or something.' He looked at me over his reading glasses. 'The food here used to be good.'

'I like pasta.' I never knew what to have, so always had the cheapest.

He was looking sadly around the room. 'Things never stay the same.'

'Did you come here with Mum?' I blurted, breaking all our family's unwritten code of not talking about my mother.

He dived back into the menu. 'Have the roast beef.' This was typical of him.

'I'd prefer the spaghetti, Dad, with a salad to start.'

'All right ...' He examined the wine menu. 'I think ... a Beaujolais.'

The waiter took our order, and we sat in our usual Trappist silence. As I studied the only other couple in the room, my father took out his pipe and filled it. 'Mind if I smoke, my dear?'

'Course not.'

'You know your brother.'

I smiled. 'He's not here.'

'By the way, I'm sorry about your guitar, my dear.'

I'd never known him to apologise. 'You didn't know.'

'I should've asked.'

'It wasn't your fault ... The teacher gave up on me. I'm not very musical.'

He put his pipe on the table and rummaged in his pocket. Then he took out a small package, handing it to me. 'I nearly forgot. For you, my dear.'

I peered at it. 'What is it?'

'A small act of reparation.'

What was he talking about?

'Open it, my dear.'

It was a gold watch.

'Weir's will change it if ...'

'Gosh, it's gorgeous! I wouldn't change it! Thanks, Dad.' I looked at him, puzzled.

'I'm sorry for that blow, my dear.'

I giggled – I do this in all life's serious moments. 'You shouldn't have.'

'I certainly should! It was the act of a cad.'

I put on the watch. It had Roman numerals and a brown crocodile strap. He must have paid a fortune for it. 'It's beautiful.'

The waiter came with the wine. My father tasted it, nodding approval. 'Nice and dry.'

The waiter poured mine. 'It is dry,' I agreed, sipping some. All wine tasted more or less the same to me. I didn't care, so long as it was alcoholic.

My father lit his pipe. When he'd got it going, he looked slowly around the room again. 'They've changed this place. There used to be a piano over there ... You asked about your mother. I did bring her here.' He looked right at me. 'We came here the night of our engagement.'

Now it was my turn to be speechless, as my father went on in a low deadpan voice. 'We met in December and got married in January. Your mother kept on her teaching at first ... but then she got pregnant with you. You were born the next winter. We didn't go out much after that – except for a Sunday walk. I used to carry you on my back. Once I carried you to the top of the Sugar Loaf.'

'I remember.'

'You couldn't.'

He smiled maddeningly. 'They were ... happy years. But I was too old to marry.'

'Dad, that's ridiculous!'

He knocked out his pipe. 'Your brother was right to call me a randy old goat.'

I sighed. 'That's because you gave him condoms.'

It was my father's greatest fear that one of us would make him a grandfather. So, although a faithful Catholic, to prevent that dread event he'd taken to supplying us both with contraceptives: condoms for Tim and spermicidal jelly for me. At one stage he even suggested Tim have a vasectomy. It was mad. Tim had no girlfriend, as far as I knew, and I could hardly drown with no water. I had read that frigidity comes from an unresolved relationship with your father, but I didn't know how to overcome this.

'I shouldn't have married,' my father went on, brooding. 'Look at you.'

'What's wrong with me?'

He sighed. 'I wanted this to be a pleasant evening, Sally Ann.'

For courage, I downed my wine. 'Tell me what's wrong with me.'

He fell into silence, then said sadly. 'You were so clever as a young child.'

I didn't answer. I knew what was coming: how I'd failed him by being on the dole, by not being a doctor. The waiter brought my salad and my father's soup. 'You wanted one of us to do medicine.'

He tucked his napkin into the top of his waistcoat. 'No, it's not that. I realise that medicine's not your bent. You're just too good for that ruffian, Kingsley Kelly and his ridiculous gallery.'

'It's a start.'

'To what?'

'To a career in the arts.'

'Hmm ... well, I always liked your paintings.'

I looked at him. Why had he never said?

'I hoped you might do something in that line.' He sighed heavily. 'It's different for Tim.'

'Why?'

'A woman will only have to support herself.'

'But Tim's ok.'

My father shook his head. 'I can see the writing on the wall.'

'What writing?'

'It'll be my task to feed his family in my dotage.'

I said nothing. There was no point in arguing. Or reminding my father that Tim didn't seem interested in girls. Never mind marrying.

'I blame myself entirely,' he went on.

'For what?'

'For my children.'

I sighed. 'Dad, you're not Jesus Christ.'

'Don't blaspheme!'

'Sorry. I only meant you're not responsible for the sins of the world. Tim, me, my guitar yes, but that was a mistake.'

He looked somewhat appeased, but between courses we lapsed into another silence. I desperately wanted him to talk more about my mother. So I sat there, gauging the right moment to ask again about her. You had to pick your moment with my father. When we had started our main course, I tried again. 'It must've been awful for you ... when Mum died?'

He gave me his panic-stricken look and finished chewing some food. 'It was a great loss to me.'

'Me, too.'

'I know, my dear.'

'I suppose boarding school was ...'

'It was the best solution at the time.' He put down his knife and fork and looked worriedly at me. 'I thought you should be with women. Was it that bad?'

I shrugged. 'You did your best.'

Talk of the past was upsetting him, so I changed the subject. But the rarity of any communication with him put me into a high gear and I couldn't sleep that night. I tossed and turned, thinking of my mother's death. How could such a young woman die? Actually school was fine. I was sent to a convent which took junior boys and Tim joined me after a year. My big hangup is I forgot my mother so easily. It hurt me that I had so few memories of her. One was of me being in bed and waiting for her to come back from town in time to say goodnight. I didn't think she'd come, then she did. 'I'm so glad you were awake and we could chat,' she had said. Then once I made her cry. God. I did something and she corrected me, so I kicked her. It haunted me to have made her cry. Then I remember feeling odd at her funeral, sort of dislocated. I seemed to be watching myself. I wondered how the people there could smile when I had lost my best friend. Of course, I was eight years old and didn't understand they were greeting their friends outside the church. And it's normal to smile then, and they weren't laughing.

Overnight everything changed and I knew nothing would be the same again. My father became a recluse. At boarding school no one deferred to me – as the elder at home I'd always considered myself grown up, but the nuns and senior girls seemed huge. Even my father, though tall, was diminished by the vast high-ceilinged convent parlour. At first I looked forward to his Sunday visits. But when he came he never hugged me. He sat on one of the hard chairs, telling me how much the school was costing. Then he'd quiz me about what I'd learnt that week. I'd have to recite 'Frere Jacques' or 'How they Brought the Good News from Aix to Ghent' – wherever the hell that is. Then I'd recite my tables, and he'd spend the rest of the visit firing questions at me: 'Twelve twelves? ... Nine nines?'

It was crazy. I remember thinking my father was so old. Why hadn't he died? And why wouldn't he go home, so I could get back to my friends. Having no mother was a sort of status symbol among them. I was different. I didn't want their pity, but I liked being different. Although I had no best friend there were interesting things to do in school, even new words to learn – words like refectory, dormitory, recreation, infirmary.

Why didn't I have more memories of my mother? Mostly I remembered her being sick and having to tiptoe past her room. A woman at a co-counselling session in someone's house told me it was probably still stuck in my subconscious. That when I was eight I blocked the emotion, which must be true because I began sleepwalking in school. And wetting my pants, which caused me terrible embarrassment. One nun was kind about it, but another was a sadist. I'd get strange fainting illnesses and spend weeks alone in the infirmary doing jigsaws. For my first year I was the good child, but then I made friends with a new girl, Brigid Dalton. We'd sit writing letters to each other at recreation. Once I wrote a pretend letter to her parents, forging the Reverend Mother's name. A novice confiscated it, and I was in disgrace. I didn't understand what I'd done wrong. The incident made me close up I'm sure. It set me on the downward path. From then on I started getting into trouble and was eventually expelled. I begged to go to a day school, but my father immediately sent me to another boarding school.

In my second last year there, Mother Rita came back from America. I'm always talking about her, but she saved me. She talked to me. She told me her mother had died too, and she understood. I started improving. I got my Leaving, and then went to college to study history, which was my way of trying to reclaim the past. But you couldn't change anything. My mother was part of history now, and I could hardly remember her face. That night I fingered her wedding ring which my father had given me and I always wore, realising that he was right in his stoical pride. It was awful for him and awful for my mother, having to leave us, but stoicism was all we had.

When I came in the next morning, Kingsley had already opened up. 'Where's the blackboard, Sally Ann?' he snapped.

I took off my coat. 'I brought it back.'

'You *what*?'

'I rubbed it off and brought it back.'

He sat down putting his head in his hands. 'Oh, my God!'

'What's wrong?'

His eyes were dead, and he spoke in a mechanical voice. 'Put your coat back on. You're fired!'

I obeyed, terrified. He stalked to the hall door and pulled it open. 'Never come back to the gallery!'

'Would you not tell me what I've done?' I asked on the outside steps.

'You've destroyed a work of art!'

'The scribbling was valuable?'

He nodded, speechless.

'The blackboard belonged to the nuns!' I argued. 'I had to bring it back.'

He slammed the door in my face and I went home in tears. How could I have done it? Of course, my father laughed to scorn the idea of the blackboard being art, but I knew otherwise. I even thought of writing to Jan Wessell and begging him to scribble on another blackboard. But I didn't know his address and was too depressed to even try. Now I was back answering my father's phone, and listening to his patients' symptoms. So my own returned. The lump in my gum had spread to my neck, and I was sure it was Hodgkins' Disease. But, as always, my father dismissed me with a callous joke about being dead in six months, and a reminder of our mad great uncle.

His humour didn't help. It depressed me more and more, plunging me into the certain knowledge of death. Once, over lunch in Mooney's of Abbey Street, I confided my fears to my friend Denis. He was Adonis-like in his blond good looks, but married so we were platonic friends.

He peered at my neck, feeling it. 'It's there all right. What does your old man say?'

I shrugged. 'I have six months.'

Denis stared at me. Then he put his arm around my shoulder. 'That's no help, Sally Ann.'

My abysmal failure at everything suddenly brought tears to my eyes. 'My father doesn't care at all. He just picks rows.'

Denis gave me a squeeze. 'I care, Sally. My God – I'd really miss you if ... you're sure?' He pulled back, looking intently at me, then saying bossily. 'You can't sit at home, moping. That's the worst thing for your condition.' He frowned for a second. 'I always thought you'd make a good journalist.'

I wiped my eyes on my sleeve. 'Did you?'

'You wrote articles for the *Irish Student*. Remember?'

'They weren't very good.' I had only done them to impress Colm, but I didn't say that. Denis was a real writer who had published short stories in *St Stephen's* and *The Dublin Magazine*, and was now working on a novel. 'I can't write. I tried a novel, but it was crap.'

'If you can speak, you can write. Another Smithwicks?'

I nodded, and he went to the bar. Coming back with two more pints, he said, 'You know, Sally Ann, I can arrange some work for you. Seamus Daly, the new editor of *The Catholic Trumpet* is looking for an arts assistant.'

I sipped my pint. 'What'd I have to do?'

'Some art and drama criticism. The odd book review.'

'Thanks, but I couldn't.'

'Of course you could!'

'I've never done anything in the line of acting or plays. How could I criticise others?'

'If in doubt, attack!'

'What?'

'Name any Dublin critic,' he went on.

'Well ... Kingsley Kelly.'

'Has he done anything? Had an exhibition?'

I shook my head. 'He knows a lot.'

'Well, go through all the papers. I'll bet you'll never find a critic who's also an artist. The two callings are different.'

So I agreed to go for an interview the next day.

The Catholic Trumpet was a right-wing weekly which was under a new left-wing editor. The office was at the bottom of Gardiner Street, on the top floor of a shabby Georgian house. A secretary in the outer office announced me, and I went into a back room where Seamus Daly was typing madly. He was a heavy man with rolled shirt sleeves, a red face and thick grey hair. He nodded at me without stopping typing. 'Take a seat. I'll be with you in a minute.'

I sat down, looking around the cluttered room. There was a smell of sweat and cigarettes. It looked like a poor paper, but it was a start. Maybe one day I could transfer to one of the bigger dailies. First I'd have to join the NUJ.

'So, you're Denis's friend?' The editor swung round, facing me glumly across his desk.

I nodded. 'We were in college together.'

I expected to be interviewed and had brought clippings of my student efforts, but Seamus Daly didn't want to see them. To my surprise, he rooted in a pile of letters on his desk. 'Let me see ... there must be something here for you.' Then he handed me an invitation. 'Write me five hundred words on that.'

It was a Paul Henry exhibition at Trinity.

'When do you want it?'

'Wednesday's copy day. Can you have it before noon?'

I said yes and he went back to his typing. That was all: I'd got the job, and walked on air.

The opening was a grand affair. In my new blouse and midi, I went along to the New Library at Trinity. The party was already in full swing so I lingered at the door, but now I was as good as Kingsley Kelly so why be shy? I went in, but guess who was the first person I saw? Kingsley stood near the entrance with Anabel. I fled.

The next day I viewed the exhibition privately. I spent a couple of days slaving over the review and it appeared in the next week's *Trumpet* under the headline:

The Paul Henry Exhibition is being held at Trinity College Dublin and then moving to the Ulster Museum, Belfast, where it can be seen until January 12th. Clearly no Irish artist could be so well known to the Irish in reproduction as Paul Henry. The blue mountains and lakes of the West, the romantic cottages, the Rousseau-like peasants working in the fields are all familiar to us. To be honest, we are sick looking at them. The muddy blue Paul Henry used is not even an accurate depiction of the West. It is interesting to note that it is a well-established fact that he was red green colour blind. Can a colour blind person be an artist at all? He painted mostly at dawn and during the hours before sunset, but his work does not even reflect the light effects of these times of day which can often be very unusual. His colours are like mud on the whole. In the catalogue, George Dawson states that he was much influenced by Van Gogh. Certainly his figures resemble Whistler's in their stillness, but his work lacks the emotion with which Van Gogh used paint and colour so that his landscape took on movement. Is there any real comparison? I think not. One is an artist of world class, the other a dauber. Van Gogh's cypress trees flare up into the sky like black flames, whereas there is no sign of any movement in Paul Henry's work. The clouds are like slabs of concrete; here one thinks of other landscape painters like Constable where the clouds sweep across the sky. The figures in such paintings as 'The Potato Diggers' are also caught in a static position; his fishermen are eternally looking out to sea, and it is easy to make the comparison with the far superior figures of Jack Yeats. Paul Henry presents us with an image of reality which is falsely romantic, he fails to portray the hard life of rural Ireland, which some of his peasants must have lived, the reality of hunger and emigration. He is a painter of visual perception in the nineteenth century tradition who fails to look beyond his subjects and find the essence or meaning of reality. Whose idea was it to mount this exhibition? Haven't we had enough of Paul Henry and his cottage art?

I thought it pretty good, but I didn't want to boast to my father about my new job. So I left the paper on the hall table and, of course, he saw it.

'Who bought this fascist rag?' He flicked through it, coming into the kitchen.

I was cooking the supper. '*The Trumpet* has a new editor now, Dad.'

'It's a fascist rag, and that's all it'll ever be!'

'Dad, you're living in the past. It's not fascist. I'm writing for it now.'

He gaped at me. 'You're what?'

'I have an article in that issue.'

He searched through it. 'Where?'

'On the arts page,' I stood beside him. 'There, "Colour Blind".'

I waited in a sort of nervous pride while he scanned it.

'Well,' he said finally in an injured voice. 'I'm surprised at you, Sally Ann.'

I had expected he'd be pleased.

'You've become a philistine.'

'A philistine?'

'Yes, I never thought you'd descend to criticising an artist like Paul Henry!' He flung the paper on the kitchen table in disgust. 'And it's ungrammatical. You have semicolons where you should have full stops.'

He slammed out of the kitchen to his surgery.

I reread my article. Semicolons instead of full stops? Why couldn't that be my style? And why was I a philistine? Why should I like Paul Henry? He was old hat. My father was too much. How could I ever succeed with him on my back? I ignored him, continuing with my career as a philistine. I did weekly articles on all sorts of topics: art shows, plays, books. I reviewed an O'Casey revival, slamming it. Hadn't we had enough of Dublin tenements? Why couldn't they put on *Who's Afraid of Virginia Woolf*? The editor never spoke to me, or commented on what I wrote, good or bad. So I assumed it must be ok. Denis was my only critic. We met for the odd drink, during which he always enquired about my health. He also said I was doing well but should get more 'chat' into my stuff. So I tried this in my next book review, on *Da* by Hugh Leonard, published by an obscure US publisher. It was a boring flop, I wrote, with a cold central character. And I wouldn't risk the hazards of the bus strike by going to see it, even if anyone were foolish enough to revive it. Then I added some 'chat' about meeting a Jehovah's Witness, hitching to see *Black Man's Country* by Des Forristal the previous week. Leonard wasn't worth a journey, I ended, and hopefully he would not bore us again, but stay buried between the boards of this book in some forgotten library, etc etc etc.

I was no wishy-washy critic, so I shouldn't have been surprised when my father yelled at me after Mass the next Sunday. 'Sally Ann! Will you come down, please!'

I struggled out of bed.

My father was fuming in the hall. He waved the paper in my face. 'I bought this outside the church. I've never read such drivel. I don't know how you ever got a degree!'

'What's wrong with it?'

He glared at me. 'Come into my surgery.'

I went, thinking him a maniac. He sat at his desk. 'First, let me say this: if you ever do anything as good as Hugh Leonard, I'll be the proudest father in the world!'

'Dad ...'

'But in the meantime, I won't stand by and let him be abused by the likes of you.'

'But ...'

'Hear me out! What right have you to criticise others?'

'I don't know.'

'Have you ever written a play?'

I shook my head. 'I've a right to my opinion.'

'An uninformed opinion!' I had never seen my father so angry. 'And what is the relevance of this bit: "... which I did last week when I saw Desmond Forristal's play, *Black Man's Country* ..." Did you give that a bad review too?'

'It was ok. Fair.'

He put his head in his hands. 'Fair! Who are you to say? What's the relevance of your argument with a Jehovah's Witness here?'

I felt crushed. 'I was told it needed chat.'

'Who told you that?'

'Denis.'

'A boyfriend?'

'No, a friend. He's married.'

'You're not?'

'*No*! Dad!'

'Well, if you insist on being a philistine, you can at least be grammatical.' My father took a pen from his inside pocket and, as I stood there, went through my article word for word, saying at last, 'In future show me what you write.'

But he needn't have worried because the next time I left copy into the *Trumpet*, Seamus Daly wanted to see me. 'Take a seat,' he said, as I entered his reeking office. He looked mournfully over his cluttered desk. 'How are you feeling?'

I sat down. 'Fine.'

He shuffled some papers. 'Look, you should be taking it easier.'

'Taking it easier?'

He quickly averted his eyes. 'Your condition ...'

'My condition?' Did he think I was pregnant? 'I've never felt better in my life.'

He looked puzzled. 'But ... don't you have Hodgkins' Disease?'

'Hodgkins' Disease ...' I felt my neck, the truth suddenly dawning. Denis had believed my hypochondriacal fears, when I had forgotten them.

'I thought you had a few months to live.'

I bit my nail. 'Well – eh – it seems to have cleared up.'

He rubbed his face in embarrassment. 'Your work is – ah – fine, but I want to employ someone more general. Someone fulltime.'

'Would you give me a chance?'

He shook his head. 'It's not in my hands, love. I thought you'd be dead by now.'

I didn't tell my father; I couldn't give him the satisfaction. Without telling him I applied for a job as a hostess with Aer Lingus, but failed the interview for wearing Wellingtons. For God's sake it was lashing rain, and I didn't realise it was the real interview, when it was. I'd been sent a card to 'call' to the Shelbourne Hotel – it had said nothing about an interview. The row of interviewers looked at my boots and then at each other. One man asked my name and a woman smiled, saying sarcastically that I'd worn sensible footwear anyway. Then they said I could go. So I didn't get the chance to give my spiel about my hobbies or where I went on last year's holidays.

Next I got a job in Murph's Restaurant in Baggot Street. But the pay was awful, and I clashed with the manageress, so I was fired again. When you're sacked as a waitress, it's time to come to a realisation about yourself. Maybe my father was right about me being qualified for nothing. I wish I could say that things have got better with him like they would in a book, but we've relapsed back to our former Trappist silence. My father's like the old woman who lived in the shoe. He has two too many children and doesn't know what to do. And we're too old for boarding school now.

VI

ALASTAIR

Holidays are hell. How is it that the worst things happen when you're meant to be enjoying yourself? Maybe it's from too much hope. I mean, the gap between illusion and reality. I don't know. Anyway, I lost Alastair when we went to France together – which was the exact opposite of what I'd planned. Although we'd split up I'd asked to go, hoping to change his mind about our future. So he took me to visit some friends in Lille, and then camping in Normandy. You'd think staying with friends might be difficult, but that was ok. The camping finished us.

Our last day was the end. I had to get back to my Dublin job, so was leaving the next morning. We'd driven all day. I'd wanted to stop hours before, but he insisted on sightseeing till after dark. We'd seen the Sherman tank at St Mère-Église surrounded by tulips; Omaha Beach with its German bunkers stinking of urine. It was too late for the American Cemetery at Collville-sur-Mer, which I really regretted. And, of course, the campsites were all full, so we ended up persuading a farmer to let us use his field. Bloody hell – just when I needed a bath. Alastair drove the van slowly over the bumps.

'Let's go on to Bayeux in the morning and skip the American Cemetery.' He had a lovely Edinburgh accent. It was a reasonable request and I could've agreed, but didn't. He parked in a corner of the field. 'I don't know what you see in graveyards.'

I didn't either, but I'd read so much about the war. Also, it was a way of asserting myself. One of the girls we'd visited was so bossy I decided that I'd handled everything the wrong way. He pulled a ragged Aran jumper over old jeans and jumped out of the van. He was tall, dark and woolly-haired with thick horn-rimmed glasses, ordinary-looking, really. But that's the reason I liked him – besides, I wore glasses too. He ran to close the gate. He's careful about things like gates, which was another reason. I suppose opposites attract.

I was meant to be getting the meal started while he pitched the tent. But, as he spread it out by the van's headlights, I lingered by the passenger door. Everything was eerie in the moonlight, sort of lonely, yet beautiful. The traffic from the nearby road was muffled, and the farmhouse hidden by a clump of trees. It could easily have been haunted. After all, blood had been spilt there for centuries: Norman, English, German, American, French. Before that the ancient tribes of Gaul – I'd spent hours translating Caesar's wars in school.

'Pass the pegs, Sally!'

I flashed the torch into the back of the van. Light fell on old jeans, rucksacks, the primus stove, but no sign of the pegs. Then it hit me. I'd left them in the loo at St Lo. I'd gone there at the last minute. The loo at St Lo was almost a tongue twister, but he'd be too mad to appreciate that. He always got unbearable when hungry, and he'd have a fit now.

'Hurry up, Sally!'

I kept looking. 'They're not here.'

'What do ye mean?'

'*Ils ne sont pas ici.*'

'Your French is awful!' He came over and, grabbing the torch, rooted impatiently in the van. 'I've to do everything!'

Snob, I thought, a first in French didn't give him a monopoly on the language, just a superiority complex. Everyone in France bowed before his fluency. It was crazy to be jealous, but I was. The farmer hadn't even minded being disturbed. '*Eh, bien! Bon Dieu! Bon appetit!*' The Frogs were sickening about their language. The hours I'd spent in the Dublin Alliance Francaise were to no avail. The day before, I'd finally got up the courage to say, '*Cafe au lait, s'il vous plait.*' But the smirking waiter had answered in perfect English. It was maddening.

Alastair was now searching the front of the van. 'Dammit! They aren't here!'

'I told you ...'

'You're awfully good at saying that!'

I grinned nervously. 'Sorry.'

'Don't be facetious!' He flashed under the seats. 'I saw you holding them at St Lo. They must be here.'

Wearily I shook my head. 'I left them in the loo. I went at the last minute.'

'Why didn't you say?'

'I told you.'

'Don't say that!'

I giggled – I do this when I'm nervous. 'Sorry!'

'It's not funny!'

I composed my face, studying the ground. Irritably he pushed his glasses up on his nose. 'Where're we going to sleep?'

'The van?'

'You have it! I'm sleeping in the tent!' He flashed the torch at the hedge behind him and then further along the field.

'An accident, *n'est-ce pas?*' I pleaded.

He didn't answer and I didn't blame him. It was my fault. I'm definitely irritating. I suppose I'm facetious too.

Alastair pulled a branch out of the hedge. 'I'll try and use twigs. You get the meal on! Lucky it's our last night!'

His words were like lead in my heart. What was so lucky about it? He was leaving me to the Paris train the next day. So there wasn't really time for the Cemetery – not if I wanted to see one of the world's wonders. I was miserable about going back to Ireland, and secretly hoped he'd stop me. It was my Casablanca complex. I'd thought the country of the Impressionists, of those vaulted country roads and Proust's Balbec would be a rubicon in our relationship. How could we not fall in love? But he'd said nothing about the future. Not even at the Quatorze Juillet dance we'd happened on and danced stumblingly through.

Things were not going well. I have to admit finding the campsites disappointing. The toilets were holes in the ground and were always crowded with Germans and Americans. We might as well have been in Bray on a bank holiday. In comparison, Bray was almost depopulated. It'd been my idea to stay in the one place and meet French people, but they were mostly rude or in a hurry, like that damn waiter.

I burned myself lighting the primus. I hated camping. There was sunburn cream, but where? *Ici le problème.* Or was it *la problème.* Ice was best, I knew from my father, but there was definitely none of that. So I plunged my hand into the cooling grass. The daisies were curled in sleep. Lucky things, able to exist without all our clobber. I often think I'll come back as a flower in the next life. If you think about it, reincarnation makes much more sense. The Buddhists were right – I was thinking of becoming one. I mean, what could be more boring than eternal life?

'The meal won't cook itself!' He was dragging a branch past.

'I burnt my hand!'

'You're always doing that.'

'Sorry!'

'Is it bad?'

'No.'

The pain was easing up. While he pared the branch and cut it into twigs, I put two fish on the pan. The eyes stared eerily up at me. I'd bought them that day in a leafy market with all sorts of stalls and live chickens running about. I remember wondering whose task it'd be to kill the bird if we bought it. Not mine. At least the fish were obligingly dead. In Ireland they had the decency to cut off their heads, but the French probably ate them. They ate the oddest things: frogs, snails, brains. Yet when I said this to Alastair, he'd called me provincial. I suppose I was. He was hammering loudly now.

'That smells good.'

The tent was nearly staked out. He was so damn efficient that I couldn't help regretting my imminent departure. But since college I was for holidays, not real life. The Irish Sea separated us, since he was teaching in England. When we first met, only Stephen's Green lay between us. It had been bliss to meet halfway for coffee in Bewley's, then a matinee in the Green Cinema. I get lonely thinking of the Chinese meals we had: Peking duck and lychees for dessert. He was at Trinity for an M.Litt, while I struggled with history essays in UCD. It was all Bertrand Russell's fault for saying that you couldn't understand the present without knowing about the past. I was an expert on things like Lanfranc, the Avignon Papacy and the Defenestration of Prague, but couldn't manage a simple relationship.

Alastair thought history bunk, like turning pebbles on a beach. The past didn't matter, he claimed, even our bodies changed every seven years. He was brilliant, so maybe I had a BA in turning pebbles. Aristotle had thought history inferior too. It related what happened, not what *might* happen. Coping with the difference was my problem. Still, the past's all you have. Alastair said I was the clinging type, and he was right. My problem was accepting everything he said, being his mattress as well as his mistress. The holiday had changed nothing in that line. Except that I was less nervous about sex now. I'd read Edna O'Brien, so knew it was difficult for others too. Although most people implied that it was the greatest thing since sliced bread, I couldn't let go. Maybe it was being Catholic. But, crazily, it upset me that Alastair used condoms. Despite my father, I wanted to get pregnant and love one man. But everything was so mixed up. When I wasn't anxious, I was jealous of Alastair's life without me. How did other people manage? You saw them in college, cooing in the library or over lunch in the Country Shop. They did a line for years, got their degrees and got engaged. Next thing they married. How did they do it? How did they know? My friend Denis was happily married. I'd tried to make Alastair jealous by talking about him nonstop, but it'd had no effect.

'It's working!' Alastair called.

The tent was yellow in the dusk. Although I pretended to hate it, I'd miss it so much. It was our only home. Maybe I'd back down and stay? What did my job matter? No, I had to show independence.

The farmer appeared at the gate, flashing a light. '*Ca va?*'

I stood there.

He waved at me. '*Ca va?*'

What should I say? *Bien*? *Merci*?

Alastair went over. '*Bon appetit!*' ... '*Bon appetit!*' came through the silence.

I buttered two slices of bread and put them on plates with the fish. They looked 'bon appetising' enough. A change from the tinned food we'd been eating. That's another thing Alastair always said, you need variety in food just as you need variety in people. A person wouldn't dream of eating the same food all the time, so why live with the same person? It was sickening. He wanted freedom, lots of women, but I'd hoped he'd change his mind. Looking back, it was crazy to be scared of being twenty five and single. He didn't love me, but maybe he couldn't help it. After all, I hadn't loved Paul Brady.

I peered into the darkness. 'It's ready!'

Alastair had disappeared.

'It's ready!'

'I heard you!' came from the tent. He came over and hunkered down beside me.

I passed his plate. 'They're big.'

'They look yummy.' He wolfed a mouthful, then spat it out.

I stared at him, then at his plate. 'What's wrong?'

'You didn't clean them!'

'Clean them?'

'Yes, gut them.'

I peered at my plate. 'Fish don't have guts.'

'Of course, they do!'

'But they're not mammals.' It was stupid of me. When I bought fish at home they were ready to eat. So I thought this was always the case – if you hadn't actually caught them.

'I'm going to bed!' He got up and scraped his plate into the refuse sack in the van. He didn't have to do that. There was cheese and bread, but I wasn't offering him any.

I picked at my fish, avoiding the area near the head. It tasted ok, but I'd lost my appetite. Men were impossible, so demanding and precious. Why had he brought me to France if he was going to be so awful about everything? I heard him pee in the ditch and then go into the tent. 'Come to bed,' he called.

I was in no hurry. I stared miserably at my fish bone, thinking the poor thing should never have left the water. Then I went over and scraped it onto the field for the birds.

He looked through the flaps. 'You're littering.'

I was too weary to answer: his superiority was maddening. Matter turned to matter, didn't it? I went to the loo on the grass. Inside the tent, I zipped myself firmly into my sleeping bag, as he leaned over. 'Give us a kiss goodnight.'

I turned my back. 'Night.'

'Sorry, I was grumpy.'

I could've turned, but didn't.

'Let's go to Bayeux tomorrow,' he said. 'Then I'll leave you to the train.'

The word 'train' finished me. Tomorrow I'd be on my own, probably forever. 'I want to see the Cemetery.'

'Seen one, seen 'em all.'

'It's the thirtieth anniversary of D–Day.'

'The tapestries are one of the world's wonders.'

I wriggled down into my bag. 'There wouldn't be a world if the Americans hadn't defeated Hitler.'

'They didn't do it alone. I don't understand you.'

That was true, but I didn't say so.

'Hitler was dead before you were born,' he went on. 'I thought you liked art.'

'I do. I'd still like to see the Cemetery.' I was being difficult, but the Cemetery had become a symbol of women's liberation, or something.

He sighed resignedly. 'I'll leave you there and have a coffee in town.'

'You won't come with me?' It was stupid but I panicked at the idea of being by myself. Some French person might speak to me.

'Sorry, don't like graveyards.' He snuggled into me, patting my behind through the bag. 'It's our last night, Sally ... It'll probably be a while.'

'I can last.'

He turned away, angry. 'I thought you'd got over your frigidity.'

That got me. 'My *frigidity*?'

'Don't pretend you enjoy it.'

'I do!'

'What do you want, Sally?'

'I want you to love me.'

He sighed. 'Go to sleep, for God's sake.'

I curled up, crying to myself. I'd never be Mrs Macbeth now. It sounded so interesting – Mrs Alastair Macbeth. Looking back, I wasn't going about it the right way. But then, was it fair to call me frigid when I thought I'd been so seductive? After a while, I blew my nose noisily. 'Last night was pretty good.'

'Hmm ...' He was nearly asleep.

I shook him, whispering, 'Macbeth shall sleep no more.'

He groaned again. How could he sleep at a time like this?

'It worked last night!' I said again.

'Yes, but not for you.'

'It did.'

'You didn't come.'

'I did ... a bit.'

'Go to sleep.'

'But what about us, Alastair?'

'We have no great love affair.'

He went to sleep, but I lay awake for hours. It was no use, he'd never love me. No great love affair. Why did he speak for me too? Once I'd shown him a poem I wrote, and he'd said I was no great writer. He was right there. Then my drawings were not so great either. What had your man Yeats said? There was perfection of life or art, something like that. I had neither. I was born to blush unseen 'beside the springs of Dove'. Wherever that was? But if I was that hopeless why did he have anything to do with me? Our holiday had been my idea, but last time he'd invited me to visit his parents in Edinburgh. I'd loved them. He had a mother at least and a father who wasn't always having hysterical fits. It was all so normal. I lay there, telling myself there was no hope. After all he'd broken it off with me three times, each time giving me a blasted poem to read. 'La Donna something' by T.S. Eliot. Sex was the important thing between a man and a woman, not poetry. Maybe it was a block, but I could never understand the poem. Why couldn't he speak if he wanted to say something? But there was only one thing I wanted to hear. He'd never said it and I'd be gone tomorrow.

I don't know how long I lay awake – hours. I'd just dropped off when I awoke to a strange noise. Someone was sniffing outside the tent. I lay in rigid fear as the sniffing moved along the tent to my feet. Was it an axe murderer? Or a ghost? After all, the ground here was red with blood.

I nudged Alastair. 'Wake up!'

'Go to sleep!'

'There's someone outside!'

'Nonsense!' He rolled over.

I lay very still. If I pretended to be asleep it might go away.

'Sniff! Sniff!' came from outside.

I thumped Alastair's back. He jerked awake as the tent collapsed. Outside a cow bellowed madly.

Alastair was right, my pilgrimage was depressing. At first I followed a coachload of noisy Americans past sentries into the cemetery's entrance museum. It had US flags and photos of the different Second World War battles and a short movie. Nine thousand, three hundred and eighty-six men were buried there. Most had died on D–Day, 6 June 1944, all cut down like flowers. Even the Americans seemed daunted into silence. I definitely was: some had been nineteen, six years younger than me.

Outside, rows and rows of little white crosses stretched endlessly over manicured lawns. I mean, you see war movies with John Wayne but nothing prepared you for those endless crosses. In school Mother Rita had read us poems about the First World War. Poems about poppies 'In Flanders fields ...' growing between crosses 'row on row'. Except there were no poppies there. I thought of her in all the oddest situations. When I was leaving school she gave me a book of Emily Dickinson's poetry. Her lines rattle round in my head:

> I felt a funeral in my brain,
> And mourners, to and fro ...

Alastair says quoting things is a sign of adolescence, but Mother Rita used to say poetry was useful furniture for the mind. Yet she didn't make us learn poems by heart. We had to criticise them, intelligently.

I remember wandering up paths that day to kill the time until Alastair came back. He was right, there was nothing much to see. Here and there the lines of crosses were broken by a Star of David. At least they hadn't separated the different religions. They were all brothers in death. 'For he today that sheds his blood with me shall be my brother,' Laurence Olivier in *Henry V*. I'd loved that film. Yet the brotherhood of man was rot. People never learn. Violence still solves everything; hate rather than love. We're still barbarians beating the drums. I mean, it's all around you – Vietnam, Northern Ireland. Before the Troubles I'd been shocked to hear that people were shot in Belfast in the fifties. Now they're shot daily. It's something I'll never understand. Bombed to bits ... for Ireland, a dying country on a dying planet. What a fate. And what a fate to have had to run up Omaha Beach. To be blasted by bullets or drown before you get there. When I'd paddled there the day before, I'd thought it like Rosslare or Brittas, except for the German bunkers peeping out of the dunes. I could never run up a beach. Yet death was the one certainty. There were only two important things I'd heard someone say on the radio. 'How well can you live, and how bravely can you die.'

I sat on the grassy verge, aching all over. Alastair had got the tent up again, but I'd been afraid to sleep for the rest of the night, imagining the cow would come back. If you were afraid of a cow how could you run up a beach? And die at nineteen, never having loved? Alastair thought I hadn't loved either at twenty five. 'If I speak in the tongues of men and angels, and have not love, I am a noisy gong or a clanging cymbal.' But that was a different type of love. Everyone wanted the 'wings on your feet' type, which was nothing to do with sex or having children. How had everything got so mixed up? Maybe in the future they'll be separate?

A dog yapped in the distance. At first I could see nothing. Then a female American voice shrieked. 'Bridie! Bridie!' A small white Scottish terrier tore up the path. It wore a little red tartan body blanket. 'Bridie! Bridie! Come back!' The little dog reached me, jumping on me hysterically. I soothed it.

'Down, doggie! Down, now!' But it kept yapping.

The woman wobbled on high heels down the path. She was oldish with lacquered hair and dressed in a suit of the same red tartan as the dog. '*Arrêtez le chien! Arrêtez le chien!*'

I reached for the dog, but he scampered away over the dead. 'Mademoiselle! *Arrêtez le chien!*'

I had a thing about walking on graves, but I ran along the grass between the rows. The dog saw me and kept on running and yapping joyfully. At last I threw myself over a grave, grabbing his collar. Then brought him back to his owner.

The woman took him in her arms, smiling at me madly. '*Merci! Merci!*'

'It was a pleasure.' I didn't know the right French.

'I have to be so careful!' she said in a squeaky drawl, clipping a lead to the dog's collar. 'She's in heat.'

I had to smile. 'There's no danger here.'

'There's always danger!' The woman looked around conspiratorially. 'But my, we're speakin' English, honey. Isn't that a coincidence? Where're you from?'

'Ireland.'

'Where in Ireland?'

'Dublin.'

'Another coincidence! My second husband's third cousin lives in Dublin. You might know her – Miss Clarke.'

I shook my head. 'I don't think so.'

'Are you Episcopalian?'

'I'm nothing, really.'

'What a shame! Everyone has to be something. Miss Clarke plays the organ in the church. You ought to go hear her.'

'Which church?'

'Have you heard of Findlater's Church?'

I nodded. 'If I'm passing I'll call in.'

'You can say we met.' She turned imperiously on her heel. 'Which way are you going now?'

'To the car park. I'm meeting a friend.'

Her blue eyes lit up. 'Your beau?'

'Well ... yes.' I backed away from the sniffing dog.

'Stop it, Bridie! Mine is buried here!'

'Gosh, I'm sorry.'

The woman's eyes suddenly filled with tears. 'He was killed on Omaha Beach. His grave is back there. I visit him every year. I was laying flowers there when Bridie ran away.' She suddenly clutched my arm. 'Would you like to see it?'

I nodded. I had plenty of time.

With the dog between us, we walked back towards the entrance. The woman kept up a constant stream of chatter. 'We were madly in love. But he was a musician, and my people were in law. They didn't think he could support me. We were going to elope ... I was in college in Virginia, Sweet Briar College, have you heard of it?'

'No.'

'He wasn't college educated. War was declared and he was drafted. That was it.'

She stopped at a Star of David. A single red rose lay on the ground before it. I read the inscription. *Philip Cohen 1925–1944*. 'He wasn't very old.'

'Soldiers never are. He used to call me from England every week. Then I heard nothing for months. There was great secrecy about the invasion. Then I heard he was killed.'

'Running up the beach?'

The woman nodded. 'He was Jewish, you see. That was the problem. My parents didn't approve, and I hadn't the courage. But he was so talented. He could sing. You've heard of Al Jolson?'

I nodded.

'Well, he did a marvellous imitation of him!' Then she started singing and doing a sort of dance with the dog. 'You made me love you! I didn't wanna do it! I didn't wanna do it ...'

I tried not to laugh.

'Before he left he bought me a Scottish terrier for company. Like Bridie here. So I've had one ever since. She's company.'

The dog pulled on its leash, growling. 'Now, Bridie, behave. We come here every year, don't we honey?' She picked up the dog and hugged it. 'The war ruined Momma's life.'

'But you married?'

'I sure did, honey! Twice.'

'Did you have children?'

'I had five dogs!' She looked sadly at the grave. 'The love of my life is under that clay. Now, honey, I'd like to be alone.'

'I'm on my way.'

'Give my regards to Miss Clarke!'

I waved, making for the carpark. She was dotty, but I'd learnt something from her. You can meet strangers in the oddest places and learn things. There hadn't been time to divorce Philip Cohen. So, of course, he became her one and only love – mourned forever.

The van was in the carpark and Alastair waved from the window. That's what I mean about him being reliable. He was always there. He wore his woolly white Aran, and smiled as I clambered inside. 'How was it?'

'It was great!'

'Hmm ... graves?'

'You should've come! I met an American woman ... from Sweet Briar College. Have you heard of it?'

He shook his head.

'It's an interesting name, Sweet Briar.'

He snorted. 'It's awful!'

'I don't know ... Two opposites – briars have thorns, yet they're beautiful. She was a bit of a nutter.'

He drove out of the car park. 'You have a knack of attracting them! We'll make the train.'

I looked at him sadly. Maybe if he died, he could be my lost love. He'd enter another realm then, like Philip Cohen, or Paul Brady from college.

Alastair caught my look. 'What're you thinking?'

I shrugged. 'Nothing.'

He pointed to a brown paper bag on the dashboard. 'I got you some fruit. And yoghurt for lunch.'

'I've no spoon.'

'I've put one in the bag.'

I was touched by the spoon.

'Got your tickets?'

I patted my anorak pocket. 'Yes.'

'Passport and money?'

I nodded, looking out the window. I didn't want to talk. I was imagining myself dead and Alastair mourning me. The tent peg wars would be forgotten. I could be the love of someone's life. But that kind of love was an idea, nothing to do with now. *Now* had to do with catching trains, with commitment and decisions. 'Life consists in action and its end is a mode of action.' I'd learn that in philosophy. Alastair was right about one thing: history is bunk. To survive you have to change all the time. You have to face things like people not loving you. Or taking trains in foreign countries when you don't know the language. It's running up a beach in a way.

As we waited together on the platform, he broke the silence. 'It won't be long now.'

I nodded nervously. I'd soon be adrift in my life. 'Tell me again how to ask if I'm on the right train.'

'You'll *be* on the right train.'

'I might want to check.'

'*Ici le train pour Paris*?' he said.

'*Ici le train pour Paris*?' I repeated.

He put his arm around me. 'You're very quiet.'

I nodded and he looked pained. 'Look, Sally ...'

I hugged him. 'I know ...'

'You know what?'

'We've no great love affair.'

The train screeched into the station, drowning more speech. I hugged him again tightly, controlling tears. Then I got on.

He handed up my rucksack. 'I'll write.'

'Me too.'

I blew a kiss from the open door, then found a free seat opposite a girl who looked like a student. I got the rucksack into the overhead rack and sat down. '*Ici le train pour Paris*?'

'Yeah,' she drawled in American, and went back to her book.

As we pulled out Alastair waved from the platform. I knew I'd never see him again, and I haven't. But I kept the spoon for years. I don't know where it finally got to. I don't know why I insisted on a graveyard instead of a work of art: I must be crazy. I used to blame myself for ruining the holiday. But maybe you invent choices if you don't have any real ones. And maybe you're not a person till you fail miserably. In a way, Alastair's in that perfect world of the past now – except there's no grave to mourn at.

VII

DONNELLY

Friday 13 April

Dear Dad and Tim,

Sorry I haven't written, but this'll be a long one to make up. I'm really enjoying my visit. So much has happened I don't know where to begin. Athens, where Richard lives, is a nice little college town, full of such beautiful young students that I'm beginning to feel old. (They look so much healthier than we do. Is this from taking vitamins?) Richard's apartment is in an old house on the main street. We stayed there for the first week, playing tennis when he wasn't working. Or else we visited friends – so many asked us to dinner because I was over. Irish hospitality's a myth compared to American.

Now we're in New York where Richard's play is going on off-off Broadway – a small theatre, something like Focus in Dublin. Guess what? I'm to be house manager! I keep telling myself it's not really happening, but your terrible dropout daughter has at last found a vocation. We arrived yesterday, taking the Greyhound bus to Port Authority, straight after Richard's class, where Donnelly, the director, met us – he's an old friend of Richard and always called that, never Joe. As they shook hands I tried not to stare. The truth is, I'd never seen a Broadway actor before! He doesn't look it, but he's a vet of Philadelphia Here I Come! *And now he's turned his hand to* directing Richard's plays. Last year they won a prize for the best off-off. He must've heard my thoughts 'cos the next thing he was staring at me, like wondering who the hell I was. Then Richard introduced us, saying I could help with the house. I joked that I knew about acting from being a daffodil in the school play when I was eleven. It fell flat because he nodded grimly, almost cracking my hand shaking it. Then grabbing my case and chatting to Richard he plunged into the Port Authority crowd.

Somehow, between snatches of gossip about Da being a hit uptown and who was acting in what, I got separated from them. As Richard's tall white-haired figure disappeared up the escalator I experienced panic at the thought of the white slave traders roaming the station. But Richard noticed me missing and, as the escalator disgorged me, grabbed my hand and said to stay close. When I coolly asked why he said it was wiser, confirming my worst theories. So all the way to the car I avoided eye contact with the passing faces. There's a great variety here: black, brown, yellow. Different from Ireland where everyone's so pasty-faced.

The car turned out to be as rumpled as Donnelly 'cos we all had to climb in through the windows. I know what you're both thinking, but that's showbiz! Anyway, it's in keeping with the roads here which mostly have potholes. It was like the bumpers in Bray, honking through the evening traffic to 22nd Street. We didn't even stop for something to eat, as the actors were waiting. But I was too excited by my first sight of the city to feel even remotely hungry. Dad, if only I had the words to describe the sun sinking behind those canyons of skyscrapers! It was pure poetry. Maybe someday I'll write about it. For the first time in my life I envied no man. It was like that line you're always quoting about 'Ulysses and his windy plains of ringing Troy.' This place is an experience and you both must see it.

Even our theatre's on hallowed ground, around the corner from the famous Chelsea Hotel which has plaques to Brendan Behan, Thomas Wolfe and Arthur Miller. Our street reeks of atmosphere (literally) with two truckloads of uncollected refuse! But that's NYC for you. There are two other theatres on the street, one called Time and Space run by a mysterious feminist group who're never there, and the other called the Borough of Manhattan Theatre (BMT for short) run by friends of Richard who specialise in American plays. And believe it or not, there are residents on 22nd Street, mostly black people on welfare who sit on the stoop of a dingy hotel all day, throwing dice or drinking from bottles wrapped in brown paper bags. With little girls rope skipping and little boys competing to see who can pee the furthest, it's reminiscent of O'Casey's Dublin. I mentioned this to Richard as we passed them but he just muttered 'O'Casey my foot'. Then pointing to a huge ad on the wall: A FUNERAL SHOULD NEVER COST MORE THAN A FAMILY CAN AFFORD, said it was his motto! (He's worried his play will be a flop). Then Donnelly actually spoke to me for the first time, calling me Susie and saying people lay senseless in the street here and nobody gave a damn – that's his favourite expression. He sort of groans it constantly under his breath: 'Nobody gives a damn!' Then Richard said my name was Sally and not to be scaring me about New York. Before I could say anything we had stopped at the theatre, imaginatively called The Nameless, and were crawling out of the car windows. Although small, the theatre has wonderfully built-in props: a hole in the roof for real rain, and dampish walls for the Irish atmosphere of Richard's play. Coincidentally, the building's owned by a Wexford man named Seán. He has a night watchman called Solomon who lives in the basement – at least I presume he does, 'cos he's always disappearing through a hole in the floor. His only other job seems to be keeping a proprietorial eye on the empty Coke machine in the lobby. You expect wisdom from someone called Solomon, but he reminds me of Ratso Rizzo from Midnight Cowboy, or of Tolkein's Gollum blinking at the daylight. I must've been staring 'cos the first time Richard's back was turned he winked and said I was a good-looking chick. God!

Well, the actors were all waiting for us, and what a talented lot they are. Stacy, the leading lady, has been an understudy for Neil Simon, and on Broadway in a John Osborne. Even the second lady has recently acted in an O'Casey production, so the street's like home to her. The leading man's Scottish and has had his picture on the cover of Time magazine dressed as a coal miner. I'm not sure if he's a part-time lecturer in Fordham and full-time actor or vice versa. He plays the moron type lead whom Stacy eventually marries to spite her macho type boyfriend, Tom; played by Donnelly – typecast I'm afraid. I know what the mention of marriage has you thinking but in real life people DON'T anymore. So stop worrying. Richard bought me a return ticket, but I'm hoping he'll ask me to stay when the play's over. I hope this is ok with you and Tim.

Re the play: I worry about my lack of experience. It's ridiculous: my only previous time backstage was when I was one daffodil and Deirdre the other. Remember our crazy paper costumes, Dad? Deirdre was working in a bank the last I heard. We met for a drink a few years back, *but it didn't go well. It makes me sad that I wasn't nice enough. It was my S. de Beauvoir stage, so say no more. The thing is not to look back. It didn't help Orpheus and that lot. The one blessing about the passing years is one grows in wisdom and maturity. But I dreaded, just dreaded making a mistake at the theatre yesterday. My duties consisted of sitting listening while the actors read their parts. I asked Donnelly wasn't there anything I could do, even cleaning up, but he didn't deign to answer me. Then Richard put a finger silently to his lips and pointed to a seat in the back row, which collapsed the minute I sat on it! I thought this funny but it made Donnelly grit his teeth!*

Donnelly's attitude made me suspect that he didn't like me. In the restaurant after the rehearsal the suspicion grew as he talked nonstop to Richard, totally ignoring my advice about his Irish accent – it's phony. Back in his tiny apartment where Richard and I are staying I knew he hated me. As we entered I said what a nice flat. Donnelly glared and said what did I mean? So I said it was a nice flat again, looking nervously to Richard. Then Donnelly growled that couldn't I see it was an apartment, not a flat? Then Richard said they called apartments flats where I came from! That made Donnelly look embarrassed ok, but he still wouldn't talk to me all night ... so I listened as the two men chatted till late about the play. They also serve, as Milton rightly tells us.

At rehearsal today Donnelly ignored me again when I reminded him that his Irish accent wasn't right. I don't know what to do to please him. He's awfully thick with Richard which leaves me a bit in the cold. Otherwise I'm happy to be living in New York for the next six weeks and to be helping Richard. It'll look good on my CV to have worked in the theatre. It was the greatest luck meeting Richard again. I remembered him from college and he said he remembered me. He's in bed now and I'm sitting up finishing this letter. I'd better close as he's yelling for lights out.

Lots of love, Sally Ann.

Friday 20 April

Hello everyone

I'm sitting in the back row as usual while Richard and Donnelly rehearse with the cast. They've been at it for a week now and you've no idea how hard the actors work. I always assumed acting was only a matter of learning the lines and walking around saying them. But they practise with a kamikaze dedication for long grinding hours in this dankish theatre – not that I mind the cold. I asked Solomon could he put on the heat but he said it was for the Eulenspiegel Society which used the theatre on Tuesday nights. I asked if that was a cultural club. He got smirky and said it was, and he'd bring me if I wanted. I said I might go with Richard – pointedly so as he'd stop getting ideas. He went off chortling hey, yeh, yeh, which is about his command of the English language. Later he came back with a smelly old coat which I had to wear so as not to offend him!

I can't tell you how exciting rehearsals are. I never feel redundant sitting in the back row. There's a wealth of knowledge and experience to be gained. My main job so far is go-for, that's getting constant coffee and donuts from the corner deli for Richard, Donnelly and the actors. I get Stacy sandwiches. She likes Margaret Drabble, so we talk a lot about women's lit. Another young actor called Jim tells me all about his problems with dominating parents who won't let him live away from home although he's twenty two! I told him what a gem you were, Dad, about letting me live amid alien corn, though there are loads of Irish in New York, and one of our actors is from the Abbey. His name's Chris Keely and he acted there in the forties. Remember him, by any chance? He invited me to the Irish Arts Centre to a ceili of all things!

I can't say much for Donnelly's friendliness. Yesterday I put my foot in it again. The actors were taking a break for a silent read, so while checking if Richard wanted coffee I whispered that the Irish would never say gotten – a phrase he uses in his play. Well, Donnelly must've thought I was talking about him 'cos the next thing he was yelling he could ask me to leave. Well, Richard didn't stick up for me, just growled that I was to get the coffee. So I walked out to the street in a daze. Usually I go the long way by the spooky warehouse to avoid the drunks. But yesterday was so dark I decided to pass them. Well, there were blood-curdling screams. I walked on, looking neither right nor left. Was someone being murdered? Raped? Should I interfere? Run for the police? What I'd always read about was happening to me. Then I heard a chuckle and looking into a black sea of faces on the hotel stoop heard: 'Hey sweetie, who's been knockin' on your head?' I laughed too and immediately felt better. On the way back I noticed some activity in the feminist theatre, Time and Space, and guess what? They were dramatising an essay by Virginia Woolf! Needless to say I went in, and needless to say it was an unforgettable experience – you know how I adore anything about Virginia Woolf. It's hard to describe what went on but basically one actor read while another actor mimed. There was only one other person in the audience, and during the interval she told me the method was experimental and the theatre got its name from the difference between male and female thought. It seems we think in terms of space and men think in terms of time. Which is definitely true in Richard's case 'cos when I got to our theatre the actors were all gone and he was chain-smoking in the lobby. At the sight of me he yelled where had I gone? That Donnelly had gone back to check the apartment! I tried to explain about 'The Moment' (which was the essay by Virginia Woolf) but he shouted louder that Donnelly thought he was Kazan, but I wasn't above being told off once in my life! He looked like he was going to have a heart attack so I explained quietly that once in my life would be fine, or even twice, but Donnelly never stopped telling me off! In fact he hated my guts and I felt in the way, etc. Well, we had it out. It was our first row. Then Richard cooled down and we took the subway home. On the way he said there was no question of me being put out of one of his plays and there'd be much more to do once the show started and I could house manage proper. Of course, Donnelly was in the apartment gloatily clicking his tongue and growling about me 'running round, running round and nobody giving a damn!' I ignored this, but when he said Richard should kick my tail I explained that as a feminist I objected to that statement. That Richard and I had an equal relationship and didn't indulge in such barbarism. Well, that's what I wanted to say but Richard dragged me off to the tiny bedroom. Later when I asked him if we could go to the Eulenspiegel Society that Solomon was talking so much about, he snored in reply, as he'd fallen asleep.

So far I haven't clashed with Donnelly today. Solomon's been hanging round as usual wondering when Richard's bringing me to the Eulenspiegel Society. I said soon, so he went away muttering that I deserved someone better than Richard! Him? God! The actors seem to be breaking up now, so I'll close.

Buckets of love to both, SA

Wednesday 25 April

Dear Dad and Tim,

Today I was given a job. The actors now rehearse without their scripts and need a prompter who is moi! I was nervous about making a mistake, even though it's the actors who're supposed to make them. I felt I'd make a mess of things, and I did. Stacy was sort of stumbling so I gave her the line. Then Donnelly snapped she'd ask for it if she wanted it! It was a misery sitting through the rest of the rehearsal wondering when or when not to prompt. The next thing Donnelly was yelling 'line please!' I've given up, just given up trying to please him.

Afterwards Stacy said I did a great job. The other actors gathered round too. Jim said he'd finally moved out of home and Dougal explained existentialism which he teaches at Fordham. He says we're all in a void and have to take a leap of faith. I said New York wasn't exactly a void, and although I could leap ok it worried me that Richard didn't believe in an afterlife. He said existentialism was all about making choices like that. Then we all had to move out as the Eulenspiegel Society were dribbling in. I asked Richard couldn't we stay and see what it was like. He glared and said absolutely not. So we wound up going to the BMT up the street. As they're doing a new play set in the Chelsea area you'd think the place would be packed with locals! But besides us there were only four people in the theatre. Richard, who gets gloomier and gloomier lately, remarked that it was his kind of audience. I said not to be pessimistic, that more people would come to his play 'cos it was better. Still, I enjoyed that play and they gave us free coffee in the interval. Dad, there's something about theatre people! Their next play is going to be a premiere of Edmund Wilson's This Room and This Gin and These Sandwiches – *how's that for a super title? I'll close for the moment,*
Yours in bliss, SA

Monday 1 May

Dear You Two,
Things aren't any better with Donnelly, but at least they're not worse. Yesterday he asked me to sit in his car to prevent it being stolen while he paid a fine. We drove miles and miles to a place called Queens where I had to wait, nearly melting, in a deserted car park. Of course he was hours longer than he said he'd be. But when he came back he at least had the grace to be apologetic. So we've established a detente as there's too much to be done with getting props and arranging publicity etc, for our opening night on Thursday. People in New York throw out all sorts of valuables, so we've gleaned most of our hand props and some of our furniture from dustbins. The set is being painted free by Mary Beth Mann, set designer for Family Business, *currently running off-Broadway at the Astor Place – a notch up from us. The lighting's being designed by Tobias Heller, a young actor and designer who has a part in* Gorey Stories, *going on Broadway in October – two notches up on us! Although neither of them would let me help I got friendly with them and was greatly awed by their dedication. Their names will mean nothing to you, I know, but in future you'll see them in lights and I mean it. I said to Richard I wished I could do something special*

like that. He said I could be a woman of letters as I was always writing them! We also had millions of programmes printed up, and we spent hours sending out flyers to four thousand addresses we stole from the Theatre Development Fund. All the critics have been personally invited. Richard spends his time tinkering sort of neurotically with the lights, so I suggested we go to the Eulenspiegel Society tomorrow night to steady our nerves. He said we could go for a Guinness with Chris Keeley in the Bronx. We did and had a great time, although the Guinness here is nothing to write home about. Still it was relaxing and steadied our nerves. We met a boy called Levi from the Irish Arts Centre who offered me a job teaching Irish. I said I didn't know any and he nearly died. Then he said I could teach them Irish dancing, and when I said I hated it he nearly died again! The last time I did any Irish dancing was with Deirdre in Irish college! Still, it was a good night and, as I said, steadied our nerves for next Thursday's onslaught.

Yours in hope, SA.

Sunday 5 May

Hello Again,

Well, the onslaught trickled in, all nine of them, all friends.

Everything was looking great. I had picked some lilacs from the park. But at the last minute Solomon dragged a bag of garbage through the theatre lobby! I got it cleared up just in time. Richard would've been mad but luckily he was already up his LIGHTS ladder and didn't see. He was too busy muttering there was a short in number two main, and he wouldn't be surprised if all the lights went out. As I frantically swept I shouted up not to be a pessimist, and he said it was his kind of lighting. The show went ok although the actors were nervous. I was nervous too, and spent the evening shuffling the programmes and counting heads.

The next night things picked up and we had thirteen, mostly friends. I should know: I counted them four times. One was a critic from The Irish Echo so I smiled at him a lot and gave him three programmes, which was more than he would've got at Da – it, by the way, has won the Drama Critics' Award for the best play of the season. Bet it never rains in their theatre! It never stops in ours! One day it was so bad I couldn't decide whether to put buckets under the leaks in the lobby or under the leaks onstage. I decided on the lobby as one of the scenes in the play was meant to be played in the rain. Solomon saw me and yelled what did I do down in Dublin when it rained? I explained it was over in Dublin, which really floored him, and we go to the movies. He naturally assumed I meant porn movies – the only ones he's ever seen. I said no, there weren't any in Dublin, which also floored him, or more than floored him 'cos he disappeared into his basement! Later, apparently touched by my cultural deprivation, he invited me to one, saying it'd be even better than the Eulenspiegel Society! I said no thanks so he gave me a free Coke instead. I don't know where he got it as the Coke machine still doesn't work.

We expected a crowd for today's Sunday matinee, but the only customers were Jim's parents. Thank goodness they really enjoyed themselves and seem to have accepted his decision. I'm sure things will pick up next week and we'll be booked out – luckily there's plenty of standing room.

Yours in hope, Sally.

Sunday 14 May

Dear Dad and Tim,

Our review has appeared in The Irish Echo! It said the play was reminiscent of Clifford Odets and should not be missed on any account! A large portion of their 16,000 readers seem to disagree though – all actually. You'll never guess who came though? Elton John – Tim'll explain who he is. I remember someone rang and booked tickets for Mr John. Apparently he came that night and I talked to him. Can you believe I never recognised him? We'd be worth something, if only I got him to autograph the programme. Then a man came by telling me he'd flown to Ireland especially to see The Star Turns Red at the Abbey. I said at least ours wasn't so far and he could take the subway! The next day an actor called Kelly Monaghan, who's worked with Donnelly and Richard before, came by. And so did a few others. There's a lot to be said for an intimate audience of one or two or three.

Our Sunday matinee was slackish too. In fact, only two people turned up. One was Alan Simpson, the famous Irish director who's in New York directing Androcles and the Lion, and the other was an Irish woman from Kells who came all the way from the Bronx in a taxi. Actually they were a great audience. Alan complimented the actors and the woman liked the play so much she promised to come back next weekend with a friend.

Richard hasn't said anything about me staying on. Lately things have been getting a bit better with Donnelly, but he attacked me for charging Alan Simpson. I said I didn't know and why didn't he say? He snapped back that I was a stupid girl and did he have to tell me *everything? I said nothing more 'cos the strain's beginning to tell on everyone. I mean we've all done our best and for what? While Richard never comes down from the lighting booth Donnelly spends every afternoon tinkering with his car which is full of strange rattles. Sometimes the rattles stop when a piece falls off, but a new noise always starts up. Once the police towed it away from outside the theatre which I thought improved the appearance of the place. Unfortunately we got it back though, and, to prevent it being towed again, Donnelly left me in it once when we were double-parked. Soon a cacophonous din started up outside which I tried to ignore. Then a man poked his head in the window and asked me to move on. He gaped when I said I couldn't drive – in America that's like being paralysed! He wouldn't go away so I finally said he could drive it but he'd have to climb in the window as the doors don't open. That got rid of him pretty quickly! I suppose he thought I was mad: after all, it's New York!*

Guess what a Cherokee Indian chief, a white rabbit and a French poodle have in common? Do you give up? Ok! They were all in the Blarney Stone, our local pub on 23rd Street tonight. Apparently they'd all drifted there after a pow-wow at the YMCA across the street. The poodle belonged to the chief, but nobody knew who owned the rabbit. We got chatting with the chief and ended up giving him some flyers, and he gave us some newspapers that explained the wrongs done to the Indians. After the chief went home to the New Jersey suburbs, I told Donnelly I was disappointed and expected my Indians wilder and something like Geronimo – I mean, who'd expect an Indian chief to own a French poodle? Donnelly actually answered that I was a romantic, and Indians today are suburbanised. On the way Richard fell asleep and I chatted with Donnelly. I asked him, among other things, about the Eulenspiegel Society. He said was that my thing? I said anything cultural was. He said that his wife had been a feminist. I said it was the first I heard he had a wife. And he said she'd left him and wouldn't let him see his kids. Which no matter how bad-tempered he is, is high-handed of her. It made me sorry for Donnelly and even like him. I must close now as Richard's yelling again about the light. Affectionately yours, Sally Ann.

Saturday 20 May

Dear Both of You,
To tell the truth, in terms of audience week three hasn't been much better than week one or two. But in terms of artistic existentialism it has been marvellous. The woman from Kells came back ok bringing her

friend. And although Alan Simpson didn't, he invited us down to see his production of Androcles *at the Perry Street theatre in the Village – I can't tell you how cosmopolitan the Village is. The show was overpowering, that is the only word. Lively and full of pizzazz with an utterly jam-packed house. It made our dingy theatre with its failing lights and scavenged props look pretty drab, and I mean it. But Alan said in spite of his theatre having money and a press agent they too scraped for an audience earlier in the run. You can't imagine how difficult the artistic life is, how dedicated you have to be. The feminists have disappeared like the Arabs into the desert, and our neighbours at BMT are having trouble with their Edmund Wilson premiere. They've even decided to scrap their next show which was to be Richard's latest play. I was gloomy about this and expected Richard to be suicidal, but he shrugged, saying his only worry was electrocuting himself. How lucky to love such a man, how lucky to be in his penumbra.*
Love, SA.

PS. Solomon gave me grisly photos of the Eulenspiegel Society in session. It's an SM club! I asked Richard why didn't he say, for God's sake, and not let me natter on like an idiot! He said he thought I knew. How's that for communication? Last night I had the most terrible Anne Frank nightmare. Apart from that, everything is fine.

Sunday 21 May

Dear Dad,

I'll probably be home before you get this letter. Truthfully, until last night, it was the same old three and fourpence. But guess what happened for our final performance? We got an audience! Yes! Yes! Even a critic from Show Business, *a magazine which gave Richard and Donnelly three awards last year! It was great to see so many people. I fingered the money like Shylock and counted heads four times to make sure they were really there. Even Solomon came out of the floor and filled the Coke machine for them. After the first scene they clapped loudly, and after the second and then all through the play. And the whole thing, which I had seen millions of times, came magically alive. The actors had always been super, but now that there was an audience to interact with, a magic thing happened, and there's no other word for it. And when it was over they clapped again and shouted author, author! And afterwards we had a party on the stage and Chris Keeley sang John McCormack songs and Donnelly sang Tommy Makem's 'Sally-O'. It was a valediction forbidding mourning. I found* myself explaining again how I had approached the part of a daffodil. Richard heard and said I was drunk, but I was just happy.

We've closed now and the next show has moved in. Uptown, Da's won the Tony Award – see how right you were about that and how wrong I was? But for us 'our revels are now ended' and what a sad, sad line that is. Tomorrow Richard will be leaving me out to Kennedy.

Your loving daughter, Sally Ann.

PS Dad, something happened before I got a chance to post this letter. But before you read on: I AM SAFE. ALL IS WELL. You know I was upset about Richard never saying anything about the future. Well, on our last night in Donnelly's apartment, I confronted him. I asked him outright was there any hope for us? He said something facetious like there's always hope if you're alive. I said no, I mean a future for us. To be specific, would he have a baby with me? He has four children who live with their mother and that's enough he said. His marriage wasn't happy as you may have guessed. Well, that finished me and I cried myself to sleep. The next morning I got up before he did and stole out of the apartment. I hate farewells so I left a note saying I was going on out to the airport by myself. It was wrong of me but I was under great strain. I felt I'd messed up again by being so blunt about my wishes re a baby. Also that Donnelly had put Richard off me. There was too much of a gap between us, age wise and culturally. Happiness would always elude me, blah, blah, blah. You know how you feel. Well, I went to Port Authority but there was no bus to Kennedy. They told me something about a terminal but I couldn't take it in. I was sort of dislocated and really afraid of New York. I thought people were following me. I walked around for a bit, stopping in an Irish bar, a Blarney Stone, for lunch. I ordered a big feed, hoping to make myself feel better. But sitting there on my own I felt awkward. I thought men were staring. Well, then a guy, younger than me, came in with his grandfather. They sat near me and we struck up a conversation. He had facial hair and jeans and a check shirt. He was so kind to his grandfather that I thought he must be ok. I said I was going to Kennedy and he told me about the bus terminal and how to get there by subway. Then he left without the old man. As I was so nervous about travelling on the subway by myself, I followed him, asking to walk a bit of the way with him. 'You're right to be careful in New York,' he said. 'I'll drive you over to the terminal.' His Volkswagen was parked nearby. It seemed harmless, so I agreed. But as soon as we were driving he said 'Why did you get into my car?' My heart stopped at the tone of his voice. I felt like a mouse before a cat. All the time I'd been afraid of black people! You don't realise how racist you are. But here was a harmless-looking white. 'You offered me a lift,' I said. He laughed sarcastically. 'I thought you wanted to be picked up.' 'Look,' I said, 'I'm sorry to have given that impression but I want to get to Kennedy. I'm flying home tonight.' He insisted we were going to his apartment. 'Please let me out!' I begged, panicking, but he wouldn't stop. He told me that he had a knife in his pocket. The car was going too fast, so I couldn't jump out. I had to think. 'Of course, I'll go to your apartment,' I said, 'it's not a bad idea at all.' But, as we had all day, could we possibly go to a book shop first? I had just remembered that I needed to buy a book for my brother who was about his age. Mention of a brother seemed to calm him, so he said there was a good bookshop with many bargains around 18th Street and 5th Avenue. We went there and I found a karate book for Tim. Browsing, I kept asking if he'd read this and that. Inside I was thinking: I should run away now, somehow lose him, but I thought it might turn out worse. I was frightened of being knifed. I mean he followed me with one hand in his jeans pocket. What was in there? We went outside again and his car had a parking ticket. I secretly memorised the number, while laughing aloud at the irony. I mean he's trying to commit a rape and he gets a parking ticket! My laughter angered him so I said sorry, that I didn't mean to laugh. Then we got back into the car and drove off. On the way back downtown to his apartment I controlled my panic by chat. 'What do you do for amusement?' I asked. He shrugged. 'Pick up girls in singles clubs'. So I asked 'If you can go there, why bother with me?' Then I said I'd never been to a singles place and would he please bring me to one. Before the apartment. Then I could at least feel as good as they were. This suggestion seemed to amuse him, so we stopped at place called Go-Go's. He bought me a drink and we sat opposite each other in a booth. I asked how did he pick up the women? 'It's all eye contact,' he said, demonstrating his technique of looking and then looking away. If the girl looked back it meant she was interested. All the time I was thinking how the hell will I get away? The irony was I'd got into the mess from being afraid. But I had to keep my head now. I asked to go to the Ladies, so he agreed to that. Miraculously there was a phone inside. So I called the operator and she got me the police. I told them he was threatening me and forcing me to have sex, but I only knew roughly where I was. I told them the name of the place. So they asked for the number of the car, which I had memorized, and the phone number there. They told me to delay him as long as I could. But when I came out he grabbed me, yelling 'Bitch! You called the cops!' I screamed as he dragged me out of the bar to the car. The barman heard but barely looked up. In the street people passed and did nothing. I remembered Donnelly's groaning that 'nobody gave a damn' in New York and thought I'd be knifed. All the way to his apartment which was down towards the Village I kept wondering how to get out. Once at a traffic light I tried to open the door, but he pulled on suddenly. 'Do that again and I'll kill you!' After that he kept the knife at my ribs. Well, we got there and I was crying. I kept thinking: I've seen his face. He'll kill me because I'll be able to identify him. He pulled me inside and up three flights of stairs, badly tearing my blouse. I tried to delay him more, saying 'There's no need for violence. I like you. Let me have a bath first.' This pleased him so he said he'd get into his robe. I locked myself in the bathroom, playing for time and trying not to cry. I ran the shower, but didn't get in. Surely help would come? After a while he banged on the bathroom door, screaming 'Open up!' Then he started calling me names. I thought I was done for. Where were the police? Surely they could trace the car owner. He kept banging on the door and finally burst it open. Seeing I wasn't undressed he yelled furiously. 'You're trying to trick me!' I thought I was going to vomit. Then the phone rang, and grabbing my wrist, he went to answer it. While he was talking, the door burst open and men with guns ran in. They were dressed in plain clothes, so at first I didn't know they were the cops. Then a women took me over to the couch, while he was grabbed and brought away handcuffed.

The police said I was lucky. There had been a few cases like this, and now they had a suspect. I was crying at my own stupidity, but they said I'd been smart to call them. I said it was only good luck. They took me to the station to file a complaint, saying I'd have to testify later in court. I said I was flying back to Ireland that night and that disappointed them, as they said he'd be let out on bail. But still they couldn't hold me as I'd done nothing wrong. Finally, as it was so late, they left me to the airport, saying they'd want me back to testify. I think I'm still in shock.

And there was another shock waiting for me. Richard was at the Aer Lingus booth, mad as hell and chain-smoking. Immediately I saw him I cried. He took one look at my torn blouse and the cop carrying my case and said 'What happened?' The cop explained I was the victim of aggravated assault. Then he asked Richard to see me onto the plane and left. I burst out crying again, thinking Richard would be angry with me. But he said 'Why do you wear that awful muck on your eyes?' My mascara had got messed. 'My blouse is ruined,' I said. 'It's *a good blouse too.' Then he said 'Give me that return ticket!' I thought he was going to check me in, but he pocketed it and we got a cab back to Port Authority. So I'm still here! It was all my own fault. I told Richard everything that happened and he agreed that it was stupid to get into the car, that I trusted people and you can't these days. I never will again. Then we taxied back into the city and made the Athens bus. When we pulled out of the Lincoln Tunnel, I was glad to be out of New York. But the skyline was gold in the evening sun. It's the most beautiful place on earth, despite everything.*

VIII

GRACIE

Grace O'Malley livened up the University of Pennsylvania
Athens campus. For better or worse her visit is still
marvelled at by town and gown alike. Dick had set up the
Irish Studies programme and was on the committee to find
an Irish writer for a semester. He said they chose Gracie for
a few reasons: she had published half a dozen novels and
had an American reputation. She was, I suspected, Dick's
ex-girlfriend, although he wouldn't admit it. He'd met her
in the wild years after he left Nettie and years before me.
Girlfriends, who shall be nameless, popped up all the time,
sending Christmas cards or asking to meet him in London.
He'd gone out with Grace for a whole summer and brought
her to the first night of one of his plays. Although she didn't
remember me I had met her in my art gallery days. Dublin
is a small place and she had gatecrashed a restaurant table I
shared with friends and drank all our wine. She was on the
wagon now, or that's what Dick thought. When she arrived
two days late I was the first person she rang. It was my third

year in America and I was missing home. So her west of Ireland accent was rain on the Sahara. 'Is that Mrs Sheridan?' she asked.

'It's Sally Ann,' I said.

Mrs Sheridan, that's Nettie, lived in a huge house across campus but that was too hard to explain. That I was his current live-in girlfriend was even more so.

'Your Dickie's daughter then?'

'I'm a friend. You must be Miss O'Malley?'

'Gracie. Where the fuck is Dickie?'

I put her language down to nerves. 'He's teaching at the moment.'

'He said he'd meet me.'

'He was expecting you yesterday,' I went on calmly. 'We went to Philadelphia airport.'

'I had to see New York! Tell Dickie to get his arse up here! I'm in some kip of a station.'

She described our nearest station and I knew the panic of looking for a taxi there. 'We'll be right up. Wait at the newsstand.'

Dick answered his office phone but he wasn't pleased about driving. He was already irritated with Gracie for wasting our whole Sunday. 'Why didn't you tell her to take a cab?' He groaned. 'I'll have to go.'

'Can I come?'

'Don't you have art class?'

I said I could miss it, and we agreed to meet at the car. It was a yellow Volkswagen, parked as usual behind our apartment – Dick always walked to the university. He's an expert on nineteenth century Ireland, probably the world expert on the Famine. He looked irritated coming into the car park. He'd been teaching so he wore his Donegal tweed jacket with jeans – even in winter he never wears a coat. Odd, considering he always insists on my wearing one.

He'd even bought me one for our first Christmas. And typically, he mentioned it now, frowning over the top of the car. 'Don't you need a coat?'

It was a snowy February, but I wore my anorak. 'This is fine.'

I got in and we drove in silence through the town. It's a place that would've been idyllic in the thirties. The big clapboard houses with their elegant nineteenth century porches weren't noisy student fraternities then. The opera house had still hosted travelling companies. There was even a theatre, and Main Street's eighteenth century facade hadn't been ruined by fast food joints like Roy Rogers and McDonalds. There are a few remaining shops, but most have moved out to the graceless mall. They've done up the old Academy building from which the university is descended, but blight has denuded it of elms. The blight is all over, although they're planting other trees. The only other remarkable thing about Athens is that it's on the Mason Dixon line. Till about 1965 the railway track divided the town. Before that any black person who wandered onto Main Street was picked up by the cops and driven back over the track. Today that's all changed thanks to civil rights, but the cargo train still trundles through, reminding me of old films where people jumped trains on their way west. Otherwise it's dull. Take my word. Dick was in a mood so I didn't make conversation. I knew he was furious at the waste of time. He's a terribly hard worker. It could be the reason he went white in his twenties, or else his unhappy marriage. I don't know. But, besides his good looks and brains, his mania for work was one of the reasons I loved him. I hoped it'd rub off on me – by osmosis or something. And since coming to America I'd gone back to my painting and worked hard, but despite this I doubted my ability.

Entering the turnpike I gripped the sides of my seat. It amazes me the way Americans are born able to drive. Even teenagers take the deadly highways so casually. You could be driving along in your little Volks when a truck the size of a house passes you out – which was the case with us now. I tensed even more, imagining us strewn across the highway.

'Is that necessary?' Dick broke into my thoughts.

'What?' I looked over.

He hissed through his teeth. 'Breathing like that.'

'I wasn't.'

'You were. It's no help.'

'Sorry.'

Lately all the romance was going from our relationship. I missed my family and friends so much. From studying history, I'd become it, and now mostly hung around the apartment when not at art class while Dick typed on his damn book. I couldn't get a job because I had no green card, and we hardly went anywhere any more. In the beginning there was his play in New York. But now I went to the movies on my own because Dick didn't like French films, only horror or cowboy: *King Kong* or *Flash Gordon* serials. I'm dead serious. Once we had this row about whether film was a literary genre. Idiotically I'd argued that it was but lately he never talked to me, only criticised. Like the remark just now about my breathing, and cutting class. I wanted to be a painter but hated figure drawing. And didn't see the need for it as my stuff was non-representational. But Dick insists that you need the foundation. He just smiled when I told him people didn't draw any more. He has a terrible habit of smiling if he disagrees with me. His eyes sort of glint. It's maddening.

Now he was glowering and he kept it up as we approached Wilmington. An interesting fact is that Wolfe Tone landed here before 1798 on his way to be a Princeton farmer. Today it's a city of vast extremes of wealth and poverty. It's not difficult to believe that it had race riots as late as 1970. It's a place you're not tempted to visit. Or, if so, there'd be no way without a car. That's another thing about America – the lack of public transportation. You can't hop on a bus like in Dublin. You're stuck in the middle of a jungle of highways. And if you take a wrong turn you might as well be in outer space. We can't seem to go down the street without getting lost – it's Dick's homing pigeon streak. Once out for a short drive we ended up deep in Amish country.

There was no sign of Gracie at the station. She wasn't at the newsstand or in the rest room. Dick checked the platform. He came back, scanning the waiting area. What if she had meant Philadelphia? Dick was right about me being vague.

He read my thoughts now. 'You're sure she said Wilmington?'

I nodded. There'd be a row next. But then we heard a Galway accent:

There's a one-eyed yellow idol to the north of Khatmandu
There's a little marble cross below the town;
There's a broken-hearted woman tends the grave of Mad Carew,
And the Yellow God forever gazes down.

It came from the bar. Gracie sat at the counter with an old black man. She was a buxom woman in her late forties, a few years older than Dick, and she had thick red shoulder-length hair and a weatherbeaten, freckled face. Worse than me in the coat line, she wore only a skimpy tight black suit, with dramatic fishnet stockings, high heels, blouse and bag. As we crossed the bar she went on reciting. Later, I was to judge her state of sobriety by different poems. 'Twenty Golden Years Ago' or 'Let the Toast Pass' meant she'd only had a few drinks. But 'The Green Eye of the Little Yellow God' or 'The Ballad of William Bloat' were danger signals.

She was on a bender but I was delighted to have found her. Dick was all smiles too. Seeing us she rose swayingly. 'Dickie!'

As they embraced, her bosom collided into him. Then she introduced her friend who nodded and smiled. She said they'd met on the train, but he looked a down-and-out. Was it safe to be drinking with him?

Then Dick remembered me. 'This is – a friend. Sally Ann Fitzpatrick.'

We shook hands. At least he'd given up calling me his secretary. He had once, in a New York bookshop, which was idiotic, considering I couldn't type.

She eyed me curiously. 'Yer the girl I spoke to?'

I nodded.

Her blue eyes were surrounded by millions of tiny wrinkles, and too much eyeliner gave her a startled clownish look. 'What are ye drinkin'? A Bourbon, Dickie?'

He shook his head. 'It's too early, Gracie.'

She waved to the barman. 'Over here, Bob.'

'We should be getting back.' Dick looked at me, saying with heavy emphasis. 'Sally Ann has lunch waiting.'

I blinked vaguely. 'Lunch ... Yes, lunch is waiting.'

'Let it wait! What're ye drinkin'?'

Dick shrugged. 'Well, all right.'

'White wine,' I said.

'Have something decent!' And she turned to the barman, ordering bourbon for herself and her black friend. I insisted on wine, as it's all I ever drink.

When the drinks were served, she leaned over. 'Lend me a fifty, Dickie. I blew everything in New York.'

He gave it to her, smiling, a bad sign. She told the barman to keep the change. Dick sipped his drink philosophically. 'You said you were flying into Philadelphia?'

Gracie sighed heavily. 'Aer Lingus kept serving me doubles. I woke up in the Chelsea.'

I doubted Aer Lingus would do that. My father had patients who regularly went on benders, ending up in St John of God's Hospital or even Grangegorman. They came to him for certificates for work, and he gave them, saying alcohol was a disease which got people in its grip. There were certain physical symptoms: a red face, yellow bloodshot eyes and a sort of puffy look – all of which Gracie had.

She sat slouched over the bar now, laughing at her companion who was requesting more poetry. She slammed down her drink, then, lowering her voice, began 'In a mean abode on the Shankill Road lived a man called William Bloat!' She went on reciting as her friend laughed raucously. Dick looked as if he was already regretting Gracie. He downed his drink and, grabbing her huge suitcase, made for the door. 'We're going, Gracie! Sally Ann, finish your drink!'

She reddened, nudging her companion. 'My friend here wants to hear the rest of the poem, don't ye?'

He nodded into his whiskey.

Dick was halfway to the door. 'Some other time. I have an afternoon class.'

They eyed each other.

'I'm going now,' Dick said steadily. 'If you don't come, you'll have to take a cab.'

He's not a man to argue with. He has this aura of authority, from teaching I suppose. Muttering, she exchanged telephone numbers with her friend. To my alarm she gave him ours – I mean she'd only just met him. Outside in the street Gracie shiveringly hugged her skimpy jacket. 'Christ! This climate'd freeze yer arse!'

'Don't you have a coat?' Dick asked typically. 'It's February, after all.'

She laughed. 'I started out with one.'

I sat in the back and Gracie got in front with Dick. All the way back to Athens she complained about the Chelsea Hotel. 'I've never seen so many bugs.'

Dick concentrated on driving. 'That's New York.'

I knew the Chelsea area well, from putting on Dick's play. But if I told my cockroach story he would only put me down. He always says I exaggerate things, but I swear to God once when I was waiting on West 22nd Street for the lights to change I happened to look down. And a cockroach the size of a mouse was beside me. The lights changed: I walked on and so did the cockroach.

'I had to get the manager up. They were flyin' round the room.'

Cockroaches didn't fly. Dick caught my eye in the mirror.

She groaned. 'When do I start giving out the wisdom, Dickie?'

'You're already late,' he said. 'I've covered your first class.'

She looked puzzled. 'Now how's that?'

Dick shrugged. 'I sent you the dates.'

'Patsy McCallow deals with everything.' She turned to me. 'He's my fiancé, the Mullingar poet.'

Gracie always called her 'fiancé' the Mullingar poet and she always blamed him when things went wrong. I suppose he was at a convenient distance. Then I noticed her shivering. 'Are you feeling all right?'

She groaned in reply, her head in her hands. It turned out Gracie was sick. So Dick made her sleep in our study the first night. But the next day she insisted she was ok and taught her fiction class. Getting ready, she spent ages in the bathroom. I waited in dread, but she came out sober and completely deflated compared to yesterday. As usual she wore her uniform – black suit and too much eye makeup which made her look like Dracula's daughter.

'Black suits you, Gracie,' I said cheerfully.

Tremblingly, she checked her lipstick in a small handbag mirror. 'I'm in mournin' for me life. You'll help, Sally Ann, if I dry up.'

'Yes, but you won't.'

To learn something about writing I had asked to sit in. I lent her my coat and we walked together across campus. The class had already assembled. They were the usual mixture of younger graduate students and older women. A student called Fred had been chosen by Dick to read his story that day. A tall, handsome boy with that healthy American look, his fair hair and skin contrasted with studious horn-rimmed glasses, reminding me of the comic strip hero, Superman. Yet there was something fussily effeminate about Fred: while most students dressed casually in jeans and a check shirt, he always wore a suit. He was a Joycean, I learnt later. This breed of academic consider every Irish writer but Joyce the dregs and spend their lives writing papers to make him seem difficult. There are Yeatsians and Beckettians too, but the Joyceans exceed them in number and peculiarity. Fred was writing a doctoral thesis on defecation symbolism in *Ulysses* – 'a shit man' was to be Gracie's definition of him. Also, he had the strangest notions of Irish history. For instance, he asked me once if St Patrick had slain the armies of Chuchulain at the Hill of Tara?

Gracie said a few words of introduction, then called on Fred. His story was absolutely corny. Rustling his papers, he began shakily, 'Eh ... It's called – eh – "Love Reclaimed".' Then, clearing his throat, went on:

> *I'll never forget the day Bar abandoned me. It was my last year in high school. I skipped swimming and came home early to practise my guitar. The house was uncharacteristically empty, but I knew she'd be in soon. She was doing some early Christmas shopping. Or she'd gone to the hairdresser to have that blonde rinse again. Why didn't she stick*

to her natural grey which I preferred? I played a few numbers, then put on a Dave Bowie record. Outside, the last shreds of day gradually disappeared, while inside a melancholy dark pervaded. 'All I have,' Bowie screeched, 'is my love of love'. I became more and more depressed, and finally switched off the record. Would Bar desert me without a word? Had our love meant nothing? We'd had days of wine and roses, of love and champagne. But were they over forever? No, they couldn't be. By eight I cooked a hamburger. She would surely be in any minute. Then I would surprise her by cooking her one. I would then make popcorn, and we'd look at late night TV like old times. But by nine o'clock there was no sign of her. My mind ran away with me. She'd come to harm. Been raped, horribly mutilated. At ten I rang the cops.

As Fred's voice droned on I looked to see how Gracie was reacting. To my alarm she held a pocket flask to her lips. God, I thought, as she rescrewed it and put it back in her handbag. Our eyes met: she gave me a 'don't you dare tell' look that I was to become familiar with. What would everyone say now? What would they think of the Irish for being such drinkers? So far we'd been able to hide her in our apartment, but tonight she'd be on her own. Who would control her then? I had an awful foreboding. The story got sillier and sillier. There was no question of Fred's friend being murdered. She had left him a note that she'd gone on a cruise or something. Listening, I got an attack of the giggles. When Fred stopped reading, we all looked at Gracie. She coughed nervously. 'Sally Ann, any comments?'

I racked my brains. 'I – thought the symbolism terrific – the parcel and that.'

Fred's face lit up. 'You got it?'

I nodded. When the others joined in, Gracie listened politely. Then, when everyone was silent, she said 'Let's talk about it in terms of structure.'

She gave a brilliant lecture on the Aristotelian plot: situation, complication; rising to climax, and finally denouement. Sick or not, she knew her stuff. The class was a great success. Everyone joined in the discussion. I asked why all stories had to have this basic formula. I mean, why couldn't there be a series of small climaxes instead of one big one, like in Virginia Woolf's *The Waves*? Lately I'd become recharged about feminism and was intrigued to learn that we were a disadvantaged class, and that we were studied in America as a separate species. So why did the male gender have to dominate a thing like plot? Locally the feminists had changed the spelling of women to wimin, and woman to womyn. So why not change in other areas?

Gracie said I was talking rubbish. 'Virginia Woolf is caviar,' she said. 'Not a writer to learn from.'

I was grateful for the caviar bit at least.

That night Gracie moved into her own apartment. It was a mistake not to tell Dick about the flask because from then on I entered into a conspiracy with her against him. While he prided himself on persuading her off the 'hard stuff' and onto a maintenance dose of wine, I knew she was drinking whiskey on the sly. But any word to Dick and I would be worse than Judas.

Around this time Dick got sick. We were grocery shopping one day when he frowned, as if in pain. When I asked him what it was he said his tongue hurt. We were having people to dinner so he wouldn't call the doctor. He kept saying that it'd go away. But all night long it got worse, swelling until he couldn't swallow or speak. He sat up, afraid to go to sleep. Although a doctor's daughter I'd never seen anything like it. I kept getting up and asking him how he was. But he'd only mumble 'Go gack to ged.'

He's a midwestern stoic and once broke an ankle without noticing. All night I dozed fretfully, dreaming he was having a heart attack downstairs. I even thought of ringing my father in Ireland for advice, I felt so lonely and helpless. At dawn I rang our dentist and he said to ring our doctor. I did, but as it was the weekend the doctor wasn't there. I left a message on an answering machine. Eventually another doctor rang me back and said to meet him at his surgery in half-an-hour. In between, I rang Gracie in desperation.

She came over immediately and peered down Dick's throat. 'It's a touch of the quinsy.'

'What's that?' I asked.

'Tonsillitis, girl.'

I could've hugged her for diagnosing something so ordinary. She came with us to the doctor who insisted that it was an allergy attack from eating cheese. Or maybe from aspirin – he didn't know which, but Dick was to write down everything he ate. While getting the medicine I remembered I'd given him a vitamin B tablet which I took for premenstrual tension. Could he be allergic to that? I felt guilty for persuading him to take it and sick from lack of sleep.

Dick seemed to get better but I still worried. It's silly, but I always imagine the worst – maybe because he smokes. Or because of my mother dying so young. I dreaded him eating and bringing on another attack, or taking aspirin. Maybe he was allergic to something growing in the yard? Everyone in the university thought I was daft – I could see them exchanging glances. No one was sypmpathetic, except Gracie. She would always listen to me with sympathy. She appeared to be doing ok in her own apartment, so I worried less about her. At first the faculty were good about inviting her to dinner, so she only came to us occasionally now.

One evening the Athens feminist community gave a party for her. It was hosted by Anna and Sue, a lesbian couple I'd met at a series of lunchtime lectures on women. The lectures were chaired by Anna, a professor who worked with Dick in the history department, and touched on everything from TV images of women to blocked fallopian tubes. Sue was a lab assistant in Wilmington, who left her job to have a child. It intrigued me that they had a baby called Circe. Apparently they'd wanted to be an ordinary family, so Sue, being the younger, had got herself artificially inseminated. It'd been a struggle to find the right doctor but they had finally. Another bonus was he used fresh and not frozen sperm – if it's anything like frozen food I understood the preference. The doctor's donors were all medical students, but the women could choose their ethnic type. To my delight they chose Irish: blue eyes, freckles and red hair. Also they'd ordered musical ability. So far Circe just smiled like any sweet little baby. I couldn't imagine her ever turning men into pigs. Or what they'd have done if she'd been a boy.

Their house was in West Main Street, one of the best areas of town. Like most American houses it had lovely hardwood floors and oriental rugs. There were spider plants everywhere and the kitchen was full of gadgets. Men weren't invited, so I went with Gracie who had unwittingly invited Fred – she went everywhere with him. It was some sort of infatuation on his part. We arrived when the party was in full swing. Hordes of women chatted in the living room, while some spilled out to the kitchen and hall. Most were casually dressed, so Gracie stood out in a sexy purple dress. So did Fred in his suit.

Anna met us in the hall. They were the first lesbians I'd ever met, so I didn't know what to expect, maybe for one to be masculine, but they weren't like that. Anna's sort of motherly with shoulder length curly hair, bleached by the sun at the tips, and lovely deep set eyes. She's always elegantly dressed. That night she was wearing floppy black evening pants and a pink blouse. Although she earns the money, they're equals. I mean, it's not like one does the cooking: they share everything. When I mentioned to Dick that this was ideal, he said to forget it – the trouble is, he can't cook anything but steak, although he does do the washing-up. But their arrangement is far better.

'Ah, Sally Ann,' Anna said warmly. 'Ms O'Malley?'

They shook hands, Anna saying 'A colleague was telling me about *On Another Man's Wound*.'

Gracie laughed shortly. 'That's Ernie O'Malley. He's the opposition.'

'She's called after an Irish pirate queen,' I said quickly, as Americans often mixed up Irish writers or mispronounced their names. '*Grainne Uaille* – it means "noble one" in Irish.'

Anna was interested in this and intrigued by Gracie's accent, saying that she spoke much faster than an American. Then, as Fred was hovering, I introduced him. 'This is Fred, Grace's student.'

'Hi!' He thrust out his hand, a gangster cigar in the corner of his mouth.

Anna didn't flinch at his grip, but looked pointedly at the cigar. Gracie sensed the situation. 'He's with me.'

Anna nodded. 'He'll have to smoke on the porch. Sue worries about the baby's chest.'

At the mention of the baby, Fred's tough act wilted and he went outside. Anna got us some cranberry punch. As well as being anti-smoking, they're anti-booze and coffee. They never drink anything but a peculiar herb tea. They're vegetarian too and dead right to take care of their health. I suggested to Dick that we cut out meat, but of course got the usual 'Forget it.'

Gracie peered at the punch. 'What's this? Blood?'

I kept my face straight. 'It's a fruit punch.'

Anna patted her shoulder. 'Full of vitamin C.'

Gracie looked at it sadly. 'I could do with some of that.'

We mingled with the others. Gracie was lionized, although no one had read her books. Later I went in search of Sue. About three weeks earlier I'd left a doll for Circe in the history department, for which they'd never thanked me. It wasn't that I expected thanks. I understood it had slipped their minds. I just worried in case they hadn't got it. She was in the kitchen, taking a tray of snacks out of the oven. She's a small Swedish blonde woman with her hair in a long pigtail. Now she looked frazzled, as she took a tray of hot snacks out of the oven.

'Hi, Sally Ann,' she said, looking round.

'Can I help?'

'You can pass these round.'

I arranged the snacks on a plate while Sue dashed about, doing this and that. Americans, I'd discovered, were marvellous cooks. By now I was better too, and had learnt to make all sorts of things from a James Beard paperback, although Dick still complained about my salads – he likes funny things on it.

'You got that doll all right?' I said after a few minutes.

Sue frowned. 'Didn't Anna write you?'

'No, but that's ok. I couldn't decide what to get. I thought you'd have enough clothes.'

'You never have enough clothes with a baby, Sally Ann. You'll find out!'

I was taken aback. 'Well, I'll ... they might change it.'

'Dolls are sexist.'

'I'll change it.'

Sue was right to be honest. If you don't like something, why not change it? People aren't honest enough. Their outspokenness was what I liked about Anna and Sue. 'Speak what you feel, not what you ought to say.'

I can't remember when, but during the party, Anna quizzed Gracie about her classes. Anna was completely committed to women, so, on hearing that the survey course on Irish literature contained men writers, she said 'I hoped you'd focus on women.'

Gracie was quite affable. 'I'm teaching the main ones – Maria Edgeworth, Mary Lavin, Elizabeth Bowen, Kate O'Brien, and we'll squeeze in Edna O'Brien.' This was a joke, as Edna O'Brien was a rival.

'Why not teach women exclusively?'

'Well, it's a survey course. There's Yeats, Joyce, Synge, O'Casey.'

'How can we ever mainstream women?'

'Not by ghettoizing them. Do you support apartheid?'

That absolutely threw Anna. 'No!'

'You're preaching it!' Gracie hesitated. 'You could teach a course on women's fiction, but it wouldn't be what you want. Mills & Boon is a definite genre.'

'I think you're being sexist.'

Gracie laughed. 'There's men's trash too.'

Luckily the baby woke up then, and Sue brought her out to the kitchen. I watched in fascination as she breastfed. It seemed the most wonderful thing to feed a baby from your own body. Even Gracie had to admire Circe, chuckling over her name. Babies have a way of bringing out the good in people. It's awe for a new life, an attempt to put the best face on terrible things. I forget how, but the conversation got onto marriage. I think Anna and Sue said they weren't legally bound or something. I said I was becoming a convert to marriage, which brought an odd remark from Anna. 'Be careful about marriage, Sally Ann.'

I was puzzled. 'What do you mean?'

'Well ... by allying yourself with Richard ...'

Then Gracie exploded. 'Sure, who else would she ally herself with?'

I thought there'd be another personality clash, but Anna said kindly. 'He's lucky to meet someone so sensitive and beautiful.'

'I was lucky too!' I knew Anna sparred with Dick at department meetings. I knew he could be acerbic. I knew that's all it was. Or maybe she thought Nettie and his children caused complications. Still, it wounded me that she didn't like Dick. And I wasn't beautiful. How could I be with glasses?

I wandered off, joining another conversation. Gracie followed me, whispering 'Let's go!'

I looked at her nervously. 'You won't overdo it?'

She gave me her word. So we repaired to the local tavern, where an idiotic thing happened. Although surrounded by laughing students I couldn't keep the tears from my eyes. Anna and Sue were meant to be my friends, probably the only friends I'd made in America – usually I was an extension of Dick. They had introduced me into a whole new world of feminism. And they'd taken me cycling into the country, before Circe was born. They seemed to like me, although Sue, particularly, was always pulling me up on what I said as if I were some right-wing person. Like I'd once mentioned something about South Africa, saying maybe they shouldn't cut off all investment – I'd read in the *New York Times* that Alan Paton thought this too. But Sue had pounced on me, as if I supported the regime. If you ask me, there's apartheid in America too: they just don't call it that. In three years I'd only met one black student, and someone told me the university had to be forced to allow blacks to attend. Another time Sue had attacked me for calling the loo the 'Ladies Room'. She asked, hadn't I read *The Women's Room*? According to her it was the most brilliant novel ever written. Sometimes feminism was too dogmatic, like the Maoists back in Dublin. If women were oppressed, so were men, paying for all the damn washing machines. Dick always worked so hard, and for years gave most of his salary to Nettie. I knew he loved his children, even if he couldn't express it. And he'd been so sick the other night. His throat wasn't entirely better yet, but he wouldn't give up cheese or aspirin. He said we all had a disease called mortality. That you lived till you died. But what if he choked to death the next time?

I sat there staring into my fruit juice. Then Gracie, who'd been chatting to Fred, noticed me upset. 'What's up with you?'

I wiped my eyes. 'It's Dick's allergy attacks.'

'Allergy attacks, me eye! It's quinsy!'

I felt better. After a while I said, trying to sound light-hearted. 'Did you hear what Anna said about marriage?'

'Silly bitch!'

'You can't call her that.' I'd used the word in the past, but nowadays it took me aback.

'Better a silly bitch than a sacred cow! Isn't she married herself?'

'They've taken vows to each other.'

'What's that, only marriage?' Gracie downed her juice in one alarming gulp. 'I don't care what anyone fucks or sucks: man, woman or goat, but I hate bad manners! A hostess shouldn't be abrasive!'

I had to laugh. Then Fred offered to go for more cranberry juice, but Gracie said 'We're going. I need wine!' She leant towards me. 'Dickie's a good man.'

It meant so much. In retrospect, I was too thin-skinned. I should've been tougher. I was a stranger in a foreign country and far from my own family, and Anna mistrusted men. Maybe she had suffered at their hands? Sue, I know, had been in a bad marriage. Luckily, I managed to change the doll for a truck.

At spring break Gracie escaped our clutches, going north to a college she had taught at years ago. Of course, they filled her to the gills with spirits. One night soon afterwards we got a phone call that she was legless in the local tavern.

So Dick collected her, making her move back in with us. He was afraid to let her out of his sight and forbade any drink.

I'd never seen anyone so poisoned with alcohol. Her eyes were black circled, her pallor yellowish, and she crept around the apartment in a worn floral dressing gown. Dick had to teach, so he was out a lot, and I ended up babysitting her again. I was fond of her and worried about her not eating. I made her eggflips – which my mother had made me. It was one of my few memories of her. Usually in the afternoons I sat in the kitchen with a book. It was old-fashioned, the pleasantest room in our book-lined apartment. Sunlight filtered through spider plants at the windows and there was a small, white marbletop table. Dick had painted the antiquated fridge and walls in different greens, and black frying pans and copper pots hung over the stove. Gracie usually joined me.

I was reading when she came in sipping her eggflip and sat down opposite me. 'I'd only drink this for you, Sally Ann.'

I glanced up from my book of short stories. 'You have to eat.'

She sipped some more. 'Ugh! Do you like America, Sally Ann?'

'It's ok.' I put down my book. 'I look forward to the summer a lot. We go to Dublin then.'

'There's no place like Ireland.'

I went back to my book.

'Sorry, I'm interrupting you.'

'No! I was finishing a Seamus O'Shea story.' I pushed over my paperback. 'What do you think of him?'

She ran her fingers through her thick hair. 'He was a premature ejaculator.'

'A what?' I thought it was some literary term.

'Surely you've had selfish lovers?'

'Well ... no.' I was embarrassed. I'd wanted her opinion of the writing, but Gracie judged every man by his sexual performance.

She looked smilingly into space. 'He was macho. I used to be covered in bruises.' She held up her arms. 'Then his wife found out.' She hesitated, then asked casually. 'How's Dickie?'

'Fine. He should be in soon.'

'No, I mean in bed.'

I looked at her, reddening.

'You get on well?'

I nodded and she lapsed into silence.

'I missed out there,' she sighed. 'We didn't like each other's bodies enough.'

'You mightn't have liked living here. Dick works all the time.'

Why hadn't Dick told me? He was like my father in the area of non-communication. I assumed our sex life was ok, because at last I could relate. I seemed to have shed my hangups because someone loved me. Maybe the cliché about finding the right person was true. Or maybe I wanted to get pregnant.

Gracie seemed to read my thoughts. 'Are ye going to marry?'

I shrugged. 'Maybe sometime. What about you and the Mullingar poet?'

'His Mammy'd have a fit. She doesn't know about me.'

Although he wanted us to marry, my father didn't object to Dick at all. I think he was relieved to be rid of me. 'I suppose we'd marry if I got pregnant.'

She gave me a sad look. 'That doesn't go with being an artist. I had a daughter – married in London now.'

'Do you see her often?'

She looked past me, saying after a minute. 'You're a talented painter, Sally Ann.' She cupped her hands. 'Talent is a little flame ... If you don't guard it, it'll go out.'

I looked away. No one had ever said that to me because it wasn't true. My stuff was too imitative. But Gracie was kind, also amazingly perceptive. I think she knew how much it meant for a person to *be* something and wanted to encourage me. Most probably we'd hit a sore spot in her daughter, because she fell into a brooding silence.

I broke it. 'You haven't finished your eggflip.'

She pushed it away. 'Would you give me a drink, Sally Ann?'

I shook my head. 'No!' I was in a quandary. One drink and she'd be lost. That was the way with alcoholics.

'Please, Sally Ann!'

I held out. 'Would you go to AA?'

She looked outraged. 'Are you off your head, girl?'

That very evening I came unexpectedly into the kitchen to find Gracie taking a swig from Dick's whiskey bottle. Before I could say anything she pointed an accusatory finger. 'Don't tell Dickie!' When Gracie moved out on her own again I knew she wouldn't eat, so I made her promise to have dinner with us every evening. In that way I could be sure she had one decent meal a day. Also, we could make sure she wasn't drinking too heavily. Well, she came for about a week. Then she came drunk one day and plonked a decanter of Paul Masson wine on the table, saying 'I'm ok on wine.'

Then Dick walked in and, taking one look at Gracie's red face, grabbed the bottle and emptied it down the sink.

She watched ruefully. 'You're wastin' good drink, Dickie.'

Dick glared at me so I poured out mine too. We had dinner in awful silence. Afterwards I walked Gracie home across campus. She didn't ask me in but yawned sleepily at the door.

'I'm sorry Dick got so angry,' I said.

'Dick's a good man. Goodnight now.' She went inside, shutting her door firmly in my face.

I had never been in her apartment. I didn't know then that Fred was inside waiting for her. Their affair was the talk of our little community. It seemed to shock everyone that he was a younger man and she an older woman. I don't know why: people accepted a young woman and an older man.

Gracie didn't come to dinner again. I missed her, but Dick was glad our life had returned to some sort of normality. Although it wouldn't be completely normal so long as Gracie was in town. He went back to his book, and I was thrown back on my loneliness. But I accepted this as part of our relationship. I'd made the decision to love Dick and now had to act on it. Happiness was meant to be the final end of man, but did it exist at all? And what was it anyway? No matter how lonely I was I couldn't admit failure. I had failed so often before – with Colm, Alastair and my terrible career. My father was only waiting for me to arrive back home, but I wanted to make something of my life. So I resigned myself to Dick's typing and became absorbed in my own work. I worked hard, attending every class and getting an A for my drawing course.

We heard Gracie was drinking again.

Towards the end of the semester we were invited to a dinner party at Fred's. He lived with an older woman, a sort of patron according to gossip, on a horse farm in the countryside. The drive down was lovely. In America they actually get a spring. I can't believe Ireland is any greener than Pennsylvania which bursts out all over. The weather was beginning to warm up and soon dogwoods would be out. We found the place without getting lost. It was like a movie set in an Elizabeth Taylor film. The house was a mansion at the end of a long tree-lined avenue. There were stables to one side and the fields on the other were surrounded by white fences. There were even horses grazing idyllicly. How did Fred manage to live there? When we arrived, everyone was having drinks on the porch. There was Max Wagoner, the chairman of the English department and his wife, Pam; a man called Felice who taught sculpture at the university; Gracie, looking red-faced and sexy in her purple dress, chatted to Fred and his patron, Mrs Davis, a hawklike older woman, with dyed gold hair and brown alligator skin. I thought at first she must be some older relation of Fred's. A great aunt maybe?

While he got us drinks, Gracie whispered to me 'Try and occupy Freddie tonight. I'm angling for your man there.' And she rolled her eyes at Felice. He was a fortyish Italian type. He had slick black hair and his shirt, open to the waist, revealed even more hair.

'What about Fred?' I asked.

'He's her gigolo.' She nodded towards Mrs Davis.

I looked disbelievingly at the older woman, dressed too youthfully in a gold pants suit. She must be the woman in his story.

She caught my stare. 'Are you a student, honey?'

I nodded. 'Of painting.'

She gave me a piranha smile. 'I thought you might be in the English department with Fred.'

'We're both taking Gracie's class.'

Gracie laughed. 'I have some real geniuses.' Sarcasm was unlike her. She was always kind and supportive, so I suspected the worst.

Mrs Davis went on sociably. 'Fred thinks there's no one like Joyce.'

'Wasn't one enough?' Gracie quipped. This brought a laugh from the others. 'He was a bloody pervert,' she went on. Gracie was pissed. I knew the signs: high colour and garrulousness. But there was no way I was getting involved in her amours, so I didn't try to 'occupy' Fred. What on earth did she expect me to do? Disappear with him into a cupboard? Several times she tried to chat up Felice, but he persistently ignored her. Finally, she fell asleep, snoring.

The dinner talk was typically boringly academic and dominated by Max Wagoner, another Joycean. He was a big German-American with tanned ash blond good looks who had learned the English language as a teenager and ended up as a professor -- a suave, preppie type who wore shirts and sweaters with little designer dragons. Anyway, during coffee, Felice casually asked him to explain the term structuralism.

Max launched into a pompous explanation. 'Well, it comes from two sources ...' He droned on, saying finally that you defined something by its opposite – no meaning exists, except in relation to something else.

'All works of literature could be said to be derivative?' Felice interrupted.

'Every system needs an opposite. Twentieth century man, for instance, is only perceived as tough compared to twentieth century woman.'

'What about deconstructionism?'

'That's from Derrida. It means "to take apart". A writer may seem to have written a comedy but it's really a tragedy.'

Then Gracie woke up shouting 'Bullshit!' There was a deadly silence. She looked sort of deranged. 'Bloody bullshit! You academics murder literature!'

Max Wagoner paled under his tan.

Dick smiled. 'Gracie may have a point.'

'Theorists, structuralists, deconstructionists! They're all the bloody same. I can't sit here talkin' gibberish.' She looked directly at Felice. 'Will ye give me a lift home?'

He looked alarmed. 'Eh ... I'm going in the other direction.'

There is meant to be no fury like a woman scorned. Gracie shouted 'You're a bumboy, that's your direction. Give me a full-blooded man!'

There was another silence. Everyone looked glacial.

Gracie was about to shout something else, but Max Wagoner interrupted. 'Miss O'Malley, AA meet in the university.'

'What are ye sayin'?' she yelled.

'I could arrange treatment for you.'

Her breast seemed to swell. 'How dare you, you Nazi!'

I got the giggles.

'Nazi! Nazi!' Gracie walked from the room with Fred running after her.

That night, when we arrived home, Dick got another allergy attack. I was sure it was from eating cheese at the party. We were up all night again and ended up going to the Emergency Centre. I told the nurse he refused to write down what he ate, so she told me to get life insurance. I now became obsessed with worry about him. I even had a nightmare that he died and was buried and I got Fred to dig him up. It was gruesome, but he still wouldn't give up things. At least for a while I stopped thinking about Gracie. Anyway, she was lost to us now.

One afternoon I was in the apartment reading when Max Wagoner rang to ask if I'd seen her. 'She hasn't been meeting her classes. I may try again to persuade her to get treatment.'

'Did you try the tavern?' I said. Lately she met her classes there.

'Yes, but no one has seen her for a week.'

I promised to tell him if she turned up. My stomach was in a knot of anxiety. Dick said there was nothing we could do about Gracie, but was it right to leave her on her own? Why couldn't we do something about her? Force her into a hospital? After all, she wasn't able to take care of herself. And why did she drink? What unhappiness had driven her to it? She was so talented and had written so many novels. How did she do it? Two drinks and I had a hangover.

Later that night there was a knock on the door. I thought it was Gracie but it was Fred. 'Sally Ann, can we talk?' I asked him in. He was wet with perspiration and completely winded. 'Have you seen Gracie?' When I said no, he wiped his horn-rims. 'You must help me find her!' I didn't know Fred well, so was surprised at his state. Apparently, it wasn't a casual affair to him. 'I love Gracie,' he said.

'She's engaged to Patsy McCallow?' I said gently.

He jumped up, pacing the room. 'She's what? She'll have to tell him it's off!'

I readjusted my glasses, amazed at his reaction. Gracie wasn't my idea of an attractive woman.

'You realise we've slept together!'

'You don't have to marry everyone you sleep with,' I said. 'Not nowadays.'

'You shock me, Sally Ann.'

If he was shocked I was more so. I had thought young Americans were all so sophisticated. But what was his relationship with Mrs Davis?

He went to the door. 'Come with me to her apartment.' We went to Gracie's apartment where the door was shut. There was no response to our loud knocking. 'I know you're in there!' Fred kept insisting to no avail.

I walked down the stairs. 'Come on, Fred.'

At that moment the door inched open and Gracie peeped out. 'I'll meet ye in the tavern in half an hour, Freddie.'

I took his arm, leading him down the stairs. The tavern was about ten minutes away. While we were waiting for Gracie I rang Dick, asking him to tell Max Wagoner that she was safe.

When Gracie came she walked swayingly over to us. 'What are ye havin', kids?'

We ordered Cokes, which reduced her to giggles.

Fred began accusing her. 'Who was in there with you?'

She held her glass up to me. 'Here's to a maiden of bashful fifteen ...'

Then Dick came in with Max Wagoner.

'And here's to the SS.'

Dick got drinks, and Max sat down, ignoring her remark. After a few polite enquiries as to how her classes were going, he pleaded 'Ms O'Malley, what about treatment?'

To my surprise Gracie patted his arm. Then Fred chipped in, saying fussily 'She's mixing with undesirable people. They short change her here.'

Gracie turned furiously on him. 'How dare you impugn the honour of my friends.'

'We're your friends, Gracie,' I said. I thought she was going to hit me. In a minute there'd be a scene. But Dick nudged me to drink up. I did and we left her. That evening Dick actually offered to take me to a French movie, the only thing on. It'd be like old times I thought. But we were on the way out, when there was more pounding on the door. It was Gracie again. We got her back to her apartment. I later learnt that she headed right back to the tavern. Of course it was too late for our movie. So, exhausted with all the drama, we went to bed. Dick was absolutely fed up. Life had become a grand opera. The term was a write off.

The next day Gracie disappeared. I worried about her nonstop, but Dick had that male ability to detach himself. It was nearly time for us to go back to Ireland for the summer, so there was a lot of packing to do, but Dick was still sick. I was afraid he'd get another allergy attack in the airplane, so persuaded him to see a specialist. Gracie turned out to be right: it wasn't an allergy but an infection. The first doctor had been prescribing the wrong thing entirely. But how had Gracie known? It was probably her canny wisdom about life, her enormous sympathy. You could tell her anything, and she wouldn't be shocked. There was nothing bourgeois about her. She could see through the pretentious Max Wagoners of this life. Despite everything I liked her much better than them. She was named after an Irish pirate queen and had her own sort of grace. I'd always miss her sense of fun.

I thought we'd never see her again. We were about a week from departure to Dublin when the Irish embassy phoned to say the New York police had Gracie in protective custody. Could we come and get her? So Dick and I went to her apartment and packed up her things. We found her passport and air ticket in a drawer, so Dick rang Aer Lingus, changing her flight to the following day. Then we drove to New York.

Gracie sat behind bars on a grim prison bunk with her head in her hands. Her red hair looked grey-streaked and tangled. Her stockings were torn, her arm bandaged, and she had a black eye and a badly grazed face. I put an arm around her shoulder. 'What happened, Gracie?'

'I'm a terrible person, Sally Ann.' Then her bloodshot eyes got angry. 'Did you see that cop out there? He said the Irish were all drunks.'

I turned to Dick. 'Look at her face.'

But she was reciting:

There's a one-eyed yellow idol to the north of Khatmandu,

There's a little marble cross below the town;
There's a broken-hearted woman ... There's a broken-hearted
woman ...
There's a broken-hearted woman ...

Dick took her arm. 'Come on Gracie, we'll get a pair of
shoes.'

IX

PEGGY AND TONY

Buying a house in Ireland is hazardous these days, especially with no money. We managed it, thanks to my friend Peggy. The four of us, Peggy and her husband Tony, and Dick and I, were in a Ranelagh pub, if I remember rightly. And the chat was going in the direction of troublesome landladies, the bane of our life then, when Peggy got her brainwave. 'Why not buy a house here?'

Dick's pint of Guinness stopped in mid-air.

Peggy smoothed her blonde hair. 'You could rent it out when you're in America.'

We weren't yet at the house-buying stage. For years we'd been 'unofficially engaged' – at least that's what my father told people. I didn't believe in marriage and Dick didn't either, but you have to allow fathers their pride. Peggy smiled at her own brilliance – she has a beautiful smile. Maybe it was some sort of mother complex but I loved her. She doesn't mind people knowing that she dyes her hair, or being overweight. Like Jack Spratt and wife Tony shrinks while she gets bigger. Tony knocked out his pipe. When the cards are down men will stick together, but Dick was lubricated enough to be taken with the idea – for a minute. Peggy's a seasoned mother of six and undeterred by obstacles.

'You need a mortgage!'

Dick spluttered into his Guinness. While I believe it's a free world, he thinks the opposite, so I expected an explosion about the cost of living, or the young generation. 'I already have one in America!' He gave her the pitying glance reserved for women and idiots and turned to Tony for reassurance.

'Rent's dead money, old son,' his friend said between puffs on his pipe.

Peggy waved at the smoke. 'Join an Irish building society.'

Dick frowned. 'I'm American.'

'Sally's Irish!' Peggy tore open her second packet of peanuts, offering me some.

I should explain that, although Peggy and Tony are old friends of Dick and his wife, Nettie, our friendship is not the less. Tony's a journalist so I expected his tacit male acceptance; I was, after all, the last of a line of girlfriends – or I hoped the last. But Peggy was another matter. She's fifteen years my senior and I had feared her judgement as an Irish Catholic wife and mother. But she immediately took my side, 'as a human being, Sally!' Peggy has none of the intolerance of our race and, like all the happily married, is an incurable matchmaker. I suspected her house idea was part of a strategy to get Dick settled again – i.e. properly divorced from Nettie and properly married to me. That I had failed in this became a challenge. Buying a house, if not a step down the aisle, was a step in that direction. I'd heard of building societies. I knew courting couples deposited their pittance in them, staking out a future. But the idea of joining one had never occurred to us. Before I met Dick I hadn't a penny over, and now he had another mouth to feed. Besides, we were suitcase people.

That evening in the pub I sipped on lager and lime, while Peggy explained the mechanisms of house-buying in Ireland. She knows all about the legal end: insurance policies, mortgages, solicitors' fees, bridging loans – topics which are Greek to me. Her 'conviction' woos you into thinking something impossible is possible. So my house obsession took root.

The next day Dick came home from the library unexpectedly early and presented me with a little blue savings book of an Irish building society. The sum of £50 was deposited inside. 'A twig for the nest,' he said, pouring himself a whiskey. 'Then I'll have to carry you over the threshold.'

By that dim and distant day, he won't be able to, I thought. I'd have attained the dignity of Peggy's proportions, and he'd be even wirier. Or else we'd both be in our graves. But the little book gave me hope.

Hope is the thing with
feathers that perches in the
Soul – and sings the tune
Without the words – and
Never stops at all.

From then on househunting became our hobby. Every fine weekend we'd windowshop in parts of old Dublin like the Liberties or one of the mucky new developments in the environs – the only two types of houses we could afford. It was a case of Scylla and Charybdis, Dick said. But he stuck to his preference for all mod cons, while I was lured by the romance of things old. In this Peggy was surprisingly sympathetic to me – I mean for a practical person. Still, in my obsession even the plains of Tallaght took on charm. I lusted after a house, any house. Unlike the birds of the air I needed a place for my plastic bags. Peggy saw an ad in *The Irish Times* for a Kilmainham artisan cottage at the amazing price of £7,000 – low enough for us to put a deposit on a mortgage and manage the fees. The little house was us. Kilmainham is south of the Liffey – the more fashionable side since the Duke of Leinster crossed the river in the eighteenth century. The house was in a cluster of quaintly-decaying cottages on low-lying land between the main road and the River Poddle. It had been painted white and looked like the child of a poor family on its First Communion day. Smoke straggled thinly from the brother and sister chimneys but you could feel the atmosphere. Centuries of Dubliners had lived there: Danes, Saxons and Gaels. I said this to Dick on the doorstep but he muttered something about centuries of grime – men, I've discovered, are low on imagination.

'Ah, come in!' A tall, dark, moustached man opened the door. There was something sinister about his tight black jeans and high cowboy boots. And the sharp way he looked us over. 'Wander round yerselves!'

The cottage consisted of an open-plan sittingroom with a kitchenette and bathroom at one end so this was done quickly. I admired the redbrick fireplace.

'All new!' the owner snapped. 'Everything's the very best. That's woodchip wallpaper.'

Dick was looking around stuffily. 'Is there a bedroom?'

'A bedroom?' The man looked puzzled.

'A place to sleep?'

He opened a large cupboard door. 'You could sleep in there, I suppose.'

Dick peered in. 'It's ah ... small. And there's no window.'

The man bristled. 'Sure, you don't need a window.'

'All we need is a double bed!' I butted in.

Dick counted his steps across the room.

I opened the kitchen window. 'There's a river! We can have a boat. It's Venetian.'

Dick was behind me. 'Venetian, my foot! It's a health hazard!'

The owner glared at Dick. 'I've a lot of people interested. It's cash, for a quick sale.'

'Won't you wait for our mortgage?' I begged.

The man twirled his moustache, softening. 'I can take a booking deposit of £50.'

I looked at Dick. 'We can manage that.

'It's non-returnable, mind you!'

Dick pulled me towards the door. 'He's a crook!' he muttered, as we walked gloomily around the area. 'Do you want to live here?'

I said I wanted to live some place.

Then Peggy picked out a three-bedroomed Georgian gem in a new Bray development. As we trooped round in the wake of the owner, a rising young banker, he pointed out the fitted wardrobe in the master bedroom, the garden shed and the handy additions in the kitchen. I began to settle in. The second bedroom would do for Dick's study, I thought, but I had plans for the third – a nursery. As yet there was nothing to put in it, but in the meantime I could be a pied piper aunt to the swarms of local children. Except there weren't any – the Catholic curate lived next door.

I'm a lapsed Catholic but never did I imagine living in a development with a priestly neighbour. But my training in history (BA, NUI) has taught me that life is a compromise. I wanted that little house. Like the pony when I was nine. Or the high heels when I was fifteen. Even Dick was bitten: I knew by his gloomy look.

That night I dreamt I was the old woman of the roads in Padraic Colum's poem. On awakening to the world and its troubles the next morning I reminded Dick that a motherless childhood had left me with a desire to be an owner. But he said his need to remain a renter was equally deep. In short we couldn't afford it.

I had got used to all the moving – you can get used to anything. We lived in Killiney one summer, over a TD in Leeson Street another, with a cat in Herbert Park another, and with my brother in Sandymount another. For one whole half-sabbatical we shivered in squalid splendour as caretakers of a crumbling tenement in Mountjoy Square. The drawingroom was the size of a hockey field with two fireplaces situated like goalposts at each end – handy for jogging but useless for keeping warm. An outside tap and toilet did for a bathroom, and the smell of something too impolite to mention wafted up the rickety stairs from the hall. Because I had found the house everything was my fault. A happily-married couple might've ended that tenancy in divorce or murder but we survived. The owner was so delighted with our guardianship he offered us the place cheaply at two hundred thousand pounds. Wasn't it the sort of house an American scholar would want to 'do up'? In my desperation with our rootless existence I flirted with the idea of saving a slice of vanishing Dublin, but Dick politely declined. He claims he's always right and I'm always wrong, but it evens out. Because if we were both right, it'd give us an unnatural advantage over others. He also says I complain too much about things, especially moving. The endless packing of books into boxes and clothes into plastic bags at the end of every summer was probably good for me. As Dick always said I was doing some of my purgatory on earth. And over the years we got to know Dublin well. It's a city with a variety of accommodation: you can pay the same for a palace or a hovel. Last year I answered an ad for a luxury flat and was shown round a flooded Leeson Street basement by a landlord in waders. As we splashed through the sittingroom I suggested that it was dampish? Whereupon he showed me the door, shouting that he was looking for a gang of girls. 'Bankers!'

'Mermaids,' was Dick's retort when I told him.

You meet all sorts renting. One landlady had rooted in our wardrobe and rearranged our furniture every time we went out. She actually evicted us because she thought my friend and her truly wedded husband were having an affair in our flat. But they had borrowed it for their honeymoon, we were having the affair. For propriety I had to pass as Mrs Sheridan, making my friends address letters to her and trying not to look too startled when the same landlady addressed me as such. It was practice for the future. I wanted to tell her we were still 'walking out' together but Dick says you have to consider people's feelings. In that case too, I suppose, he was right. He also says I go on too much about psychology and that, but I'm a believer in self help books: *Your Erogenous Zones* or *The Action Approach* or *How to be an Assertive Woman*. I once read that if you imagine something you desire, it'll happen. So, as the reality of years of wandering stretched before me, a picture formed in my mind's eye. A picture of a whitewashed cottage set beneath a green hill with wild roses creeping through the latticed windows. Inside, the huge range was always lit, and outside the old orchard always creaked with ripe apples. It was silly for a born and bred Dubliner to want a return to the land, but I did.

Meantime we had to return to America. Reading *The Irish Times* over breakfast, Dick said 'What are you thinking about?'

I looked up sleepily – I often have problems with sleep. 'I'm not thinking. I'm reading the paper.'

'You're staring into space.'

I studied my half of the paper.

'Come on, why so pale?'

I sighed heavily. 'I was thinking it'd be great if we had a house. We wouldn't have to pack everything.'

He rustled his paper. 'Peggy's been at her mischief again.'

'She hasn't said a word.' She had regarded the lost Georgian gem as defeat in a skirmish rather than the battle.

'She's giving the government a rest and turning her attention to me.' He took my half of the paper. 'God help the country if she were in power.'

The country would be in less of a mess, but I didn't argue. After a bit, I broke the silence. 'Where'll we live when you retire?'

He was buried in his paper. 'I can't afford to retire,' he said at last.

'Some day you'll have to, and houses will be exorbitant.'

'Then I'll take to the heath like Lear!'

Remembering that no mention is ever made of Mrs Lear, I vowed to abandon all hope. Dick's children were now alarmingly producing their children. It was like compound interest. Without knowing the bliss of motherhood I'd become the equivalent of a grandmother. So we could barely afford a wheelbarrow. I'd tell Peggy this when we next met.

Hugging me goodbye at the airport the next week Peggy whispered 'Now, come back married!' Dick hadn't untied his first fateful knot, so I was to fail her in this – the failure of hope over experience, with acknowledgments to Dr Johnson. But by selling the car, depositing Dick's book royalties, and going nowhere, we did manage to save nearly £1,000 towards our house. I gloated over the money like Shylock.

A plan hatched in my brain. Another half-sabbatical was due the following January. I would be dispatched ahead to make straight the way like John the Baptist – i.e. find a flat and pay the deposit and advance rent. For this I'd be given about £1,000. What if I bought a house with it? Dick would get mad, but as we weren't married he couldn't divorce me. It'd be a *fait accompli*. Our savings were enough for the deposit balance and Peggy had promised to get the mortgage. Her relative had given blood to save the life of a high up building society official and because of this he could refuse Peggy nothing. That's how things are done in Ireland.

Our university library gets Saturday's *Irish Times* two weeks late. I always read the book reviews and articles by Maeve Binchy *et al.* But for the next four months I scoured the housing ads: there was nothing under £20,000. The cheapest houses were in the developments mushrooming in north Dublin. I'd resigned myself to being up to my ears in muck when I saw an ad: '5-roomed cottage, 35 miles Dublin, central heating, telephone, £15,000.' With Christmas hangovers, it took a week for the Dublin estate agent to answer the phone: Rowley Cottage was still available. It was beyond Kells and 'way off a bus route' a sleepy voice warned. Still, I was undeterred. What was the use of all my assertiveness reading if I couldn't steer our fate? With central heating and that rarity – a telephone – the cottage was a giveaway. Tenements without bathrooms were double that in Dublin. With our savings we could afford a deep freeze and a car. I'd learn to drive – up to now I'd put off the evil hour.

I made an appointment to view with Mr Kelly, the Kells co-agent. My first problem was getting there, but Peggy came to the rescue. She was so delighted Dick had at last agreed, that I couldn't disenchant her: she might have baulked at what I was doing if she knew. We set out early, but by the time we saw the Celtic cross in Kells the light was waning. It's a bustling country town with narrow hilly streets. We grabbed some fish and chips for lunch and, on asking directions, were told the estate agent was around the corner. We turned several, finally happening upon it by accident in a building society's branch office. Apparently Mr Kelly wore two hats. He was wearing slippers and a striped three-piece suit when he came out of the inner office. The combination was as odd as his red country face and badly dyed brown hair, but I stopped myself staring.

'Mrs Fitzpatrick, I presume?' He addressed me in a sing-song voice, as if I were Livingstone.

'Ms Fitzpatrick!' I tried not to flinch at his iron handshake.

Then he shook hands with Peggy. 'You're the mammy?'

'We're friends!' I blurted. Peggy wasn't that old, but didn't appear to mind.

'It was Rowley Cottage you wanted, Mrs Fitzpatrick? I'll get the keys.' He pulled on big rubber boots. Then he squeezed his burly frame into a skimpy overcoat and stomped after us to the street. Because his car was laid up, we used Peggy's mini.

'The cottage's only a stone's throw.' He squeezed into the back.

A pretty long throw. As we left the town for the countryside, I figured the ad was way out too. It had claimed the cottage to be thirty-five miles from Dublin, but Kells was over forty, and no sign of us arriving.

Mr Kelly kept up a running commentary. 'Ah, yes, Mrs Fitzpatrick, ye'll like the country.' He let out a melancholy sigh. 'De owner o' dose fields on yer right is rooned. Rooned. Brought it on himself.'

'How?' I asked.

'Mortgaged dem at a million. Didn't he open de papers next day to find land fallen by a turd.'

'God!' I said.

Peggy shook her head, but our guide chuckled chestily.

'Is Rowley Cottage much further?' I asked nervously.

'Another few miles. See dat house on yer left?'

It was a gaunt grey mansion set in lush fields. I thought it'd make a painting.

'For sale for years.'

'That's hard luck!' Peggy took her eyes off the road.

'Serves dem right! Way overpriced,' he muttered. 'Cromwellians ... sure who'd want to live out here?'

For some reason he was putting me off.

'Is Rowley Cottage long on the market?' Peggy looked in the rearview mirror.

'A time! A time!' A cautious note crept into his voice.

'It's a good asking price,' I said. Then, catching Peggy's glare. 'Eh – I mean it's fairly good – for the country.'

'Hmm ... mind you, the owner won't take a penny less dan fourteen and a half.'

Already I'd saved five hundred pounds. We fell into silence as hedges skimmed by and an occasional worker saluted as we passed. There was something odd about Mr Kelly, something contradictory. He wasn't exactly trying the hard sell, but maybe the cottage was owned by Cromwellians too. From my historical studies I knew Old Rowley was the nickname of Charles II. Three centuries separated us from his rule and presumably he'd been better than Cromwell? But time is nothing in Ireland – they're still fighting the Battle of the Boyne. Perhaps he simply had another customer in mind? This filled me with dread.

'Rowley Cottage doesn't sound Irish,' I pumped.

'It's de hunting' lodge o' Rowley House. We'll be comin' to it now.'

We drove on and on.

'That's Rowley House!' our guide suddenly shouted. 'Through dem gates. We're round the next bend.'

A red-coated girl rode down the tree-lined avenue. Horses are in the Irish blood, and she became a vision of my future life. We rounded the next corner and there, nestling between the navy blue sky and the green humpy fields, was my cottage. A mucky path led to the red front door. Mr Kelly heaved the hall door with his shoulder. It wouldn't budge, so he tried again.

'Damp!' Peggy eyed the house knowledgeably.

He slapped the corners, pushing again until it creaked open. 'De owner bought it for his daughter, but she wouldn't live in it.'

'Why?' Peggy looked at him sharply.

'Couldn't stand the loneliness.'

We followed Mr Kelly into the drawingroom. It was a biggish room with a handsome redbricked fireplace and a broken bay window.

'Someone should repair that!' Peggy said.

'It's only a breath of air!' Mr Kelly pulled his coat round him.

'All we have to do is turn on the heat,' I said. 'Where's the switch?'

'Out beyond.' He pointed to a couple of rickety sheds in the garden.

We walked through the two bedrooms, the cosy breakfast room opening into a tiny kitchen with a huge old-fashioned sink. Peggy turned on the tap, which clanked and spluttered, but no water came.

'The water's turned off,' the agent admitted.

I remembered the trouble we had with no water in Mountjoy Square.

'Can you turn it on?' Peggy demanded.

He rubbed his chin worriedly. 'Tank's in the attic. Ye need a ladder.'

Peggy looked suspicious. 'They should leave a ladder here then.'

'The big house supplies the water for now. Eventually, ye'll have to dig a well.'

That water didn't come through the taps like magic had never before occurred to me. But we were in the country now and different laws applied. The lack certainly explained the stench from the bathroom. When the toilet was flushed that would go. And the bath was fine and big – Dick would like that.

It was dark outside. We could hardly see the gate separating our garden from a picturesque barn. The garden was a jungle, but two fields were to be thrown in with the cottage. A rickety apple tree grew in one, and thistles, lots of thistles.

'Two fields?' Peggy tried not to look impressed.

'Dere's always a bit o' land trown in with a country house. Ye could build another house dere.' He gave a short laugh, muttering under his breath. 'If ye could get anyone to live in it!'

Peggy gave me a hug. 'We'll come and live in it!'

Mr Kelly looked puzzled.

'Where does the sun come in?' I asked. An important question when buying a house.

He looked as if he'd never heard the word. Or had forgotten what it meant, which can happen in an Irish winter.

'The sun?' I repeated.

He peered upwards at the inky sky. 'No sign of it now! Or the moon!' He shivered under his coat, stamping his boots in the muck. 'Come on back to town, and I'll show ye a nice semi-d.'

I said that if I wanted a semi-d, I'd buy one in Dublin.

We went back inside and, as we lingered again in each room he rattled his keys impatiently. I ignored him, suspecting the reason for his attitude. He wanted to sell us something he'd get commission on.

'Tell ye what, girls!' he said at last. 'I have to see a man down the road. Lend me the car!'

I was thinking of the idiocy of grown women being 'girls' when Peggy gave him her keys. As he roared off into the night, the house lights went out.

'A fuse!' Peggy diagnosed.

We couldn't find the fuse box. It was pitch black, so to cheer ourselves up we lit the kindling in the breakfast room grate. Almost immediately smoke puffed back into the room. I almost choked, but Peggy calmly quenched the twigs with her high heel, saying the chimney needed cleaning. I was grateful for her presence. For in the ghostly darkness I felt a sudden chill. It was eerie. We were miles from anywhere.

Peggy tapped the breakfast room wall. 'The first thing you do is knock this down. Extend into the kitchen.'

Before I could answer a light appeared at the window and behind it a bony figure with mad eyes and wild white hair.

'Look!' I whispered.

The door creaked open and an Englishy voice screamed. 'Out! Out!'

I made out a dishevelled woman in jodhpurs and anorak.

'I'm Ms Fitzpatrick.' I stood my ground. 'And this is my friend, Mrs Peggy O'Hara. We've been shown the house by Mr Kelly of Kells.'

Her fury changed to understanding. 'You're viewing the cottage?'

'I'm buying it.'

She fiddled nervously with her hair. 'Forgive me, Mrs Fitzpatrick –'

'Ms! Fitzpatrick – Sally Ann.'

'What a lovely name! I'm Dorothy Blake from Rowley House. I have to watch for burglars. We'll be neighbours!' We all shook hands.

She held the light to my face. 'Wouldn't it be wonderful if someone like you bought the cottage! Come up to the house for a drink!'

'Could you turn on the water?' I asked.

Mrs Blake ran to the garden shed and pulled out a ladder, which the three of us lugged into the house. She positioned it under a ceiling trap door and disappeared into the attic. 'Tell me when it comes on!'

We stood by the kitchen tap.

It gurgled dryly, but nothing happened. Then there was a loud crash. We ran into the hall to find my new neighbour dangling from a large hole in the ceiling. Her riding boots flailed wildly and the ladder lay on the floor.

'Hold her legs!' Peggy shouted. 'I'll get the ladder!'

'No! No! Stand aside!' Mrs Blake jumped to the floor, getting up at once and dusting herself down. There was white plaster everywhere. I stared in horror at the hole.

'Good Lord!' was all Peggy could say.

'My husband will repair that!' Mrs Blake announced cheerfully. 'We'll leave the ladder. Come and have a drink.'

'I need one,' Peggy muttered.

We left Mr Kelly a note on the door, and the three of us climbed the gate and walked up the avenue between the two properties. The dark was oppressive. Mrs Blake's wobbling torch seemed the only light in the universe. The big house loomed gauntly ahead. The world of the Anglo-Irish was foreign to me. I only knew from books they had leaking roofs. But what if Cromwellians had lived there?

What if my rider had been a ghost? Sometimes my imagination ran wild. We crossed a farmyard, then a stableyard.

'Say hello to Rufus,' Mrs Blake stopped to nuzzle a pony looking over a stable door. 'He's a sweetheart.'

'Do you have many ponies?' I asked.

'Six. I run a riding school.'

It explained the horseback rider. The pony butted her affectionately. 'I couldn't manage without him!' She petted his nose again. 'The country can be lonely, Sally Ann. You must be sure you like it.'

I said an artist is never lonely. My worry was what to do if I ran out of milk.

She waved me into silence. 'I'll lend you a horse!'

I pictured Dick's face as I galloped off to Kells.

We came to the house at last. She led us through huge old kitchens, a hall with an antique rocking horse, into a shabby but stately drawingroom. There was a haunting elegance about everything, a sort of faded beauty. Turf smouldered wetly in the grate, so we kept on our coats. Mrs Blake had a nearly empty bottle of whiskey but she insisted on sharing it. Huddling over the fire we at last managed to warm up. Mrs Blake told us the story of her life. How she'd been born in the house. How her brother was killed in the second world war. How the roof had caught fire a few years ago and how the neighbours had formed a human chain from the well. How she had sold the cottage to pay for a new roof. But now she had a problem with dry rot and she was planning to extend the riding school to pay for that. I suggested adding art classes and English for foreigners to the curriculum. By the second drink we had decided to go into business together. A neighbour 'called' while we were there, returning Mrs Blake's 'call' – something I thought happened only in Jane Austen. When I lived in the cottage maybe I could 'call' on someone too. It had been a perfect day: the countryside, the intimacy of the drive with Peggy, finding my house and now stumbling on this world. By the time Mr Kelly came back I decided that by buying the cottage I was gaining not only bricks and mortar but a way of life.

Peggy's only worry was that I'd tell someone before she could pull her strings with the building society. If it got out about the two fields someone would snap it up. She was serious about Tony and herself building a bungalow there when their children grew up. For the moment they might park a caravan for weekends. Even Tony got infected and took the next Saturday off from his paper to vet the house. As we drove and drove there the atmosphere thickened with tension. But he'd fall in love with it when he saw it, I told myself.

'We're halfway to Enniskillen?' he said after another bit.

When we got to the cottage Peggy and I walked the land. The thistles would be the first to go and she'd give me plants for a garden. But Tony was preoccupied with the roof, staring oddly upwards. 'Sally Ann!' he called. When I came over, he was still circling the cottage. He stopped to knock out his pipe. 'You see that bulge in the roof?'

I noticed a sort of camel's hump.

Peggy came over. 'An architect has vetted it!'

'I don't care who's vetted it. She'll have trouble with that roof.' He shoved tobacco into his pipe. 'And see that crack down the side?'

'Can't we fill it?' I asked tiredly.

He went inside without answering.

I found him staring at the ceiling hole. 'Mrs Blake's husband's fixing it.'

'He'll have a job.' He hunkered by the hall skirting board. 'Sally, put your thumb nail into this.'

It was like butter. 'Eh ... what's wrong?'

'Dry rot.'

'It feels wet.'

'The skirting boards are riddled with it. And see that stuff!' He pointed his pipe at a white substance growing out of the walls. 'Rising damp. And there's ground damp in the kitchen.'

My father always said houses were like people, there were good houses and bad houses. But he never said that like people they had diseases. 'Maybe we could turn on the heat?'

He shook his head vehemently. 'The place is a disaster!'

I looked at the rotting boards, at the garden with its thistles and dreary sheds, the ragged fields, seeing them now through his eyes. It was like a balloon bursting or falling out of love as a teenager. Suddenly you see a person, a thing, for what it is. The place was a ruin. I'd been cracked to think we would live here. Dick got mad if a bulb blew or the toilet got stuck. But would I find another house in time?

'Think what we're saving?'

'And two fields?' Peggy had come inside.

'They don't want fields! They want a house on a bus route! And you'll save much more if you don't buy it, Sally.'

As he marched out the door I looked miserably at Peggy. She indicated that we were to follow so I locked the door behind us, and all the way to Dublin pondered on her capitulation. She'd been so for it but had completely caved in. I mean she'd given me the 'conviction' to do what I was doing. But Tony was the boss all along. I suppose he was right: you can't argue with buttery skirting boards. I had rheumatism from even touching them. In a way it'd be a relief not to be always travelling in the dark. But did Tony suspect what I was doing? As we hit the city streets again I felt relieved. Country life wasn't everything. I was a Dub, and although the fields were lost all was not lost. I had a week before Dick returned.

After the Kells fiasco Tony and Peggy applied themselves to finding a 'sensible' house. It'd be too boring to describe everything I saw. Suffice to say I'd almost bought a redone Bray bungalow when the agent sold it over my head. I'd resigned myself to a box in Clondalkin when my brother heard of a Ranelagh artisan house, circa 1880, going for a song. It was built of that mellow Dublin brick and in a cul de sac behind a Victorian square. The only drawback was you had to pass a row of cottages with graffiti such as 'Provos ok' and rude things about the Queen of England to get to it. There was no garden, the halldoor opened onto the street, and an extension had been built in the back. Usually small old Dublin houses don't have bathrooms, but this did – outside. The house needed a lick of paint but it was great value. Artisan houses down the road were going for £35,000 and ours had a doll's house charm. I couldn't see any evidence of disease. On the whole its hundred years had worn well. I had to act quickly. The agent wanted £23,000, so I offered £22,000, and we settled for £22,750 – in retrospect, I might've got it for less, but there wasn't time. I gave him a £1,000 deposit and rang Peggy to arrange the loan. Our savings would be enough for the deposit balance.

Dick kissed me at the airport a couple of days later. 'You found a flat ok?'

I nodded. 'We're staying with my father for the moment. Darling, I've a lovely surprise!'

He looked suspicious.

'I've saved you over £13,000!'

'Don't tell me you've been shopping?'

'Yes, for a house!

He looked dazed. 'A house?'

'It only cost £22,750, and houses in the next street are going for £35,000. I'll run for a taxi!'

He dragged his case tiredly after me. 'Don't tell me it has a bit of character,' he groaned in the back seat.

'We can see it on the way. I have the keys!'

He had jetlag so mightn't see the drawbacks. Also it was too dark to see the graffiti. I fitted the key on arrival. 'It needs a lick of paint.'

Dick said nothing, and nothing, as we walked around. He just stared at a ceiling stain and at a gaping hole in the stairway – neither of which I'd noticed.

'What do you think?' I asked as he stood in the tiny yard.

'I'm looking for the back garden.'

'You're in it.'

He went into the bathroom. 'Where's the washhand basin?'

'It's right there!'

There wasn't one. I'd never even noticed.

He faced me in the kitchen. There was a weary look on his face. 'You bought this hovel?'

'I paid a deposit ... £1,000 ... I can get out of it.'

'You live in it! I won't!' And he slammed out of the house.

As the taxi roared off I stayed put. For the second time in a week my world had collapsed, except this time more seriously. I walked upstairs, seeing it for the first time. The carpets were hideously patterned and the wallpaper was ghastly. It must've looked even worse to Dick who, as an American, had no appetite for squalor. I thought I was so right, but was I? Was a house worth this? Worth losing Dick? Had my mind lapsed, a 'plank in the reason' broken? I didn't know. I just sat there dazed. Loud knocking aroused me.

'Honey bunch!' Dick shouted from the street. 'I'm back!'

I opened the door to him and Tony – both tipsy. Tony looked around him. 'Hmm. Not bad!'

Dick let out a shriek of laughter – he always laughs when sad.

I felt tears coming. 'Peggy can tell them we don't want the loan.'

'Then I won't be able to carry you over the threshold!' Dick grabbed me, carrying me out to the street and then back into the house. 'I suppose,' he gasped, collapsing on the floor. 'I suppose ... this means we'll have to get married?'

'No!' I said, but he was lying on the floor.

I turned to Tony. 'Is he ok?'

'He needs to sleep. I'll drive you over to your Dad's.' And he heaved him up and helped him out to the car.

Dick didn't back out. 'Love in a hut,' as the poet says, may be 'cinders, ashes, dust' but it's better than renting. We now have proper neighbours. I got my little house 'out of the wind and the rain's way.' But my troubles were only beginning. Since we've moved in Dick's been very gloomy. He's forgiven me all right but there've been all sorts of fees. We've no money for furniture, and there's no washhand basin. Also there's a ghastly hole in the stairway, although Tony's helped with that. I love when he comes. Then I don't feel so awful when Dick finds something else wrong. I live in dread of him finding things wrong – and hammering. We've done it up by degrees, slow degrees. But I often wonder if the whole thing wasn't an obsession, like the Kells house. But if you can't hope what else is there in life? And it's true if you imagine something, it can happen. I cheer myself up, imagining improvements. A nursery maybe? Dick says he's nervous about going through all that again. I feel that he doesn't mean it, and distract myself by working on the house. I've even learnt how to point bricks. Before I'd never have noticed if a house had proper gutters, now I know if they're leaking – ours are. There's a bit of damp too, but what house is free of it in Ireland? The whole country's dripping wet. Dick calls it a bog, but he's more committed to me now. Also I'm to add a postscript: while he was pulling off a century's wallpaper I was working on my painting. He says why couldn't I paint the house, but I told him that's man's lot – a joke. If I painted he'd start finding things wrong. He's become house proud so I do the outside brickwork.

I nearly forgot another postscript: they're trying to sue us for the Kells ceiling.

X

MONA

When Mona opened her eyes she was in pain and a tube was in her arm. What time was it? A minute ago she was lying on the operating table. How had she got back to her room? A nun was sitting by her bed. She knew it was a nun by the dowdy blue habit, but she thought she must be hallucinating because the nun was reading a movie magazine with Robert Redford on the cover.

'It's a healthy boy, pet.' The nun's voice came from the end of a long tunnel. Mona focused on the silly little veil, but it wavered away. The next thing Mona felt herself being injected. 'The baby's fine, pet.'

The baby, of course, she'd had a baby. Mona drifted into a dream about her son, Danny, who was ten now and on hard sums. Tonight's geography was to mark the Nile on a blank map of Africa. It wiggled across the ceiling towards a peeled patch for Lake Victoria. She pointed to it excitedly. 'All day, I face the barren waste,' Frankie Laine's voice blared as she ran to the lakeside, 'without a taste of water.

Cool, clear water.' She was glad of a drink, but before she reached the edge a wind whipped the glassy surface into a foaming tidal wave which surged towards her, getting bigger and bigger and drowning her in a great watery wall. She awoke in the nick of time. Slowly she took in her bandaged stomach, the tube connecting her to a drip, the curtains drawn around her bed, the cats' chorus of crying babies down the corridor. The baby? Where was it? There was no cot beside her, so perhaps it had died. Someone had mentioned a baby dying. But no, the nun said it was all right. Where was the nun now? There'd been talk of a cup of tea. Her body felt as if it were cracking in two. If she called out, the Foxrock woman in the other bed would want to help. She could hear her talking bossily now. 'Maeve Binchy's new novel is marvellous.'

'I like her journalism,' another voice answered. 'She's the funniest writer in *The Irish Times*.'

That was Sally Ann from down the corridor, some kind of artist. She'd come in the night before and borrowed magazines from the other woman in the room. Mona remembered their conversation. The younger woman had looked in on her, asked if she wanted anything. She was having some tests for infertility. The Foxrocker was called Astrid something or other – it sounded like the name of a boat. She'd had a premature baby and gave you blow by blow. Mona knew the type: Renault 4 car, meals on wheels, mohair-suited husband, nannies, children bandy from riding lessons. A life of glamour, while hers had been spent wading knee deep in nappies. Terry's insurance had specified a ward but they'd put her in semi-private. Getting out of the hospital without a chequebook might be a problem, and explaining no baby clothes. She hadn't bought any yet, and now she was out of cigarettes. As she reached for her bell, a glass shattered onto the floor.

'Are you all right, Mrs Reilly?' Sally Ann popped around the curtains.

Mona didn't want to get into another conversation. The younger woman wore a huge fluffy pink dressing gown. She had dishevelled black curly hair and, with gold granny glasses at the end of her nose, reminding Mona of a character out of *School Friend*. It must be thirty years since she'd read it.

'I'll get Sister,' the girl said.

A few minutes later the nun pulled back the curtain. 'So Mrs Rip Van Winkle's awake at last. Are you in pain, pet?' She checked the overhead drip. 'We'll get you comfortable.'

Mona nodded and the nun went away. In a few minutes she came back with a nurse carrying a syringe on a dish. The nurse injected her, then placed a bedpan in the bed. 'Try and use this.'

Mona shook her head.

'We must get your bladder working.'

'No, I'll get up!' Mona tried to haul herself up by gripping the bedhead, but the pain was like a train across her body. When she was finished with the bedpan, the nun came back with a cup of tea.

Rattlingly, she placed it on a trolley which she pushed to the top of the bed. 'Slowly, now. Too much will sicken you. Nurse will bring the baby. She'll help you breastfeed.'

While in labour, Mona had been told to focus on an object in the room. Now she focused on the nun's crucifix. It rested on her chest and was almost level with the end of the bed. A twisted body on twisted wood. 'What time is it?'

'It's one o'clock. You've been asleep all day.'

A young nurse came in with the baby wrapped in a blanket. Hysteria bubbled inside Mona like vomit. 'Take it away.'

The nurse started cooing at her bundle. 'But he's a dote!'

Mona turned away. 'Take it away!'

The nun waved the nurse out. 'It's normal to be depressed, pet.'

'I'm not depressed!' Mona threw the teacup at the curtains. It clattered off the floor, spilling tea everywhere. 'I don't want to see it. Or you! Or anyone!'

The old nun blinked.

'My husband's left me for a whore. Why don't you give it to her!'

'Now, now, don't fret.' The nun wiped the floor with tissues.

Mona sobbed into her pillow. Her whole situation had been caused by religious people who knew nothing. 'Have faith' the red-faced parish priest had said when she went to him about Terry's first affair. 'Forgive us our trespasses, as we forgive others' he had preached, ushering her out after the second. It'd always been the same. Terry wasn't mature enough for marriage or children. He'd gone on a drunken binge after their first child, on another after their second, and now he was gone altogether. Good riddance. Why the hell hadn't she died? She'd lost enough blood.

It seemed years since the day before yesterday. The pains had started at breakfast. Not wanting to frighten the children she'd hurried them out to school before dialling 999. The guards had screeched up minutes before the ambulance. They'd helped her into it, then arranged for her neighbour to look after the children. When they'd offered to contact her husband at work she'd lied that he was in England. It was weeks before her time, so no Dr Cunningham. He was fishing in the west, they'd said, leaving her to bleed. They kept trying to contact him, but couldn't. By that night she knew by their worried looks that something was wrong. After hours of labour there was no baby. Then at the last ounce of her strength, her own doctor had hurried into the delivery room. After an examination he'd said calmly 'Mona, I'm doing what's best for you and the baby. I believe in bringing useful citizens into the world.' Nurses had swarmed round her performing the rituals. She was whizzed down the corridor into the lift, out into another corridor, and into theatre for a Caesarean. Bright lights were shone in her face, masked figures leant over her, jabbing away the pain.

Dr Cunningham turned into corrugated iron. 'I'll give you a lovely bikini slit, love.'

It had sounded like an ice-cream from Cafolla's.

Mona stared up at the cracked ceiling above her bed. The last couple of days had been a nightmare. Maybe she'd wake to find her whole life had been a dream. Anxiety gnawed at her. God, the baby ... but she was too weary to go through all that again. Why didn't they warn you about the pain of childbirth? Was it some sort of conspiracy on the part of women too? We're child fodder, that's all, battery hens. Why did they leave her so long in labour? But at least the baby was all right. She wanted it to be all right, she just didn't want it.

The nun came back, followed by another nurse, beaming with cheerfulness. She pulled a trolley beside Mona's bed containing items of ablution. The nun found a pink nightie in her locker. 'How pretty! Now sit up.' The two women helped Mona out of her hospital gown. Then, as she lay in rigid exhaustion, the nurse sponged her down and put on the clean nightie. As the nurse took the trolley away, the nun went back to her locker. Why was she poking now?

'I can't find a comb.'

'In my handbag.'

The nun combed Mona's peroxided frizz. 'You'll feel better when you look better.'

Mona couldn't remember anyone combing her hair. She watched them change the bottom sheet, plump pillows and tidy the bedspread. When they drew the curtain she panicked. 'Please leave them.'

'But you'll have company!'

'I don't want company!'

Then Sally Ann came through the curtains with a tray. 'Time for tea.'

The nun took it, turning to the girl. 'I hear you're going down in the morning.'

'I'm having a test for infertility.'

'Make sure you fast after tea!'

Mona glared at the plate: two slices of plastic white toast. She sipped some tea, avoiding conversation. The girl might stay longer if she got any encouragement. Why couldn't she count her blessings? She didn't know when she was well off. Sally Ann lingered by the bedside. She took a paperback out of a pocket in her copious dressing gown.

'I brought you something to read; *Resurrection* by Tolstoy.'

Mona thought she must be a religious nut. 'No thanks.'

The girl went on jabbering. 'It's about a noble who got a girl into trouble in his youth. Then she's convicted of murder and he goes to Siberia with her. The message is that sometimes your mistakes are the means of your salvation.'

Mona didn't say anything.

'I'll leave it ... in case you might read it. Can I get you anything else?'

Mona hesitated, whispering 'Would you have a cigarette?'

'My husband will have some. He'll be in this evening.' The younger woman left, drawing the curtains behind her.

Mona thought the book looked heavy. She wanted to be left alone, feeling no part of the conspiracy of birth which bound women together. She could forget she ever had children – except you couldn't, that was the trouble. She should ring her neighbour and find out if Danny and Lisa were all right. Lisa had started school, and for the first time in ten years she had a moment to herself. But now this. She didn't know how long she'd lain there when she heard footsteps, the scrape of a chair, wheezy breathing.

The nun was back with her magazine. 'Can I sit with you?'

Mona pretended to be asleep. If they could only plug her into some permanent life-support system. She didn't want to be responsible for anyone again, least of all herself. If she had a cigarette she might be able to cope.

'If I were king,' the nun murmured. 'If I were king, it's a far, far better thing I do.'

Mona opened her eyes. Jesus, the woman was senile.

Suddenly she flung down her movie magazine. 'There's nothing in it about Ronald Coleman.'

'He's a bit past it.'

The nun bristled indignantly. 'Past it? Didn't you see *A Tale of Two Cities*?'

Mona watched her curiously. Odd for a nun to be into films. She was ancient, yet she seemed to be still working in the hospital. 'Wasn't that Dirk Bogarde?'

The nun waved dismissively. 'If you'd seen Ronald Coleman waiting for the guillotine you'd never forget it. Remember *Random Harvest* where he lost his memory?'

'I didn't see it.'

The old woman rolled up the magazine. 'You're too young. Will I bring the baby, pet?'

'Can't it wait? I need to sleep.'

'Yes, get some rest. Can I get you anything else?'

'I'd kill for a cigarette.'

'Smoking's forbidden here!' She tidied Mona's bed. 'Besides, you're not well enough.'

Mona knew that she would have to see the baby. The nun had called her young, but her whole problem with Terry was age. He couldn't make love to her because she was thirty nine and fat, and he needed someone young and thin. For the past few years they had tried but it never worked, until ... until. When he'd almost lost his job from the stress of sexual frustration, and starvation loomed, she'd agreed to the last affair. So long as he didn't tell her about it. But he'd moved the little bitch into the house. They were to share everything, like communists. When Mona had threatened to go to England with the children Terry had responded by saying it was a good idea, that the threesome wasn't working. What did he call it – the *ménage à trois*. It had become a madhouse, so he drove her to the boat, bought the tickets and comics for the children. Cool as you like. What kind of man was he? Jesus, that crossing with the two of them vomiting, changing to the train in the dark, Euston in the grey morning, porters shouting, the children crying, the station cafe full of deadbeats, then queuing for stale tea. She thought she'd have the courage for it, but she hadn't. She'd devoured the London papers and finally got a night job in a Slough Wimpy Bar and lodgings in a guest house. They'd all got sick from the food and there was no television. Danny had nowhere to play, but only when he started sleepwalking did she wise up and come home to occupy their Clontarf bungalow. But the child was disturbed now, wet the bed and was backward in school. A psychologist told her his creative side was too dominant. Why the hell couldn't he learn to read properly?

The nun fingered her beads. Easy enough to pray when you believed life was as simple as going to the pictures. People had the stupidest ideas, herself included. When she first met Terry she'd thought him the image of Marlon Brando in *The Young Lions*. She'd seen the film as a teenager in that re-run cinema on the quays. Mona went into another dream about Terry. It was before the children because they were cycling to the Enniskerry waterfall. The hedges were jewelled with blackberries, the sky a miraculous blue. 'Oh, Mary, we crown thee with blossoms today,' she sang lustily. 'Queen of the Angels, Queen of the May.' A car honked, and she discovered herself clad in the briefest of bikinis. Gaily she waved back. What did it matter when you had the figure? She raced after Terry, breathless. At the Bray turning she lost him. Where was he? Would she ever find him again? In the distance she heard a noise, and suddenly there he was. His hair was as blond as their first meeting, his shoulders as broad. He'd put the kettle on and was waiting by the waterfall for her to get the meal on. So she unpacked his favourite picnic of hard-boiled eggs (shelled), a pinch of salt and Jacob's Original and Best Cream Crackers (buttered).

'I'm so thirsty!' she shouted, over the roaring water.

'It's time for elevenses, pet,' a voice said.

Terry never called her pet. Besides, his back was to her, but she recognised his red woollen jumper. She tugged at the sleeve, but he turned his back. 'You have the children! You don't need me,' he shouted and she was left rolling unravelling wool into a ball which got bigger and bigger, and too heavy to manage. At last she caught up, having ripped the whole jumper. 'Look at me!' she thumped his back and she got the shock of her life to find herself staring again into Robert Redford's baby blue eyes.

'Go away!' she shouted. He arched an eyebrow and floated off behind the curtains.

'Now, Mrs Reilly!' A hand brushed her forehead. 'You didn't drink your tea.'

Mona knew she was talking rubbish but she couldn't stop herself. When she awoke again it was dark. She was alone. Where was the nun? Perhaps she'd been an hallucination after all. No, she was real, but it was a lie that love existed. Maybe your secret love could be forever with a stranger in paradise, but it didn't happen on earth. Here you got pregnant and that led to children, and they were nothing but little leeches bleeding you of life and youth. Even sex was a total sell: the pleasure was momentary, the position ridiculous and the cost ... the cost was her life. She groped for the bell and rang it, noticing an opened packet of cigarettes and a box of matches beside her hand. Who had left them? The nun? Sally Ann? The woman in the next bed was gone. Before she had time to light up footsteps came into the room. A young nurse pushed another bedpan under the blankets. 'The baby's doing well,' she said casually. 'Are you still depressed?'

'I was never depressed.'

'Bonding's the hospital policy.'

'Why don't you policy off! And take this thing with you!'

The nurse took the bedpan and left.

'Wait!' Mona called, and she reappeared through the curtains. 'I'm sorry ... a nun was getting me a cup of tea.'

'Sister Mercy's the chaplain.' That explained things. Yet she hadn't mentioned religion. 'We'll be giving out a cup of tea at six o'clock.' The nurse turned to go. 'Can you last till then?'

Mona nodded. She got out of bed and made her way to the bathroom in the corridor by holding onto the wall. In the privacy of the toilet she sneaked a cigarette. The nicotine flowed through her veins relaxing her. Sally Ann must've left them. She'd be having her operation sometime soon. Then Mona made her way back to bed and read a few paragraphs of *Resurrection*. It'd give her something to talk about. The book seemed to be set in a prison and was all the usual stuff about forgiving your brother; not seven times but seventy times seven. Impossible commands. She snapped it shut, trying to doze. Nobody could understand how badly she felt. She'd never forgive Terry. She wished the child well but she hadn't planned it. It was a fit of drunkenness, that's all. When she came back from England, Terry had moved out to a flat with the girl. Then one day he'd had a row with the little bitch and made love to her instead. Of course, she got pregnant. It was like the old days when she got pregnant if Terry looked at her. How would Sister Mercy like that for a slice of life? The name suited her in a way. In school, their English teacher had been called Mother Mercy. It was a coincidence. 'Girls, "there's a Divinity that shapes our ends, rough hew them how we may."' Something had certainly ended her shape and rough hewed her end. She hadn't always been fat. In her dancing days she'd had a good figure. She was a culchie who came to Dublin in search of a man. It was Palmerston on Saturday nights, the Metropole or Old Belvedere on Sunday nights. The dances had been like a religion. She went on the bus, a headscarf over her curlers, smoking all the way. There was never any difficulty about getting a lift home. But at twenty nine she was still single. 'Mona'll get married when she finds a man who can keep her!' her father had boomed. Money was all her family ever thought about and keeping up appearances.

All looked lost until she met Terry. He'd been standing at the Metropole Bar one evening and offered to buy her a drink. She could still see him, laughing, in a houndstooth sports jacket. Later they danced and he'd sung 'The Way you Look Tonight' while driving her home. It became their song. 'Lovely, lovely ... never, never change. Keep that breathless charm ...' She had been taken in by his Englishness and good looks. Blond hair and brown eyes were unusual. She'd bought everything, the whole spiel: he'd even been to university, another world to her. He worked in an advertising agency where he had sophisticated friends. Of course, her family had hated him from the word go: London-Irish and worse – a lapsed Catholic. Was she sure he hadn't been married before? 'You'll regret it, Mona!' they had warned. But before she had time to, Terry was coming into the bank to enquire if she'd got her period. They had married in Kildare Street Register Office. It was a terrible blow to her family. Why couldn't they have accepted Terry? He was a little different but that was what had attracted her. The Irish were so insular. You were suspect if you came from the next parish. Her marriage had cut her off from her family, friends and church. Now she had nothing. She'd gone back to mass, but the parish priest had said she'd have to confess before a tribunal of bishops. She'd committed a reserved sin by marrying out of the church. When Terry left, all her father could say was that she must have denied him his rights. They'd done a U turn now that she might be short of money. Terry was the hero. *His* rights? What about her rights? It was all over between them. If she complained Terry threatened to stop paying the mortgage, after all the work she'd done on the house. The little sexpot was too lazy to paint or sand floors. She couldn't cook either. Maybe she'd poison him with her wild rice. Mona lay in the dark, crying.

'How's Mrs Reilly this morning? Did you have a good sleep?' The nun was back.

'Can I smoke a cigarette?'

The nun shook her head. 'It's not allowed.'

Mona started crying, she couldn't help it.

'Smoke it quickly then! Mrs Barrett-Byrne is gone home. I'll look out!' The nun disappeared behind the curtain, while Mona inhaled deeply. Again the nicotine relaxed every muscle. Non-smokers had no idea how good it felt.

'I'll open the window,' the nun said. Then handed her a photo of Ronald Coleman.

Mona thought it was one of those collectors' items from long ago. 'He's old-fashioned now.'

The nun snapped back the photo.

'I – I meant handsome ... in an old-fashioned way.'

Before she could say anything more the day nurses breezed in and helped Mona out of bed and out to the bathroom. Mona thought it was a ruse to get her to see the baby but the nun waited in the bathroom without comment. You took natural functions for granted but now bending was agony. Why didn't anybody warn you children would lead to this? When she came out the old nun was looking in the mirror.

'Did you never want to get married?' Mona asked, washing her hands.

The old face wrinkled into a smile. 'I had a vocation ... everyone is called.'

'I wasn't.'

The nun wagged a scolding finger. 'You know the story of Martha and Mary?'

'One did the dishes.' Mona pulled a comb through her tangled hair. 'I look a sight.'

'We have a hairdresser who comes in.'

'I do it myself.'

The nun looked interested. 'What do you use?'

'Polyblond – I get it in the supermarket. I can tell you one thing: you missed nothing in marriage.'

The nun drew herself up to her full height. 'Are you giving up without a fight?'

Before Mona could answer a nurse came in to help her back to bed. When she'd gone she lay there exhausted. The old woman was cracked, but she must be lonely carrying that photo around. You never thought of nuns having no one. Bad and all as he was she had Terry for eleven years. They'd been all right together till the children came, even then there were good times.

Waiting for breakfast she dozed off and suddenly Robert Redford was running up the hospital corridor. He stood over her bed, producing a bunch of red roses from behind his back. The chancer had shaved his moustache but she wasn't going to be fooled again. And why was he staring? Couldn't he see she was a woman in pain? Someone should brain him. 'Curiosity killed the cat!' she warned, lifting her arm, but at that moment two nurses dragged him away, saying 'Breakfast, Mrs Reilly?' Afterwards they gave her another injection. Did they think she was some sort of pin cushion? She was so sore that she had to lie on her side. Sometime later she found herself in a dream about her days in Slough. It was always the same dream. She and the children were lost in a station. It was vaulted and grimy with fetid, filthy tunnels leading nowhere. She wandered down one looking for a timetable or a guard but couldn't find either. Their footsteps echoed hollowly, frightening Danny and Lisa. Suddenly she came to the end and a train screeched in front of them. Hastily she gathered the children and got on but suddenly millions of policemen piled out of the engine and grabbed Danny. As they hauled him off she sobbed helplessly. 'He's my child! He's my child!'

'We're taking care of him, love.'

Dr Cunningham was standing by her bed. He examined her stitches. 'You need blood, love. Blood.'

They hitched her to another bottle. The rest of her day consisted of more sleep, disturbed by visits from a physiotherapist and an intern who took blood. Someone mentioned a psychiatrist but Mona pretended not to hear. Before lunch two nurses walked her around her bed. At mid-afternoon there was a snack she couldn't eat. She felt only a vast indifference, assuming that she'd hear if her neighbour had any problems with looking after the children. The hospital seemed to have given up worrying her about the baby. She'd have to see it soon, she knew that, just as she'd have to face the months without sleep, the endless nappies.

In the evening Sally Ann returned. 'You got the cigarettes?'

Mona smiled. 'Thanks'

She sat down beside her. 'I was worried in case you'd set yourself on fire!'

'I've had plenty of practice. Are you ok?'

'Yeah. It was nothing.'

'It was an operation.' Mona reached for the Tolstoy novel. 'I'm enjoying this, by the way,' she lied.

'Isn't it good?' Sally Ann leafed through it. 'He's terrific on character. Listen to this. *One of the most widespread superstitions,* she read aloud, *is that every man has some distinguishing quality: one is kind, another cruel, a third wise or stupid, or energetic, or apathetic. Men are not really like that. We may say of a man that he is more often kind than cruel, more often wise than stupid ... Men are like rivers: the water is the same in one and all, but every river is narrow here, more rapid there ...'*

Mona interrupted her. 'Did the doctor say anything?'

'He advised me to adopt.' The younger woman burst into tears.

'Listen, you might be as well off.'

Sally Ann wiped her eyes. 'I know you're feeling terrible.'

Mona pretended to be sleepy so the younger woman left. It was either a feast or a famine with children. Still, it'd be awful not to be able to conceive: it was something she'd never thought of. Her children were her one blessing. Without them she'd have nothing to show for her life. Why had she gone crazy now? What had Sally Ann said about a character being like a river? Maybe she'd hit a narrow spot? It wasn't fair to take things out on a tiny baby. But how was she going to cope with him?

The next time the old nun came she wore a black raincoat over her habit. She peeled off black woollen gloves. 'You're looking better, pet.'

Mona panicked at the word 'better'.

The nun took a Dunnes bag from her basket. 'I got you this.'

It was a Polyblond rinse. 'You shouldn't have.'

The nun peered short-sightedly at the instructions. 'You'll feel better when you look better.' She took some baby clothes from her bag. 'Mrs Barrett-Byrne left you these. Her baby died.'

Mona felt tears coming as she fingered a white matinee coat, the matching bootees, several babygrows. She'd forgotten how tiny new babies were. God, what had got into her? What sort of woman was she? She inhaled deeply, looking at the nun. 'You must think I'm terrible?'

'I do not!'

'Can I go down to the nursery?'

The nun busied herself, picking up the clothes. 'Doctor said not till you're strong ... But we could have a peep?'

Mona hauled herself out of bed. 'Ok.'

They walked slowly out to the corridor. Halfway to the nursery Mona had to stop. She felt completely drained of strength. They went on and at last reached the nursery. It was full of cots, but only two were occupied. Mona stopped by the first, assuming the bigger blond baby was hers. Both of her other children had been fair.

But the nun beckoned from the other cot. 'Over here!'

This baby had a shock of black hair. 'Are you sure?'

The nun pointed to the tag on the tiny wrist. 'Reilly.'

Mona studied the helpless, sleeping bundle. 'He looks Spanish.'

The nun bent over the crib. 'He's as Irish as Sarsfield!'

The baby wrinkled his nose like a little old man. He made a fist with his tiny hand. Mona touched it. Was he really her child? He was too beautiful. And how did he get so dark? With all that hair? Maybe Terry did have foreign blood way back? She looked worriedly at the nun. 'He's very small.' It was a miserable world to be born into, Mona thought, but the only available one. If your own mother didn't want you, who the hell would?

'Have you thought of a name, Mrs Reilly?'

A name? She'd vaguely thought of some. She looked at the old nun, then down at the baby. 'Ronald,' she said. 'I'm calling him Ronald.'

XI

MAUREEN AND BRIAN

Ireland would make a feminist out of a stone. It's an absolute patriarchy. I'm dead serious. Take Brian de Burca: he's an older friend of Dick's and a famous historian. In college I used to be dazzled by his ilk. But I had not yet entered the groves of academe through the back door of marriage and observed such luminaries from a distance – at a lecture or on TV where Brian had his own history programme. So imagine my surprise last summer when he behaved like some sort of sultan to his wife, Maureen. The six of us – Maureen and Brian, Peggy and Tony, and Dick and I – were in a Galway hotel for a long weekend where Brian's bullying started at the first breakfast. He's a burly man with wire glasses, a red face, a scholarly mane of white hair combed over a bald patch, and a Shavian beard. As always he presided at the top of the table. I sat on one side with Tony and Dick on the other, while the two other women chatted obliviously at the far end. As always Brian was telling a story – this time about Parnell and the famous

Galway mutiny of the Irish Parliamentary Party. With his captive audience he was like some ancient Irish *seanchai*. He was in tiptop form, but suddenly, in between the porridge and the fry, interrupted his monologue with a shout. 'Maureen, the Flora!'

This was for his cholesterol.

Maureen is a waifish woman with wispy grey hair and a beautiful bony face who always wears tweeds and a twinset. She was chatting to Peggy and did not immediately turn round, which made Brian apoplectic. 'Maureen!'

Her forehead puckered with anxiety. 'What is it, dear?'

He snorted. 'You ignored me!'

'I didn't, dear.'

He still glared and she paled in agitation. There was an awful silence and nobody knew where to look. At last Brian relented, holding up the butter dish. 'You know what my doctor said about butter.'

She immediately jumped up. 'Oh, yes. Flora! I forgot.'

He smiled, saying with heavy emphasis 'I was trying to tell you that!' Then to Dick and Tony he had the gall to say 'You've got to keep women in line.'

It was meant to be a joke. I watched Maureen's birdlike figure hop across the diningroom, looking to Peggy and silently mouthing the question 'Why didn't he go himself?'

She raised her eyebrows philosophically and reached for her orange juice. I wanted to protest, but was getting no support. For all her talk, Peggy's a weak reed when it comes to any confrontation. I discovered this at the Kells house and nothing had changed. Lately all she talked about was dieting but I was relieved that she was thinking about her health.

It was Tony, the peacemaker, who broke the silence. He was even wirier, and had a bit of grey in his dark hair. 'You were telling us about Parnell's finaglings in Galway, Brian?'

My father would've loved to be with us, as he's an expert on Parnell.

'Ah, yes!' Brian cleared his throat, going on in his highish voice. 'The Clare people wanted nothing to do with O'Shea in '85. So he was out in the cold politically. Chamberlain's Central Boards scheme had failed.'

'What was that?' Tony interrupted.

'An early version of Home Rule,' Dick said sleepily.

'Which Parnell wanted nothing to do with!' Brian always pronounced the name *Par*nell instead of the more usual Par*nell* of today. He glanced irritably at Dick now – he couldn't stand anyone to know more than he did.

At that moment the waitress plonked a plate of toast on the table. Brian grabbed a slice, buttering it thickly, despite his heart. He signalled the girl back. 'I'm afraid we'll need more toast than that!'

I guessed that she was on school holidays and had probably never seen anyone so eccentric.

'More toast!' Brian bit off a bite, munching hungrily.

'Yes, more!' Tony said.

'Toast!' echoed Dick.

As I always say, the men stick together. The girl nodded slowly then, pushing her heavy glasses up on her nose and went off. She was probably wondering how grown adults could behave in such an idiotic way. Tony and Dick were giggling moronically now, while Brian was grabbing yet another slice. To show my disdain I said to Brian 'You were telling us about the Clare election.'

Brian left his beloved toast on the plate. 'Ah, yes – where was I? Yes ... O'Shea had no intention of being fobbed off. He started to get nasty, so Parnell had to keep him quiet.'

'What was he nasty about?' Tony held him up again.

'Katharine O'Shea was Parnell's mistress,' Dick said, bringing the usual glare from Brian.

'Ah yes, Kitty, the mot,' Tony said.

'She was never called Kitty!' Brian snapped. 'That was an invention of the Irish.'

'Of the press, surely?' Dick enquired, irritating Brian again.

Brian was holding up his hand for silence like a traffic policeman. When assured of our attention, he continued. 'There's dispute about O'Shea's knowledge of the affair. It's one of those things impossible to pin down.' He shrugged. 'Some historians claim he knew everything from the start. Others that he didn't.'

'Parnell built a cricket pitch in Katharine's garden,' Dick said. 'He stabled his horses there. Surely, O'Shea noticed that?'

'Maybe he was short-sighted,' Tony quipped, getting a laugh from Dick.

The two of them sat there giggling. It was corny.

Brian looked irritably towards the diningroom door. 'Where has that woman got to?'

There was no sign of Maureen.

Brian went on with his lecture. 'Where was I? Yes ... in '85 Parnell had to get O'Shea elected somewhere – the reason will never be clear. First he tried Armagh, but the northerners wouldn't have him. Parnell, by the way, always underestimated the north. Next he tried one of the Liverpool seats but the Liberals wouldn't hear of that.'

Then Maureen came back with the Flora, completely out of breath. 'There you are, dear.'

'You took long enough!' was all Brian could say. Then, frowning importantly, he continued holding forth.

I wanted to protest. I tried to catch the other men's eyes, but received no acknowledgement. They were all the same. If Dick behaved like that he could starve for all I cared. Why hadn't he said something now in support of Maureen?

Brian was busy spreading Flora on yet another slice of toast – he'd eaten nearly the whole plate. 'Finally,' he was saying, 'a vacancy occurred in Galway, for which Parnell proposed O'Shea. The party was outraged, but Parnell rammed O'Shea down their throats.'

'To keep him quiet?' I asked.

Brian looked at me over his glasses, 'It's impossible to know.'

Tony reached for the teapot. 'Parnell was in O'Shea's clutches.'

Brian held out his cup. 'He was in Mrs O'Shea's.'

'He loved her,' I said.

Brian gave me an irritated look. 'It was a bad day for Ireland when he met that dumpy dowager.'

'It's always the woman's fault,' I said. I couldn't help it.

No one spoke.

'Tea, Sally?' Tony held up the pot.

'I'm on coffee, thanks.'

Brian's breathing was short. 'Parnell was surrounded by mad women. His mother was eccentric. His two sisters, Fanny and Anna, fanatics. Emily, the third, a constant drain on his purse.'

He was definitely a misogynist – no wonder there were strident feminists.

'What about O'Shea's affairs?' I persisted.

Brian looked as if he was going to blow a fuse. The whole table was silent.

'He was a well known philanderer,' I went on.

Brian spluttered into his tea. Dick glared again, but I ignored him.

'I suppose it was all Dervorgilla's fault too,' I said. 'The Normans would never have invaded us except for her.'

Brian was put out, but I didn't care. Why should women be blamed for everything that went wrong in the world? And why couldn't I have opinions too? I had a history degree, after all.

Then Brian said in a quiet voice 'as a matter of fact, nothing is known of O'Shea's affairs. And Mrs O'Shea was no help to Ireland. The divorce put paid to Home Rule. Because of her we got 1916, the Civil War and Ireland became insular, backward and self-centred.'

'God save Ireland!' Tony suddenly sang.

Dick joined in a duet. 'God save Ireland, said they all!'

A waitress carried a tray of 'full Irish' fries to our table. She slammed down a plate at every place but Brian's.

'I ordered poached eggs!' he said.

This brought no response from the waitress.

'Maureen!' Brian shouted down the table. 'My eggs haven't come! And we need more toast!'

The two women were now huddled in conversation about the benefits of porridge.

'They won't be long, dear,' Maureen said.

Another silence descended, during which Brian fumed, frequently looking towards the kitchen. Then Tony asked 'What happened to O'Shea.'

Brian was slightly appeased. 'Well, after the fuss in Galway he refused to vote on the second reading of the Home Rule Bill. In June of '86 he walked out of the House and never came back. It was the end of his public life.'

Tony was hacking a rasher. 'Did he give a reason?'

'Not publicly.' Brian turned again to the kitchen. 'There are different theories – he'd found out about Parnell and Mrs O'Shea. Or that the affair was known about in high places and would make him the butt of gossip ... Where's that girl? We need more toast!'

'Toast?' echoed Dick and Tony.

You'd never believe they were grown men. Another waitress flitted by, ignoring us. I didn't blame her.

'I have to do everything myself,' Brian finally said. Then he threw down his napkin, got up and stormed out to the kitchen, disappearing inside. He was a character. Dick told me that he once forged a letter from Parnell, claiming it was genuine, to confuse a rival. I imagined a row going on in the kitchen, but he came out in a few minutes, carrying a mound of toast on one plate and two slithery poached eggs on another.

Dick and Tony fell on the toast, shouting 'Let the toast pass!'

The whole table broke into laughter. It was idiotic, but I had to laugh too.

Before breakfast was over Brian sent Maureen back to their room again – this time for his tablets. I said nothing, realising it was marriage Irish style. Women here were nothing but servants to men. They spent their lives going on messages for them, or else bearing children. Thank God I'd married an American. We'd done it on the spur of the moment last year in a Wilmington register office. Two friends had been witnesses. I was given a mysterious brown paper package courtesy of the State. I thought it contained contraceptives but it was a book called *Vanishing Bride* and some stain-removing products. Afterwards, we had lunch in the Hotel du Pont in Wilmington – table d'hôte. Our marriage was completely different to those of our Irish friends. Dick always helped with the housework, unlike Brian who exploited his wife.

Brian was friendly now with everyone except me. He laughed at Tony and Dick who were fencing on the hotel stairs. But as I passed him in the upstairs hall, on the way to brush my teeth, I knew that an invisible gauntlet had been thrown down between us which was to remain for the whole weekend.

The hotel was on an Atlantic inlet between Galway and Mayo. The sextet planned to tour Galway one day and Mayo the next. An expedition to Renvyle strand was voted for that morning. As we had no car Dick and I were to split up among the other two couples, as we had done on the way down. I made sure to get into the back of the O'Haras' Fiat, leaving Dick to travel with the de Burcas.

'You'll need a cardigan. Sally love,' Peggy bossed, getting into the front.

'I'm fine.' I was wearing a shirt and jeans.

She tied a headscarf over her bleached hair. 'Go and get your cardigan.'

So I, a woman of thirty two, obeyed. That weekend Maureen and Peggy bossed me all the time. I think they forgot that I wasn't their daughter, or especially young any more. In a way I enjoyed it, not having had a mother. I sat happily behind Peggy and Tony that morning watching the west's wild fuchsia flashing past and the sheep grazing morosely. We passed a couple of woolly corpses, and waited several times as they loitered on the road in front of us. So it was lunchtime when we arrived at Renvyle.

The whole weekend was dominated by food. If we weren't eating we were planning meals or digesting meals. As soon as we rendezvoused on the strand the men were hungry again. So we three women went in search of forage. I would've preferred to stay and hear Brian hold forth on Oliver St John Gogarty's nearby house, now a hotel, but I dutifully followed the women.

'Gogarty's wife sued the locals for stealing after they were burnt out.' His high voice carried over the strand. 'She won one case and lost another. Even though the furniture was in the people's houses ...' Then Brian launched into another story I couldn't hear about Gogarty's role in the Free State Senate. Brian's knowledge was encyclopedic and he never tired of sharing it.

The cluttered country shop sold everything from tyres to tea. I went round by myself while Maureen and Peggy kept together, their figures reminding me of Laurel and Hardy. As they looked for sandwich stuff they were deep in chat about country food prices.

I watched an old country woman fill her basket with packet soups and biscuits. Then I put a barmbrack in our basket as Dick really liked it, but Peggy took it out. 'You can't make sandwiches with this, Sally, love.'

'Oh, ok.' Who would want to, for God's sake? But why was my presence required if I could make no decisions?

After lunch there was to be a swim. But this was voted unsafe for an hour so we huddled on the soggy strand, waiting. I can still see us, like a modern version of that famous Monet painting – I forget the name of it: Brian in his little straw hat with his feet bare and trousers rolled up; Dick in his plaid shirt and turned-up Levis, as usual smoking; Tony wearing an American baseball cap against the non-existent sun and sucking a pipe; Peggy and Maureen discussing a knitting pattern. Children played with buckets and spades nearby, watched over by their parents, while at the water's edge bathers shrieked as they dashed into the icy Atlantic.

It was a typical Irish summer's day – miserable. A cold wind blasted us, whipping the water into vicious little waves which lashed the rocks. Dick always complained about the Irish climate, so I always stuck up for it and even pretended it wasn't cold. In a way I liked grey summers: I was used to them. That day I wore my bikini under my jeans. To delude myself further I rubbed sun oil on my arms. The smell of it mingled with sea spray brought back memories of being on a beach with my mother. Lately I thought of her all the time. I found myself staring at women whose age she'd be now, wondering what she'd look like. Her hair would be grey, she'd have wrinkles. Would she be thin like Maureen or heavy like Peggy? She'd got thin before her death, but that was cancer. Then, one day, she went to hospital and never came back. The beach was one of my few strong images of her. My father was always too busy working so she would bring Tim and me to rented seaside houses – at Brittas or Donabate. One year we were poor so she took us for a week to Butlin's holiday camp where an extraordinary thing happened. There was a ventriloquist who was meant to be entertaining the children with funny shows and that. Well, he was a paedeophile and actually felt me up. I don't think it did me any damage, as I was too young. One day he brought me to a variety concert and had me touch him. I thought it rather odd but never told my mother. Then another day I was in his chalet looking out a window. The next thing my mother was running up the path and came in and grabbed me. Or at least I think she did. I asked Dick if the man could've possibly molested me and I'd blocked the memory. Could that account for my nervousness about sex? But he said he wasn't a Freudian. If I was screwed up, which he'd never noticed, it was probably Catholicism. That retarded people by about five years. Thank God I was an atheist now. Still, I'd always felt inadequate. Last year I'd gone to a sexuality workshop. I knew Dick would laugh the idea to scorn so I told him it was a meditation group. At first I was quaking with nerves. But there were other women there. First we were lectured on the causes of frigidity and then did exercises to get over inhibitions. This involved studying the shape and variety of the vagina. It amazed me that they came in different sizes. We'd examined our own and each others' with the help of mirrors. It was really embarrassing. Then we were told about masturbation techniques, and how to arouse a man. One lecturer said all troubles came from suppressing emotion. They said you had to discharge it, not bottle things up. The best thing for anger was to beat a pillow. Later I told Dick who said it was all Balzac.

'You don't need oil today, Sally, love!' Peggy interrupted my thoughts. 'There's no sun.'

'It's insulation for my swim.' I kept on rubbing, thinking it was lucky people couldn't read your thoughts. Peggy would think me cracked, they all would, but you were stuck with yourself. You could change your personality but not your basic character, according to one of my self-improvement books. My brother, Tim, was always quoting Popeye 'I yam what I yam.' I had to accept myself too.

Tony shivered, looking at the water. 'Isn't that our Minister breasting the waves?'

A dark-haired man in togs stood at the water's edge, gingerly dipping his toe in and immediately leaping back.

'It is,' Brian said.

Dick laughed. 'A typical politician.'

'What's he Minister of?' I asked.

Brian peered over his glasses. 'Trade and Industry.'

The politician suddenly ran up the beach, out of the way of splashing girls. Our group burst out laughing. When we'd recovered, I said 'I wish he'd do something for women.'

Peggy looked up. 'What do you mean, Sally?'

'I mean abortion, divorce.'

She gave me a funny look.

'Bread and circuses, my dear,' Brian sighed – at least he was talking to me again.

Dick lit a cigarette. 'It'll come. People are pushed by events.'

'Why is abortion bread and circuses?' I persisted.

'It's a smoke screen,' Brian said, 'to distract people from real issues.'

'But it's 1982!' I argued. 'Women all over the world have abortions.' I looked for support to Peggy and Maureen, but they gazed at the politician, refusing to be drawn. The Minister was slowly approaching the water again.

Tony puffed his pipe. 'How many women take the boat weekly?'

'I'm not sure.' I said. Tony was always willing to discuss things. 'But women have the right to choose.'

'They certainly do,' he said.

Dick sighed boredly. 'The government should address the problem.'

'We're having a referendum,' I reminded him.

The politician now dipped his fingers into the sea, making the sign of the cross. Hugging himself, he walked out a couple of steps. Then, seeing a wave, he ran back. That started Dick and Tony on their duet again. 'God save Ireland, said the hero! God save Ireland said they all!'

I had to laugh. When their noise had died down, Peggy said 'But what about the child being aborted, Sally Ann? Isn't it a human being too?'

I was drawing on the sand with a stick. 'It's human tissue.'

Peggy was outraged. 'It's a human being!'

'Why not baptise the menstrual flow?' I argued.

Maureen looked over. She was huddled in a rug and her face was pinched with cold. 'A human being exists when the sperm penetrates the ovum.'

Dick groaned. 'I have several children who haven't made it.'

Tony laughed. 'There's time yet.'

'It's running out.' Dick was like my own father about his children.

Then Brian interrupted. 'A man could never have an abortion.'

I thought I was hearing things. 'A man wouldn't have to!'

Even this brought no response from the women. God, they couldn't even stick up for their sex. Then the politician passed our group, breathing hard and slapping himself – as if he had been swimming. It was so silly. We'd been watching him all the time, and he'd hardly wet his toes.

'How was the water?' Tony enquired.

'Brutal,' shivered the Minister, slapping his chest.

This reduced our group to more laughter. I sat staring out to sea. It wasn't funny. How could there ever be any progress with his type in power? If he couldn't even go for a swim how would he bring about change? And why did men always make decisions for women? Finally I got up and took off my jeans, saying 'I'm going for a swim.'

Peggy looked at her watch. 'It's not an hour yet, Sally, love. You'll get cramp.'

'I won't.' I ran to the water's edge.

In a way I didn't blame the politician. Swimming is something I don't like much either, which is probably why I've never learnt properly. But it's a point of honour for me to get wet at least once a year, especially if I'm at the seaside. It didn't feel right not to. The cold that day took my breath away. I plunged down, kicking wildly, and after a few strokes ran back to the edge where Dick stood shivering in his togs. His white hair and brown skin were in contrast to the pale Irish. After seven years, we were still together. Love was a mystery. The songs were right. He cautiously dipped his big toe in the freezing water.

'It's not bad when you're down,' I lied.

His teeth were chattering. 'It's not bad for the fish!'

I ran off along the strand at the edge of the water but he called after me.

'What is it?' I arrived back beside him.

He jumped out of my way. 'Don't splash me! And for heaven's sake, cool down a bit!'

'Ok.' I splashed off again to keep warm. In the distance I saw Brian undressing under copious towels. Men were all the same. They thought you were quarrelling if you expressed your ideas. Actually I don't know what I think about abortion. I could never have one either. Yet I think it should exist. My mother had been pregnant with my brother when her cancer was discovered. I'm glad I have my brother, but she should have had the choice of an abortion. Women were expected to be such saints. My American feminist friends were right about men exploiting us. They blamed us for everything: Eve, Dervorgilla, Katharine O'Shea. Dick even jokingly blamed me for the Irish climate, saying 'Your dank country' etc. I always blamed myself for the house too. If something went wrong with it, which it usually did, I got paroxysms of guilt about buying it. But on the whole it had worked out well, and Dick was moving his library over, by degrees. I still worried constantly about his health. If he got a stomach ache it was my cooking. If he sneezed it was somehow my doing too. Looking back along the strand I saw he was down and swimming strongly. He'd probably get a cold now, but the Atlantic was an international ocean.

I don't know whether it's the relief of getting out of the water but you feel terrific after a swim. I did that day. My irritation at Brian was washed out of my system.

Our next stop was Kylemore Abbey, the famous Benedictine girls' boarding school. It's a chocolate-box castle on a lake with a Paul Henry mountain behind it. Besides the school there's a cafe and pottery shop. While Dick and the others were looking around the Abbey I visited the pottery with Maureen. She runs her own craft shop in Dún Laoghaire so was interested in seeing what they had. As we stopped to admire a vase she surprised me by saying 'Did you ever think of getting a job, Sally Ann?'

'I'm a painter.'

'That's a hobby, surely? I need someone to help in the shop.'

'I'd be glad to help you, but I don't want a job.'

'Everybody should work.'

'I do work! Painters paint.'

She walked around the shop. I followed her small, tweedy figure, telling myself not to be annoyed. That she was being kind to me. After all, she wasn't the only one who thought me a layabout. My father, who knew I worked five to six hours a day, was always saying 'Art is wonderful therapy, Sally Ann.' He meant well, but he never had any faith in me. Tim, my hippy-happy brother, was doing well now as a commercial artist, but was still the butt of my father's criticism. I would be too if I lived at home. Except for Sister Rita, long ago, Dick was the only person in the world who believed in me. I'd never have managed without him. The only trouble was I had no real talent. I was too imitative.

As we went outside to find the others, Maureen said 'A pity you haven't your sketchbook here, Sally Ann.'

I nodded agreeably. The Abbey was chocolate boxy and the last place in the world I'd want to sketch.

'They're waiting for us in the cars!' She wrinkled her eyes at the edges, saying as we hurried over 'Why don't you display your paintings in my shop?'

'Thanks, that'd be great.'

At least there was no ill-feeling between us. She wagged a finger. 'You might earn some money. Nothing too abstract now.'

'I do earn money! And all my paintings are abstract – one is being considered for the RHA exhibition.'

The lie just popped out. How is it you never grow up? You're always the same idiot inside.

She gave me a long look. 'You're aiming high, aren't you?'

I shrugged, as Brian honked from the car.

Maureen got into the back, as Dick was in the front with Brian. As usual, I got in with Peggy and Tony. Clifden was next, and all the way there I smarted at her remarks. It hit me that for all my talk about women's lib I was financially dependent on Dick, while she was independent of Brian. I'd never make a living as an artist.

While Dick and Tony sneaked a drink in the bar, and Brian snoozed in the car, we women went foraging again. This time for fish, because Brian didn't eat meat. But talk about looking for coals at Newcastle, or whatever the cliché is, there wasn't a fish to be had at the harbour, or anywhere in the town. We learnt of a factory on the coast so it was voted we try there.

As we waited for Tony in their car, Peggy turned to me. 'I'm surprised you approve of abortion, Sally Ann.'

I was taken aback at her tone.

'I hope you wouldn't consider having one.'

'I certainly would.'

Her face blotched in anger. 'Well! I'm shocked!'

I had upset her. 'If I was raped I'd take the morning after pill.'

She shook her head. 'But it'd be yours too.'

'Not if I was raped.'

She looked at me in puzzlement. 'It's unusual for a pregnancy to occur after rape.'

I didn't want to argue, but I couldn't help asking 'What if you were having a defective child? Say it had no brain?'

To this she had no answer.

'Irish society discriminates against women, the unhappily married, homosexuals.'

She frowned. 'Don't tell me you approve of homosexuality?'

'I certainly do!'

She picked up the folded newspaper, pursing her lips.

'According to Freud, everyone's homosexual,' I went on. 'If you're not active, you're latent.'

She glared. 'I've never thought much of Freud.'

'Well, you're in the minority!'

She rustled the paper irritably. 'If you don't mind I'd like to read the paper.'

Silence fell like a curtain between us. Actually I didn't know if Freud said it or not, someone did. But he was right about so many things. He said that you fell in love with your parents and spent your whole life searching for them in others. It was important to be loved, then other things fell into place. I glanced over at Peggy who was still reading. I shouldn't have argued with her. She didn't know any homosexuals. She'd never met anyone like Anna and Sue. If she came to America I'd introduce her to them. Now she was irritated with me. She was probably thinking I'd got liberal ideas in America, had had loads of abortions. Or made some sort of choice not to have children, when the opposite was the truth. I'd just never produced anything. Dick and I had tried. With Nettie he had only to walk through the bedroom, but I always got my period. I had adhesions, the doctor had told me. And he couldn't even be sure about that, although he'd seen my insides on a TV screen. 'I can't say you have blocked tubes, but I can tell you one thing: it doesn't look good.' Dick was relieved when I told him, I knew. There was no one else to tell. I'd longed for my mother or even a sister to talk to. When I had a laparotomy, my father came to see me. He sat there for ages, looking puzzled. 'Why on earth do you want children?' he asked at last, which was a reflection on Tim and me.

But I imagined this child I couldn't have. Would it look like Dick, or me? I knew I'd missed a great joy. Yet sometimes I was relieved. I could do my painting; at least that's what I told myself.

We drove for miles in search of the fish factory, finding it at last. They normally exported everything to France and were put out at having to sell to us, mere natives, but Peggy was persuasive, so they did. We ended up with enough sole to feed an army. Finding a picnic place was next. We drove along the coast, but something was wrong with everywhere we stopped – no shelter, or an unsuitable view. Once Peggy spotted a fat horse in a field and waved the other car down.

'It looks pregnant,' she said, getting out.

Although inexperienced, I had to agree. It stood perfectly still with legs outstretched, as if doing the splits.

Maureen looked worried. 'I think we should go for help.'

Peggy climbed onto the crumbly stone wall. 'It's about to give birth any minute.'

Brian came up and wanted to eat immediately. The other men nodded assent, but Peggy was adamant. 'That animal's in need.'

Brian blinked at the horse. 'It looks all right to me.' The horse had now lain down, its legs stretched straight out. 'Besides,' said Brian, 'Animals can cope. It's nature, after all.'

'That's what they say to women! I'm going for help!' Peggy set out across the field. 'Coming, Maureen? Sally Ann?'

There was a cottage two fields away. The three of us trudged across the soggy fields, but for naught. Two old men listened, nodding and smiling, then politely dismissed our fears. So we had to leave the poor horse to its fate.

'They probably eat children out here,' Peggy raged on the way back.

After more driving we came to a scraggy field with rocks going down to the sea. Litter was strewn in one corner with ashes from a previous picnic. But at least the place had some shelter. So Tony and Peggy immediately set up the stove and I was given the task of chopping onions, peppers and tomatoes for frying. To my amazement Peggy ordered the men to set the table. Brian spread the tablecloth and Tony and Dick put out the cutlery. They were very proud of themselves. Then Peggy pointed to a brown stain in the middle of the cloth. 'Look where you've put it!'

It was on a moist cow pat. I've often wondered what people see in picnics. We could've been comfortable in a restaurant. It was a cold evening and everybody was starving. Brian hovered hungrily around although Peggy kept telling him furiously to go away. She was mad about her tablecloth. But the fish were cooked at last and I was elected to serve it onto plates.

As I did, Brian crept up and snatched one.

Peggy shouted. 'Put that back!'

He ignored her.

'Brian!' She made for him with a spoon, but he ran to his car, his white hair wild.

He had locked himself in and was eating hungrily. The rest of us were served at last, and ate our food huddled in a group near Brian's car. He had the nerve to open his window and announce. 'The fish was cold!'

Peggy was unruffled. 'Serves you right for grabbing!'

In that weather it was difficult to keep anything hot. I can't remember how the chat went exactly. I think we must've been talking over the career of the vacillating politician at Renvyle, or the government or something. But, as we were finishing our coffee, Peggy said to me 'I've been thinking, Sally. In abortion a case of assault would be an exception.'

'It wouldn't be the woman's fault.' I was glad we were friends again.

'Of course it wouldn't,' Dick said, joining in. He didn't know we were referring to a previous conversation, but he had heard the word 'assault'. 'Tell them your Butlin's story, Sally Ann.'

Dick and I often think of the same thing. So the coincidence of me thinking of the Butlin's incident that very day didn't surprise me. It often happens with us, so I told the group my story, without much trauma, because really it hadn't upset me. I was too young. They were all amazed that the ventriloquist had been in charge of the children.

But Brian suddenly blurted. 'Little girls are always asking for it!'

I was too shocked to say anything, as he continued 'My sister used to accuse a neighbourhood boy of interfering with her. So my mother made me follow her home from school. Well, the fellow was there all right, waiting on the corner, as she'd described. It was assault all right. They went into the garden of a deserted house. I looked over the wall, and what did I see?'

Everyone was agog.

'She was interfering with him! Thirteen, and unbuttoning his fly!' He shook his head.

I was furious – for all women, and myself.

'I'm a liar then?' I said.

'I didn't say that!' Brian was red in the face.

'Well, I must be.'

He finally got his breath. 'How do you put up with this one, Dick?'

Dick looked embarrassed, and the women, as usual, looked away.

'We'll have her shot, Brian!' Tony went over to the stove. 'More coffee, anyone?'

'You'll have to boil more water.' Peggy busied herself with filling it.

I went down to the rocks, pretending to go to the loo. I had to get away from the others. They all thought me humourless, or something like that. Maybe I was, but inside I was boiling. Why had I got so upset? Because women would never speak that way about men, I told myself, and Brian should know better. He was meant to be enlightened, a professor. How would things ever change for women? I sat on a rock for ages, hoping to imbibe some of the Connemara peace: the plopping water, the smell of turf on the wind, the swallows swooping and diving. Where had they come from? Like us they were getting ready for winter migration.

As we drove back to the hotel through Connemara's mysterious mountains, the sky was an angry red and I knew by his glare that Dick was angry with me. Of course, Brian was only being funny. I had spoiled the day by getting angry. I always put my foot in it. Dick travelled with Brian, and was probably apologising for me now. I dozed in the back of Peggy and Tony's car. They weren't against me, I knew, just too tired for conversation. So I wandered in my mind. All holidays turned out disastrously. My French one had ended my relationship with Alastair. For years I blamed myself. I cringe, thinking of my former selves. Sometimes they flash before me like scenes in an old-fashioned movie. I was a pain. In college I had camped it up to hide my nerves. I thought I was in a Camus novel – except I didn't know any French. I even remembered arguing that Jane Austen was a bore. Why didn't she write about something important, instead of *who* married *who*? God, I was thick. I even fancied myself a journalist. Now I was trying to be an artist. Maybe that would turn out the same. I'd never know who I was. No wonder Alastair couldn't love me. In a way he'd become my Michael Furey. Did he ever think of me? Probably not, but I forgot people too. Paul Brady was dead for years now. I'd never forget that terrible funeral. For solidarity, I didn't want a Christian burial either. I didn't want to be buried at all. I couldn't stand the idea of bugs crawling on me. I'd be cremated and used as an egg timer. There was some point in that. But why had Paul done it? Life was so beautiful. 'It's a great big peach, Sally Ann,' Mother Rita used to say. 'Take lots of bites.' Then I reminded myself to ring her when I got back. It was Sister Rita now. She came from somewhere in the west and was the kindest person I'd ever known, one of those really good people. She'd made such a difference to my life. But such is human nature, I used to go round calling her names. I was so embarrassed to have feelings. I'd shocked my friend, Deirdre, once by running her down. Deirdre was from the west too. She'd never grown up, really, lived in the past. Yet I could've helped her. The last I heard she was doing a night degree in UCD. Where was she now? Life's a journey really, the poets were right about that, and friends fell by the wayside. God, it was 1965 when I visited Deirdre in the west. We'd cycled in those lovely fuschia-lined lanes, seventeen years ago, over half my life. Now I was thirty two and still alive. Because of my mother I had never expected to be old. I kept imagining diseases, yet here I was.

Back in our room Dick wouldn't speak to me. He got into bed quickly and turned out the light. I undressed in the dark. 'I'm sorry.'

He didn't answer. It's typical of men, never wanting to discuss things.

'Please say something.' I could hear his thoughts ticking. He was thinking me a pain.

Finally he sighed. 'It was a bit heavy.'

'I didn't plan it.'

He turned on his side. 'Go to sleep.'

I was forgiven, but lay awake for hours.

Peggy called me at the crack of dawn for a sauna with her and Maureen. By the time I'd staggered sleepily downstairs in my dressing gown, the two women were sweltering in the oven. They both wore swimsuits, but I was naked, continental-style.

Peggy's daughter was pregnant, and the conversation focused on the event. Fragments penetrated the steam to my sleepy brain.

'It'll be a new lease of life for you.'

'Your grandchild must be two by now. Are you all right, Sally, love?'

I nodded woozily.

'Take a shower now. We had one before you came down.'

The heat was unbearable, so I went. I loathe showers and was miserable standing under that one. Yet it might cool me down. The others certainly looked cool.

I went back to my perch.

'It's awfully hot,' I said to Peggy.

'You'll feel marvellous afterwards, Sally.'

I went for another shower. Stepping out of it, I realised something was wrong. I was going to faint. How had this happened when the others were completely unaffected? I managed to put on my dressing gown and stagger towards the hotel stairs. I reached them and collapsed. I don't know how long I was there, but I opened my eyes to see Brian de Burca's red face. 'My dear girl!'

I closed my eyes. God, why him? He put his arm under my shoulder and hauled me to a sitting position. Then he thrust my head between my knees. 'Keep your head down, that's the girl.'

I felt awful. Why him?

'What happened?'

Tears came – I couldn't help it. 'I had a sauna. Look, I'm sorry about yesterday.'

He sat down beside me on the stairs. 'Don't try and talk.'

'I was humourless.'

'When?'

'During the picnic.'

'I don't know why you're sorry. I was the boor!'

In a few minutes, I felt myself recovering. This used to happen to me in boarding school years ago, but not since. What was wrong?

'Can you make it back to bed?'

I nodded, and he helped me up, saying 'Sitting in an oven couldn't be good for anyone.'

Together we walked to the bedroom. Halfway I joked 'I'm not even a proper feminist!'

'You're a passionate feminist, Sally Ann.'

'I know you only like docile women.'

He snorted in reply. I was unable to say any more. Near my bedroom door he said 'Basically you were right about Katharine O'Shea.'

'You're the historian.'

'Don't interrupt! Katharine O'Shea was blamed for Home Rule which hadn't a chance of getting through. Gladstone and Parnell were both living in fantasy.'

'What was Parnell really like?'

'Now that's a silly question. What is anyone really like? There were many Parnells. There was Parnell the country gentleman, Parnell the political strategist, Parnell the mad scientist, Parnell the lover.'

We came to my bedroom door but Dick had gone down to breakfast. 'Get into bed.' Brian looked at me over his glasses. 'I'll send Maureen up with a cup of tea. Another thing ...'

'What?'

He cleared his throat, looking at me over his glasses. 'The artist is the true historian. In a hundred years they'll be looking at paintings to know what life was like at the end of the twentieth century.'

I got into bed, laughing. 'They won't be looking at mine.'

He folded his arms. 'I thought your Christmas card showed great ability.'

'You need more than ability. You need talent.'

'You've got that.'

I sighed tiredly. 'Not enough.'

'You're a stubborn woman, aren't you?'

'Know thyself – Plato.'

'Not Plato! That was written in the temple at Delphi. And you don't know anything at your age! Now get some rest. I've a surprise for you later today.'

Later Dick came up with Peggy, who brought my breakfast on a tray. She put the tray on a table and anxiously perused my face but Dick said I had probably drunk too much wine. When he left she stayed, sitting on the bed. 'I'm sorry I got cross yesterday. You must think me right wing.'

'No ... I don't.'

She gave me her wonderful smile. 'Will you stay in bed?'

'No, I'm fine, except for nausea.'

She grabbed my hand. 'You're not –?'

I laughed aloud. 'God, no!'

She looked disappointed. 'That's alright then. Children aren't everything. You have artistic gifts.'

'Oh, we've tried.'

Her face lit up again. 'Have you?'

'Nothing ever happens.'

She thought for a moment. 'Try a pillow under your hips.'

I nodded, not telling her about all the tests I'd had.

Brian's surprise was a visit to Moore Hall, the ancestral home of novelist George Moore. Tony and Peggy wanted to go shopping in Louisburg instead, so there were only two of us to show around. Wearing his straw hat, and with a huge walking stick in hand, he led us up the long ferny avenue, as usual talking all the way.

'The Moores were originally an English family who claimed descent from Sir Thomas Moore ...'

I listened in fascination as he told us all about the family. Chauvinist or not he was the most interesting person I'd ever met. He hit a thistle with his stick. 'The novelist's father was elected to parliament in 1868.'

'Before Parnell?' I queried.

'Parnell was elected in '75,' Dick said.

Brian controlled his irritation at the interruption. 'That Moore was a supporter of land reform – one of the few landlords who were. Despite that, the IRA burnt the house.'

They sure had. We came out of the green gloom of the avenue to a spectacular ruin. The big granite house was a roofless shell with bricked in windows and weeds growing inside. Still it was hauntingly beautiful. The four of us were like characters on a Chekhov stage set, lamenting a lost world. There was no one else about. Brian pointed out a plaque the IRA had erected in reparation for their deed.

I went up the wide steps to the non-existent door. 'What a pity to burn a place like this.'

Brian was following me. 'That's patriotism for you.'

'Vandalism,' said Dick.

I wandered round the weedy outside by myself, while Dick chatted to Brian inside the ruin. In Ireland people talked about the past, yet had no respect for it. The beautiful house had been a symbol of oppression to the people. Now its brooding presence was a scar on our country's psyche.

Fanaticism got you nowhere, but it was still going on. Parnell's time was gone now, as ours would one day be. He wouldn't have wanted this destruction. It was done by the thinking of the time. People were stuck in their own rut. In the future our Stone Age laws would seem as ludicrous as the burning of this house. Change would come. It was only a matter of time. We still had Rome Rule, but give us another hundred years.

Dick was waiting for me at the ruin, smoking.

'Isn't it great?' I said.

He smiled, and we followed Brian and Maureen down the avenue. They were ahead of us arm in arm: Brian, Churchillian with his hat and walking stick. I thought how happy I was. Brian was right: it was impossible to know anyone. Like heaven, marriage is a house with many mansions. 'Frankly,' Brian's voice carried back, 'Moore wrote like a woman.'

Hmm! I thought.

XII

BIRTHS, MARRIAGES AND DEATHS

Two nuns were in the drab community room. Although for recreation, the floor was covered with hard lino and the ugly Victorian furniture looked uncomfortable. By one wall a glazed bookcase held musty tomes and there was no friendly clutter. It was early summer, so sun from the tall windows overlooking the terrace cheered things up a bit, but not much. Sister Rita sat reading the *Irish Independent* at the centre table. As usual, Sister Clement hogged 'her place' by the cold storage heater. Short-sightedly she poured over *The Irish Times*, singing bits of a hymn: 'Oil in my lamp ...'

'Anything in the *Times*, Clemmy?'

The older woman didn't look up. 'Give me oil in my lamp ...'

'Could I have a bit of your paper, Clemmy?'

'I want oil in my lamp.'

Resignedly, Rita tried to find something of interest in her paper. Thirty odd years in the convent had taught her patience. But Clement had had the *Times* for the last half-hour. She wasn't even reading it. She was singing, and tunelessly too.

Monday was Rita's morning off from lecturing at Carysfort and she looked forward to a quiet read of the papers. Usually she had the room to herself. But in a Mother House you could never be sure who would come out of the woodwork. The young nuns taught all day in the new building but the old tended to wander down from the infirmary. She could take the papers to her own room, but there was a vague house rule against this and she was meant to be the superior. So instead she made a cup of Nescafé Blend 37 with a kettle in her room – the nearest thing to brewed coffee she could afford – and carried it downstairs. There was a house rule against this as well but she ignored it. It was her prerogative as superior to ignore petty rules.

She folded her paper, replacing it in the middle of the table. In five minutes she'd have to go and draft a letter to the minister protesting about delays in the secondary school curriculum reform. The Conference of Secondary Sisters had appointed her as spokeswoman, and just as well too – someone needed to shake things up. The department had been talking about change for years but every year brought the same old excuses. Teaching sisters, she would point out, welcomed the principle of non-sexist education ... but where were the teachers of woodwork for girls' schools ... no woodwork and mechanical drawing. Who would make this possible? And, more important, where were the long promised changes in the Examination Board?

A low mumble broke into her thoughts. Clement was fingering her beads, the paper lying unread on her lap.

'Are you finished with the *Times*, Clemmy?'

'Am I what?' The old woman looked comical with a brown, springy wig under her navy blue veil.

'*The Irish Times*,' Rita shouted. 'Have you read it?'

'I haven't seen it.'

'It's on your lap!'

She scrunched it up. 'Here! Take it!'

Rita crossed the room, catching the glare of disapproval at her jogging shoes.

'How are you feeling today, Sister?'

'Terrible ... terrible.'

Rita stood over her. Clemmy's health was always terrible. To be honest, she was a terrible hypochondriac. 'Are you taking the new medicine?'

The old nun dragged her gaze from the jogging shoes, smiling sourly. 'Ah, sure, it's useless. I'll have to suffer. Eh ... are those shoes comfortable?'

'Yes.'

'They look queer.'

Rita didn't answer. She'd given up her battle for civvies, and now always wore the short blue habit and veil like the other nuns. But nothing would persuade her to give up comfortable shoes. She was called 'The Running Nun', which is apt, she thought, because I never stop. She returned to the table and sat down. *The Irish Times* was full of the usual alarming number of factories closing. The world news was cramped characteristly onto one page. She began reading an article about Nicaragua.

'It's very near,' came from across the room.

Rita didn't look up.

'I said it's very near, Sister.'

Rita sighed, rustling the paper. Could she not read in peace? 'What is?'

'The end of the world.' The old nun muttered worriedly 'Jesus, Lord, have mercy.'

'People have always thought that.'

Sister Clement shook her head. 'All the old prophecies are coming true.'

'What prophecies?'

'Grass will grow on the railway lines ... Men will look like women ... And there'll be plagues.'

'I haven't noticed any plagues.'

'Look at all the cancer!'

Rita kept her patience. 'There was always cancer.'

The old woman laughed bitterly. 'You think that because you're young.'

Rita smiled to herself. To be called young at fifty two was stretching it, but the average age in the convent was rising. There had only been one vocation in five years. To survive at all they'd had to sell most of their land to builders, bit by bit. Marx was right about economics ruling everything. Things had changed so much with inflation. It had been more significant than Vatican II. Since John Paul II that seemed to be almost forgotten. The winds of change were nothing but a wheezing bellows. The church was retrenching, and the Pope certainly didn't think much of women either. The battle seemed in vain.

She skipped to the leading articles: one on the Middle East, another on the coming Abortion Amendment Referendum. Judging by the letters to the editor readers were getting hysterical about wanting to change the constitution to forbid it. She glanced through them. One suggested that a 'No' victory would open the door to divorce – signed by a man, naturally. What if one of them became pregnant? Church teaching might shift then. They might stop ranting about sex, and concentrate on the gospel of Christ. Abortion was wrong, although not on all counts. She was anti-amendment and would definitely vote 'No'. But it was a woman's problem, and women were moral agents being dictated to by celibate old men and young men too.

She read another letter. It suggested that a pluralist society would be the death of Catholic Ireland. What rubbish. Pluralism was the only hope for such a benighted land. Divorce would eventually come. The church would have to accept the inevitable, something it had never been good at. 'All institutions are corrupt', a priest had once told her, 'and the church is no exception.' Unholy Babylon, Dante had called it, and it was the same today. But that wasn't a reason for leaving it. No, she hadn't jumped over the wall. Unlike others, she'd won that battle. Her late thirties had been turbulent, a time she didn't think or talk about. There had been too much pain. Her forties had been a little easier, except in the physical sense. And even now 'the heyday of the blood' showed no sign of taming. Hamlet had definitely been a young man, a young prig.

She looked over at the old nun. Had she known the same sexual craving? The hunger for the love of a man? The terrible doubts? Nuns of the previous generation denied the body's existence, accepted things and were probably the happier for it.

Sister Clement caught her stare. 'We were warned, but we wouldn't listen.'

'Stop worrying, Clemmy.' Maybe happiness wasn't everything.

Rita scanned the back page columns. No one she knew born, married or dead. She turned to the ads in the personal columns. Then her glance darted back to a death notice:

SHERIDAN: Sally Ann (née Fitzpatrick), 21 June 1983, at the Rotunda Hospital, Dublin. Also her infant son. Beloved wife of Richard (Dublin and Athens, Pennsylvania, USA): deeply regretted by her loving husband, father and brother. RIP. Remains arriving 5 o'clock today to Fanagan's Funeral Home, Aungier Street. Funeral tomorrow, Tuesday, 11 o'clock to Glasnevin Cemetery.

It had to be Sally Ann. The age was right and the husband's name. Rita read the notice again. No, there could be no mistake. But there was no Mass. The Rotunda probably meant childbirth. God, how awful. The poor child.

Trembling, she put down the paper and looked over at the wigged nun. 'Remember Sally Ann Fitzpatrick?'

The older woman went on mumbling the rosary.

Mechanically Rita jotted the funeral time in her pocket diary. 'Remember Sally Ann Fitzpatrick, Sister?'

The mumbling stopped. 'Who?'

'The Fitzer, they called her.'

Sister Clement shook her head.

'You must remember her? She was in the boarding school ... left in the late sixties. 1967.'

'Fitzpatrick?' the old nun mused. 'Was she a daffodil?'

Rita looked worriedly at the old woman. What was she talking about? Had she gone completely senile?

The old nun looked cross. 'You'll mark the table with that mug, Sister!'

Rita put her mug on the floor. 'Sorry ... it's cold. You taught Sally Ann domestic science and art.'

'Did I? ...' Sister Clement rubbed the polished mahogany table in front of her. 'The table's badly marked!'

Rita looked through the window to the garden. What did a mark matter? The grounds were at their best this time of year. In the distance she heard the hum of grass being cut. The chestnut trees were in full dress. The white flowers always reminded her of candles on an old-fashioned Christmas tree. 'She got honours domestic in the Leaving. Art was her other good subject.'

'You've a wonderful memory, Sister.'

Rita had a special reason for remembering Sally Ann. The girl had saved her sanity, been her one success in a year of humility and failure. 1967, the year she'd almost left the order. The year of Maggy May's shoplifting. Had Sally Ann heard that telephone conversation in the hall? It was something she'd never know now. The girl had been too tactful ever to mention it. She had been a problem then, but good-hearted, with a special insight. Rita used to help her with her Irish in the evenings. On one occasion Rita had been particularly blue and taken it out on Sally Ann. She had scolded her for not understanding something. 'You're a very bad student!'

To her surprise, Sally Ann had got upset. 'I did my best. Irish isn't my native tongue!'

'I know it isn't!' Rita had been ashamed of her anger. 'Sorry, I'm not myself today.'

Sally Ann had given her a long look, saying slowly 'I am Duchess of Malfi still. My Dad told me to say that.'

The student had consoled the teacher. But there had been ructions about the shoplifting spree. How had it leaked to the archbishop? Only the three people involved knew of it, but Rita had been summoned to the Mother General and dismissed from her post as Superior. Everything was her fault for being too liberal. There'd been no trial. No right of appeal. She'd been sent back into the ranks and ordered to wear the habit at all times. JC, as Archbishop McQuaid was known in the diocese, hadn't even done her the courtesy of addressing her in person. He'd followed his usual practice of writing about her to the Mother General. People claimed he was kind to the poor, considerate to ex-priests, but he was a boor. Rita had been made to work in the convent's kitchen. She had had to accept it or leave. The next year she was sent to the order's new comprehensive in Tallaght. It was meant to be a further punishment, but instead it had been her salvation. There she'd met parents, women far worse off than she was, women in the pits of depression from broken marriages, abandoned women, battered women. So she started night classes and a support group.

Then her book came out to good reviews, and the Carysfort job came up. And ironically she was back in the Mother House as Superior. She'd come full circle.

Rita looked for comfort across the bleak room. 'You don't remember anything about her?'

The wigged woman looked up crossly. 'About who, Sister?'

'Sally Ann Fitzpatrick.'

'Not a single thing.'

Rita felt a sickening anger. How could she fail to remember her? Sally Ann was always in trouble with Clemmy – for talking or acting the clown in sewing class. On one occasion Rita'd had a note slipped under her cell door, marked 'Personal and Private'. It turned out to be a confession from Sally Ann to the attempted murder of Sister Clement. As usual she'd been acting up in class and Clemmy had given out yards, saying the girl would be the death of her. Then, immediately after class, the girls had seen Clemmy getting into the Waverly Ambulance. They didn't know she was a hypochondriac who was always arranging little rests in hospital.

Sally Ann had got an attack of scruples. It was funny, but Rita had looked sternly at the girl. 'Sister is all right.'

'It'll be my fault if she isn't.'

And now Sally Ann was dead, while Clement was still complaining. Rita looked through the window and tears filled her eyes:

> It is not growing like a tree
> That makes man better be ...

'Why were you asking me about the Fitzpatrick child?' Clemmy suddenly shouted. 'Is she in the paper?'

Rita folded *The Irish Times*. 'Yes, she's in the paper.'

'Is she getting married?'

'She died.'

'The Lord have mercy!' Sister Clement went back to her beads and Rita picked up her mug and left the room.

Deirdre Kelly sat typing in her office in UCD Belfield where she worked for Eoghan O'Connor, Professor of Modern and American Literature. A telephone rang on her desk.

'Department of American Literature, Deirdre Kelly speaking.'

'Is Eoghan there, please?' an American girl asked.

Deirdre recognised the voice. 'Who's speaking?'

'It's Erin Devlin, Miss Kelly.' The girl was a little sheepish.

'The professor isn't in yet.'

'When are you expecting him?'

Deirdre bristled with irritation, the neck of some people. 'I don't know,' she lied.

There was a tense silence.

'I've got a slight problem,' the student went on. 'I'm booking my flight home ... and need to know the date of my thesis results.'

'As you're probably aware, Miss Devlin, your thesis has been sent out to external examiners, and we won't know anything till we hear from them.'

'Weren't they given a deadline?'

'No,' Deirdre lied again.

'I thought there was a deadline.'

'I'm afraid you're mistaken.'

'Will you ask Eoghan to call me?'

Deirdre slammed down the receiver. She dabbed her perspiring forehead with a hanky. The cheek of Miss Devlin calling the professor by his first name. Maybe you could sleep your way to success in America, but not yet, thank

God, in Ireland. American students were all the same. They thought they owned the world. She'd noticed the professor's eyes lingering on the girl's jeaned backside. She was always 'popping' in to discuss her stupid thesis. What was it called? *The Greening of the American Novel* – a discussion of the Irish influence on F Scott Fitzgerald. Deirdre had always eavesdropped on their talks. But maddeningly the professor had started taking her down to Ashton's of Clonskeagh for tutorials. Deirdre knew what went on afterwards. They went back to a Rathmines bedsit. She could see them threshing around on the narrow bed. All bedsits had narrow beds and lumpy mattresses. She knew from experience.

Deirdre had rung Ashton's once, pretending to be his wife, then hung up before he came. She wanted to worry him, so he'd break it off. It hadn't done any good. Then Deirdre wrote a poison pen letter:

> Your filthy flirting with Eoghan O'Connor is known of. Don't think you can get away with this behaviour here. Ireland is still a Catholic country. If this doesn't stop you will be reported to the appropriate authorities.
>
> *Signed, WITHOUT PREJUDICE*

Erin had come in giggling the next day. 'Will you take a look at this, Miss Kelly! Isn't it a riot? Eoghan in yet?'

She'd gone on giggling. The brazen bitch! But the professor had been badly shaken. Deirdre remembered his hand trembling, as he lit a cigarette after reading it.

Deirdre put a new page into her typewriter, smiling at the memory of his haggard look. Yes, she'd hit home there. At least she'd put a stop to Ashtons. There was some satisfaction in that. Now she'd better get on with the professor's article. He'd be in soon, and she'd only typed a page. Her concentration wasn't the best this morning. On the bus to work she'd read of Sally Ann Fitzpatrick's death. She used to check the engagement columns for news of girls from school. Now it was the births. Then she'd seen the name Sheridan in the death columns. God, it boggled the mind. The Fitzer gone, dead. Blast it! A typo! She corrected it and typed a few more lines. Sally Ann was only her age. Another typo! Blast! She took out the page and wadded it. She prided herself on her typing but today was a dead loss. The idea of going to a funeral was upsetting her. Especially one with no Mass. What was that all about? Why the hell couldn't Sally Ann get buried in the normal way? Why did she have to upset people, even in death?

Maybe there'd be girls from school there. They'd all be looking at her, criticising what she had on. Still, maybe not. She got up and poured some coffee from the Kenwood machine in the corner. It was running low so she made some more. The professor needed a constant fresh supply. It was a habit he'd picked up in California. And it was her job to keep him happy. No, her privilege.

Back at her desk, she took a Mars bar from a packet in her drawer and ate it hungrily. It was her third this morning. And she was meant to be on a diet. Lose three stone, her doctor had ordered. All very well for him. She couldn't help being fat. It was her metabolism. And today was different. Food was the only thing that consoled her.

If Sally Ann could die, Deirdre could too. The idea scared her, especially when she'd never done anything with her life. Oh, she'd scraped through a night BA degree. But she hadn't married, loved anyone or had children. Still, she had kept her faith, while Sally Ann had married in a register office, damning her soul. You wouldn't envy her that. And it wasn't true that Deirdre had never loved anyone. Didn't she love Eoghan? Of course, the feeling between them was unspoken, like all deep feeling. He ran around with students all right, but he always came back to Miss Kelly, who never misunderstood. And Eoghan was more distinguished-looking than Sally Ann's husband, who was too skinny and already white-haired.

Only last Christmas she'd met the Sheridans in Kildare Street. Although laden down with parcels, they had invited her for a drink in Buswell's. She remembered it was crowded, and they'd had difficulty in finding seats. Then Richard had taken orders.

Deirdre asked for a gin and tonic, while Sally Ann ordered orange juice.

'I'll have that too!' Deirdre was embarrassed.

'Have what you want!' Sally Ann said, giggling. 'I'm on the dry.'

'For a change,' Richard had quipped, disappearing into the crowds at the bar.

The two friends had looked at each other awkwardly.

'Remember when you'd only drink Guinness?' Deirdre said at last. '*Vin de pays,* you called it.'

'Did I?' Sally Ann giggled again. 'I was an idiot.'

Deirdre was too polite to agree.

'I think it's great we can change, shed our former selves.'

'Colm Connolly is Lord Mayor now.'

'I know.'

Deirdre looked at her furtively. 'Remember you had a crush on him.'

'Yes,' Sally Ann said.

'Do you ever hear from him?'

'I'm married.'

Deirdre had cleared her throat. Sally Ann was the type to be unfaithful. She was probably an alcoholic too. 'Eh – have you given up drink completely?'

She patted her tummy. 'No, it's this ... isn't it great?'

Deirdre had mumbled congratulations.

Sally Ann looked at her guiltily. 'Anything can happen, Deirdre ...' She held her hand on her tummy. 'This after seven years.'

Deirdre sniggered. 'Remember when you were a Maoist?'

Richard returned with the drinks. 'A Mini Mouse.'

Sally Ann looked at her for a long minute. 'We tried to help the homeless.'

They sat in the Christmassy smoke, discussing names for the child. Thomas, if it was a boy, after the famous playwright, Richard Sheridan's grandfather. Frances, after the playwright's mother, if it was a girl.

Deirdre had thought that it was insensitive in the presence of a single person to boast about having children. Married people were all the same. If they weren't going on about babies, it was their damn house. Sally Ann had mentioned buying one in Ranelagh which they'd renovated. Richard had laughed in the same good-humoured way as he'd laughed over the baby.

Deirdre went over to Professor O'Connor's machine and poured more coffee.

God, I'm light years away from a house deposit. Why do things always work out for others? What was so special about Sally Ann? She'd always had it easy, never suffered. Her mother had died all right, but her father was a wealthy doctor. Then she found a lovely husband, a jet set life. What had she done to deserve all that? I have to drag myself in here every day. Still, to work for a man of Eoghan O'Connor's calibre ... everyone didn't have that privilege. He was so dedicated to work, yet he understood her need for an occasional day off. When he came in, she would mention a close friend had died. Seeing her upset state his brow would furrow with concern. He would pat her paternally on the shoulder. Their eyes would lock in unspoken love. His arm would remain round her, lowering to stroke her bottom ...

She was having her favourite fantasy. The professor's fiery blue eyes met hers for the signal to go on. She nodded assent. He locked the door quickly. Then, as she pulled down her tights, he pulled the rug into the centre of the room. She lay down on it. And, as usual, he lifted her loose tent-shaped dress over her hips. Deftly he stroked her breasts, between her legs. 'Oh, Eoghan,' she murmured, coming immediately. 'Deirdre, my dear girl!' He penetrated her with joy, remaining inside her until she came again and again.

Deirdre took another Mars bar from her drawer. Night after night in bed she imagined what life would be like if she was married to Eoghan. What would they say in Galway? Maybe his wife would die and make it possible? She munched hungrily, enjoying her fantasy, as the professor rezipped his trousers. 'We can't go on like this, Deirdre.'

She looked at him sadly. 'Your wife has found out?'

He lit a cigarette, inhaling deeply. 'I don't care about her. It's not that.'

'What is it then?'

'I have to see you in a more private place. Not here. It's too sordid.'

Tears of gratitude came into Deirdre's eyes. 'We could go to my flat. I'll fry you a steak.'

He took her hands in his. 'We'll work something out.'

Then the office door opened, and Professor Eoghan O'Connor appeared in reality. He was a squat, balding man with the unkempt look and red face of an alcoholic.

Deirdre dabbed her eyes with a hanky. 'Good morning, professor.'

'Morning, Miss Kelly.' He nodded grumpily, going straight to his desk. 'Any phone messages?'

She could see he had a hangover as he flicked through his post. 'Eh, no!'

Flustered, she put a page in her typewriter. It was nearly twelve and she'd done nothing. Wearily she began typing the article. It was the same old thing, day after day. What was the point? When the one man she loved never noticed her? He was in love with that bitch, Erin, but who slaved for him? Covered up his drinking, his affairs?

'You're sure no one rang, Miss Kelly?'

Deirdre stopped typing. 'I'm sure.'

He was probably with Erin last night, and they'd parted fighting. That was why he wanted to know if she'd rung to make up. The thought of them together was too much. She started crying again, not caring if he saw.

At last he looked over. 'What is it, Miss Kelly?'

Deirdre's shoulders shook. 'A school friend has died.'

He came over to her. 'I'm sorry. Were you close?'

Deirdre nodded through her tears. 'I'll need tomorrow morning off for the funeral.'

'Of course! Take today off too.'

Deirdre managed to stop crying. 'But there's your article to be typed.'

'There's no hurry about that.'

'Well, maybe I'll go home then.'

'Do, Miss Kelly.' He went back to his desk, forcing a smile at her.

Deirdre gathered her things and left. Halfway down the corridor she remembered she'd forgotten to wash her coffee cup. She couldn't leave it there all night. It might attract bugs. She'd slip back now and get it, casually mentioning the coffee was fresh.

She reached the door, pausing for a minute as the professor's voice came from inside.

'Erin, darling? ... I knew you'd ring me. Your thesis results? ... I told you not to worry. You're a straight first ... Of course, not! The expert in sour grapes wouldn't give me a message. I've got rid of the tub of lard for the day and hopefully for tomorrow. Some friend has done me a favour and died.'

Deirdre slunk back down the corridor.

Colm Connolly was at a Monday afternoon committee meeting. He was still handsome. His brown skin was deeply tanned from a recent holiday in Portugal. And if anything, he looked more distinguished with greying hair. He had perfected a frown of concentration, which he wore now, for the endless meetings he'd had to attend since his inauguration as Lord Mayor of Dublin. Life was a round of functions: receptions, prize-givings, charity events. But today's meeting was a discussion on the government's recent introduction of water rates. As a Labour Lord Mayor he was against them, but he'd have to vote to retain them. Dammit, they were in a coalition now and the people were refusing to pay. A politician should please the people. Stringent economic policies were fine but they didn't get votes. Fianna Fail would only reap the benefits at the next election. Fine Gael would be out, and what would happen to Labour then? He was on a sinking ship.

'These penal rates are another dishonest ruse of a conservative government' an opposition councillor's voice droned on.

Colm re-adjusted his chain, looking at the speaker with intense interest. But he was thinking of Sally Ann Fitzpatrick. All morning, since reading of her death in the paper, he'd been trying to summon the courage to phone his wife, Una. It wasn't that he was upset. God no. He'd seen Sally only once since college, and then he couldn't even be sure it was her. It was all too long ago. When was it? 1969?

... no '68, after the Gentle Revolution. God, they'd all been mad, and that den of internationalists in Sandymount. Sally had been so damn intense ... and so sexually uptight. Pity she was caught in the raid. It had been a near thing for him. A drugs charge would've hurt him politically. You didn't realise these things when you were young. It hadn't done Sally any damage. Ah no, she had nothing to lose. Now she was gone forever, but you couldn't live in the past. He was curious to know if a woman could still die in childbirth. It looked like that from the death notice. And he wanted Una to come to the funeral with him. It'd look good to be seen together. Old college friends might be there, potential voters.

He'd ring home at the coffee break.

'The Labour Party are insensitive to the people who elected them' a councillor droned on. Jesus, would he never finish. Colm couldn't bring himself to forget last weekend's row. Lately he and Una had been getting on better, even talked of ending their trial separation. But when he'd brought the kids back from Dawson Street to their home in Mount Pleasant Square on Sunday night there'd been a pregnant girl sitting in the comfortable basement kitchen. Cool as you like, she'd offered him a cup of tea. Then Una had come in, blithely informing him that the stranger was to occupy the top floor flat. Indefinitely, it seemed. His study, dammit, personally painted and soundproofed against the children's noise. He could work in the Mansion House all right, but he wouldn't always be Lord Mayor, and anyway he'd decided to move home for the weekends at least. He felt lonely in these huge rooms. The view of Dawson Street was great, but it was like living in a museum. The private apartment was full of heavy antique furniture and the kitchen was most inadequate. There was nothing homely about it. But when he'd admitted all this to Una, she'd shouted 'It's too late now!'

Colm shifted in his chair. He flicked a piece of lint off his mohair suit. The councillor's voice was giving him a headache. One word had led to another, and he'd stormed out. He hadn't rung since and neither had she. Una had over-reacted about his last affair. Couldn't she accept that it was over? Her whole trouble was a refusal to grow up. Philanthropy was fine in college. It went with all the protest. It was acceptable to be idealistic when you were young. It was good for your image later on. But to be still collecting stray cats in your thirties was too much. And last month she'd really embarrassed him by picketing the Dáil with a group of women against the referendum. He was against abortion being illegal too. For God's sake it was a woman's right to decide about her own body. Hadn't he paid for two abortions? Of course, Una didn't know that. But it wasn't the thing for the Lord Mayor's wife to appear on the front page of *The Irish Times* – in jeans, for God's sake.

This blasted feminism had incensed him and driven him from his home. Why did he seek the company of other women? Because Una was obsessed, that's why. It was all her fault – she could talk of nothing but women's lib. She knew he had to approach these things cautiously. Ireland was still predominantly rural. And rural values prevailed, except for a minority in Dublin, consisting mainly of the media. Besides he had his career to think of, especially now when the party was thinking of him for the vacant seat in Dublin South. He had a good track record. As a councillor he'd done solid work for housing in the inner city, and might now reap the benefits. If he wasn't picked he might try for the Senate at the next election. Senator Colm Connolly sounded all right ... not bad at all.

'I sincerely hope my resolution will be passed unanimously.' The councillor sat down. There was coughing and shuffling as someone else got up to speak. At that moment, Eddie Nolan, the small, bald Labour Party secretary, leaned over, whispering to Colm 'It looks like we'll be here all day. Remember, there's a meeting tomorrow at ten.'

Colm frowned. 'I've a funeral.'

'We're discussing the by-election. This is your chance, boy.'

Colm didn't hesitate. 'Ok, I'll be there.'

Across town in Westmoreland Street Mona sat in Bewley's Cafe waiting for her friend Barbara. All around her was friendly noise and chatter. Across the table a man read *The Irish Times* with the death notices visible, but Mona didn't notice them. She was too busy hoping the man would go. Then she'd have the table for herself and Barbara. They always met here on Tuesday afternoon, at least ever since Ronnie was born. Her son had been an ill-wind that blew some good. Poor little fellow. To be responsible for another person's happiness at that age! But Terry had literally taken one look at him and come home. He said it was easier financially; he was sick of mess. But Mona knew it was the power of prayer; the old nun who had looked after her in hospital had promised to intercede for her. The important thing was that now they both tried. She could cope much better because of co-counselling. She'd heard of it from that girl she'd met in hospital. 'Mona, there's a group of people who can help you,' she had said. 'They advise each other. I'll ring you.' What was her name? It had slipped her mind.

Mona had been sceptical, but sure enough the girl phoned with the number. 'Ring them, Mona!'

She did nothing for weeks. Then one day she dialled and asked for information. There was an introductory meeting in a house in Clontarf that very night, so she went.

Mona smiled, remembering her nerves. They had all sat in a circle and each person was asked to say something they were happy about. Mona had quaked, and when her turn came had said simply 'I'm happy to be here.' Then they had separated into twos. For ten minuts she had poured out her troubles to Barbara. Then Barbara had done the same to her. It was like confession.

Next they sat in another circle. Each person was asked how they had found counselling and how they had liked being counselled. Then they had sung a song and gone home. Mona had thought the song idiotic. It was 'Pack Up Your Troubles.' But the next morning she'd felt so much better. So she agreed to do an introductory course. Terry had been amazed at the change in her. And now if she got too sensitive about anything Barbara helped her discharge her emotion by expressing it. So she didn't bottle things up. That had been her trouble in the past, also expecting too much of marriage. Now she was into meditation.

'Hello, Mona!' A tall, thin woman with red hair sat down opposite her.

At 5.30 that evening, tall and stately Brian de Burca waited outside Fanagans, the undertakers in Aungier Street. It was the rush hour and a handful of people stood about, awaiting the hearse. No one knew quite what to do. He, for one, had never attended a funeral like this. Wasn't Sally Ann a Catholic? Good Christ, it was awful. Poor Dick. The girl had been a handful on that holiday but you had to admire her guts. Luckily Maureen had seen it in the paper at lunchtime and they could be here.

Maureen stood beside him, dressed in a suit and sensible brogues. Her wispy grey hair was hidden by a hat.

Brian paced up and down the pavement, then whispered to her. 'I wonder what's keeping them?'

'It's the rush hour, dear.'

He cleared his throat and stuck his lower jaw out. 'I can't believe it ... I can tell you one thing. I know how I'm going to vote in the abortion referendum.'

'How, dear?'

'As Sally Ann would've wanted.'

Maureen looked sadly down the crowded street. 'That's against it, I'm sure. Remember Connemara? She got quite worked up.'

Brian paced again. He could see her sitting on that beach, arguing with them all. She was too young to die. What had happened?

A large woman stopped him, smiling sycophantically. 'Hello, Professor de Burca.'

Brian recognised her from somewhere. 'Where have we met?'

'In UCD.'

'Ah, you were a student?'

'Yes, but I work there now. I'm Eoghan O'Connor's secretary.'

'That's where I've seen you. How's Professor O'Connor?'

'He's been working hard on a new book.'

Brian despised the man, an alcoholic and philanderer of the worst sort.

The woman sighed lugubriously. 'How do you know Sally Ann?'

Brian stuck his chin out. 'I'm a friend.'

'Of her husband?'

'Of both.'

The woman dabbed her eyes with a lacey hanky. 'We were best friends in school. She was so delighted about the baby.'

Brian perused her irritably. Why did she pick on him to talk to? He didn't want to talk about it, and surely they weren't contemporaries? You could never tell a woman's age. Sally Ann looked years younger, *had* looked.

Maureen tugged his sleeve. 'Here they are, dear.'

A huge black hearse pulled up with a coffin inside. Then another limousine. Dick, a tall young man, and an older man piled out. That was Dr Jack Fitzpatrick, the amateur historian. He had met him at a reception in the National Library. He must be her father. It was a small world. Then Peggy and Tony O'Hara drove up in their old Fiat. Thank God they were here.

Brian went over to shake his friend's hand. 'Dick, my poor fellow.'

In London on the morning of Sally Ann's funeral, Alastair Macbeth heard the postman. He grabbed his glasses and ran downstairs. He had aged very little. His woolly hair was a bit thinner, but he wore the same thick horn-rimmed glasses. By this time he was usually gone to the University of London, where he taught French literature, but today he was waiting for a letter. He was expecting to hear from his girlfriend, Penny, who had gone to a kibbutz for three months.

On the hall floor there were two letters: one from the bank and one with an Irish stamp, but nothing from Penny. He turned over the Irish letter. No address on the back. Who could it be from? He hadn't been in Dublin for nearly ten years. Could it be from Sally Ann? If so, he wouldn't reply. Christ. What was the point? The past was the past. He thought of her now and again, but the whole affair had been a mistake from the word go. The bloody woman had clung to him like someone drowning. Still, he was curious.

He ripped open the letter and read the signature – a voice from the past. Slowly he read the rest. Sally Ann dead. Good grief. He stood there, stunned for a few seconds. What had gone wrong? He wadded it and stuffed it into his jacket pocket. He was already late, so grabbed his jacket and briefcase. Today there was a department meeting and he had to be in tiptop form. He couldn't afford to get upset about the past.

Running for the tube he thought it was as well Penny hadn't written. Maybe she'd changed her mind about marriage. Become more independent. How many times had he told her he wasn't the marrying sort? He didn't want to settle down. Why couldn't he meet the independent type you were always hearing about? The new junior lecturer looked a possibility. Maybe he'd ask her for a date this weekend. But as he waited on for his train, Alastair couldn't stop thinking of Sally Ann. He smiled to himself, remembering their camping trip. She wasn't much of a cook or good in the sack. But somehow she'd always be Ireland to him. She was so damn daft ... He saw her on that railway platform. She'd hugged him so tightly that last time. He'd wanted to see her again but had thought it best to end it. It had gone on too long already. He'd meant to finish with her when he left Dublin, but never had the strength. She had kept hanging on. He should never have agreed to that holiday, but having agreed he should've driven her to Paris. He could have done that at least. But what was the use of regretting things now?

The train screeched up and he got on.

Grace O'Malley was on her second double gin and tonic in the Palace Bar. For years it had been her breakfast haunt. They knew her here, and contacted Pat if necessary. It was private in the back room, and they let her in early if she needed a cure. She needed something this morning. You couldn't go to a funeral on an empty stomach. She read the death notices again. What the hell had gone wrong for Sally Ann?

All morning Grace had thought of nothing but Athens, Pennsylvania. Dick could be a right intolerant shite, always calling her an alcoholic, but Sally Ann was all right. She'd cooked her so many meals ... and those disgusting eggflips. Grace smiled at the memory. It seemed so long ago now, but it was only a few years. She'd never cross the Atlantic again, although it had been good money. Freddie Ferris still wrote to her. The fellow was cracked. He'd come over to visit her once, and she'd had a terrible time hiding him from Pat. She giggled, remembering the ducking in and out of doors. God, she'd had a hell of a time in bed with him. But it had certainly pissed Pat off. Their relationship almost didn't survive it.

The door opened and a journalist from the *Independent* came in. 'Gracie! What are you drinking?'

Grace gathered her bag. 'No thanks, Jim. I'm off to a funeral.'

'Have one for the road.'

Grace hesitated. If she didn't go now she'd be there all day. But then she wouldn't have to face Dickie and all those people. Christ, she couldn't face people. Not without a drink. 'A gin and tonic,' she said.

Tony and Peggy were finishing breakfast on the morning of the funeral. Peggy poured herself more tea. She sipped it, staring through the window to their well-tended garden. It was early summer, so the geraniums had come out in pink and red flowers. This year the apples would be good. She must weed the vegetable garden at the weekend. Sally Ann had shown an interest in gardening. Was that why she had wanted to live in the country?

'Remember that house Sally nearly bought.'

Tony was behind the paper. 'Sally was a dear girl, but crazy.'

'It was a good idea basically.'

'You're crazy too.'

'There was land going with it.'

Tony rustled his paper. 'I couldn't see them growing cabbages.'

Peggy stared sadly into her teacup. It was hard to imagine Sally gone. Now they could have no more arguments. She smiled to herself at the memory of their heated discussions. Perhaps she'd been too intolerant of her, but Sally liked a good argument. She needed someone to bounce opinions off, a mother figure. Poor pet. There was no harm to her. And she'd made a good job of things really. It was a marriage made in heaven; such things existed. 'They did all right in the end.'

Tony looked up puzzled. 'What?'

'The Ranelagh house was fine.'

'The bookcases made a difference.' He folded his paper with a sigh. 'All things are basically tragic.'

'Cheer up!' Peggy gripped his arm.

He shook his head. 'It's not good.'

She got up and started clearing the table. 'I think we should call and see if Dick's all right.'

Tony looked out at the garden. The grass needed to be cut. There was plenty of weeding to do. He'd be busy all weekend. 'Let's not intrude. He'll be with her family.'

Peggy went into the kitchen. Sally Ann had told her she didn't communicate much with her father. There was only a younger brother, a Bob Geldof lookalike, the same untidy hair. Dick would need company. He'd looked dreadful at the funeral home yesterday evening. She'd tried to get him to talk about it but he wouldn't be drawn. She certainly didn't blame him for that.

'I'm going to call before the funeral,' she said. 'Come with me if you like.'

Tony sighed. 'Grief is a private thing.'

Jim Nolan backed his Post Office Toyota van into the narrow cul de sac of artisan houses. He was now fulltime, but had given up letter deliveries. These days he worked only on parcels. He looked completely Mod and wore an earring in one ear. He still read, and attended a 'Writing for Pleasure' class in the Adult Institute in Mountjoy Square on a Tuesday evening. He had completed several short stories, but, as yet, he hadn't had anything published.

He braked to avoid a child playing ball in the street. It was always a bitch to get out of here. Already this summer he'd delivered umpteen sacks of books to the Americans in the corner. Sheridan was the name – must be terrible bookworms. Where did they fit them all in in that tiny terraced house? He reminded himself to collect the empty bags this time. The mot usually answered the door in her dressing gown, half asleep. Thank God she didn't recognise him. At first he didn't remember where he'd met her. But then it clicked: that pub in Greystones. It must be well over ten years ago now since he left her there to pay for the drinks – he knew by the eldest's age. It was something yours truly wasn't particularly proud of. He remembered the gold granny glasses and those dark Afro curls. He still fancied her, and last week he'd given her the eye, but she'd giggled. Very funny, some would be glad. Anyway she was pregnant, and hubbie was usually hovering in the background. Just his luck.

He hopped out and rang the bell. Then dragged the heavy canvas sack from the van. No one in. That was unusual. He banged the brass knocker. Still no answer. Jaysus, it wasn't his day.

He scribbled out a note on a delivery docket and popped it in the letter box just as the husband yanked the door open. He was tall, thin and white-haired, and held a glass of whiskey in one hand.

'Another c-c-country c-c-cousin?' He stared groggily at the sack. 'T-t-travelling light? C-come on in.'

Plastered at ten in the morning. So much for the intellectual classes. 'An Post, mate, delivering your books.'

'On post?'

'The p-post office!'

The man gulped his drink, swaying dangerously. 'Well, d-do me a favour.'

'Sure.' Jim heaved the sack forward.

'Dump them in the canal.'

He was really crocked. 'What?'

'Dump them!' The drunk made to slam the door, but Jim put his foot in it. He knew the type – down to Rathmines first thing tomorrow, claiming his property.

'Let me leave them in the hall. Good man! I'll get the bag later.'

Obstinately the man held the door shut. 'Take them away.'

'Listen, mate! I'm not bringing them back!'

'G-give them away then.'

'Ok, I'll leave them on the pavement.'

The man hiccuped from behind the door. 'D-d-do that!'

Angrily Jim looked at his watch. Christ, it really wasn't his day. If he left them they'd be stolen, and yours truly would get blamed. The only thing was to haul them back to the depot.

The American peered out, his brown eyes blinking.

'Look, mate! I'm only doing my job.'

Slowly the eyes comprehended. 'Y-your job? Sure.'

The man opened the door and stretched to help with the sack. Instead he took a header onto the pavement and lay face down. There was broken glass and whiskey everywhere. Jim wondered if he should call an ambulance.

He rolled the man onto his back. Blood oozed from his grazed forehead. 'Are you all right, mate?'

The man opened one eye, nodding.

Jim gripped his armpits and hauled him up. Together they staggered into the house and onto the sittingroom couch. The man took out a hanky and dabbed his forehead. 'M-must've missed my step.'

Jim watched to make sure he'd stay put. He looked around the little room. It was full of pictures and had been recently done up. 'I'll get the books off the street.'

He dragged the sack in, then carefully picked up the scattered glass. When he came back the American had his head in his hands. 'Is there a bin?'

The man pointed to a wastebasket in the corner.

'Don't worry about the sack. I'll be back for it.' He crossed the room. 'Eh, is the wife out?'

The man didn't answer.

Jim lingered in the doorway. 'She's out shopping?'

The American looked up, suddenly sober. 'My wife is dead.'

'God, I'm sorry.'

'She died in fucking childbirth.'

'Can I make you a cup of tea?'

The man looked amazed. 'Tea? I'm going to plant her in an hour.'

'Coffee then?'

The American staggered up and swayed towards the door. 'I can't go to a funeral on coffee. I'll pour us both a Bourbon.'

Jim eased him back onto the couch. 'Let me make you a coffee.'

'Ok, coffee to s-sober up-p.'

Jim went out to the kitchen. The floor was red-tiled like the rest of the downstairs. A long pine table took up a wall, and there was a pine dresser with neat rows of white cups. Hanging spider plants and pictures on the wall added to the cosiness. It was hard to believe she wouldn't be coming back. He found the coffee and put on the kettle. Then went to the pantry for cups. The sink was full of dirty dishes, and an opened packed of Cream Crackers littered the draining board. God, what if Nora died? He took her, the children, their life, so much for granted. Yet was unfaithful if he could. Most of the time he went round resenting her, accusing her of nagging him. Only this morning they'd had a row about money. He left their Bray semi-d at seven in the morning and wasn't home till seven in the evening.

When he came back, the American was wiping his eyes. Jim gave him the coffee.

'They lost the baby too.'

'I didn't know it still happened.'

The man laughed shortly. 'Anything can happen. That's what she used to say. Well, she was damn right!'

Jim didn't know what to say. 'Was it the labour?'

'She had a headache. I said, take aspirin.'

'What else could you say?'

'It was a bad headache. Finally I rang her father ... he's a doctor.'

'What did he say?'

The American looked at him dazedly. 'He sent an ambulance immediately. I held her hand. At Portobello, she said "Dick". Then had some sort of fit and passed out. She was dead on arrival.'

Jim didn't know what to say.

The man went on dully. 'They said to leave everything to them. But they couldn't save the baby. Do you have any kids?'

'Four.'

The man put down his coffee cup. 'I have four by another marriage. I didn't want another. She did. And now ...' He put his head in his hands. 'I wish I'd had it cut off.'

'You can't say that!' Jim was at a loss for words. Dammit, he was only the postman. 'You know what they say "Better to have loved and lost ...".'

The man's hands were still on his face. 'Now go! Please go!'

Luckily the doorbell rang. Jim went to answer it.

A middle-aged couple stood on the pavement. 'We're Tony and Peggy O'Hara. We wondered if Dick needed a lift.'

Jim ushered them into the sittingroom.

'Are you a relation?' The woman asked cheerfully.

'I'm the postman.' Jim slipped quickly out to finish delivering his parcels.

It wasn't a big funeral. Dr Fitzpatrick, his son-in-law, and son followed the hearse in a large, rented limousine. They were followed by a couple of cars. No one spoke in the rented car. Dr Fitzpatrick's thoughts were slow and mechanical. He looked worriedly at the man who had married his daughter. He was so grateful that she had met a decent man. Now the younger man looked out of it. He stared blankly ahead of him as if he'd imbibed a bit, which was no harm the doctor thought. Yesterday he'd refused tranquillisers. They'd always got on well – by keeping their distance. The doctor had tried to explain to him that Sally Ann's death had been a fluke. Eclampsia was one of the three major hazards of pregnancy, but it was usually preceded by pre-eclampsia which could be controlled. As far as he could determine she'd had no early symptoms like oedema or albumen in her urine. At seven months her blood pressure had suddenly shot up, bringing on toxaemia and causing fulminating eclampsia, which had killed both mother and child. He knew her husband blamed him. People always blamed doctors. As if they were the Almighty. Maybe if she'd been in a hospital they could've saved one of them. But she wasn't, and there was nothing to indicate she should've been. It had happened. It was a fact. You had to deal with facts. And death was a fact of life. He was always telling people this.

As they passed Christ Church Cathedral a man blessed himself. Dr Fitzpatrick was consoled by it. People had done it all along the route. At least it wasn't raining, there was nothing worse than a wet funeral. Dick had surprised him by insisting Sally Ann hadn't wanted a Christian burial. He'd got quite worked up about respecting her wishes. But the doctor had argued that it was only some passing whim. He knew his daughter. She was always getting crazy ideas. She had got married in a register office, without even consulting him, but she was still a baptised Catholic and entitled to the consolations of the church. He didn't really care about the civil marriage, but he wanted her buried properly – with her mother. At last they'd compromised, the husband agreeing to a priest at the graveside. A mass could always be said later, the doctor thought. Now he was grateful for the funeral, for things to do. He had a déjà vu feeling. Everything seemed external to him, as if he was witnessing someone else's tragedy, not burying his child.

He knew he was in deep shock. He'd sat up all night reading poetry. It was all he could do. He looked at his red-eyed son. Poor Tim had taken it badly, but at least he'd had a haircut and wore a suit. He'd shown some respect for his sister.

Tim caught his glance, frowning. 'You ok, Doc?'

The doctor nodded. His children had always been a puzzle to him. What sort of people were they? Since they became teenagers they'd been strangers. Did he really know either of them? You walked into a room one day and your child glared at you. They called it adolescence. Although from the Latin, 'adolesence' was a modern word for a modern generation who spoke a different language. He'd tried to instill a love of poetry into them, but had failed. Still, they'd been such lovely little children.

Dr Fitzpatrick blew his nose noisily. 'We're lucky with the traffic, Tim.'

Tim looked away. 'Yeah.'

The boy was crying but the doctor could think of nothing to say. God's will be done. He, at least, had to carry on. He'd done it all his life. You knew not the day, nor the hour. But he expected to see his daughter again. His wife too ... a doctor had to believe. He had never expected to have children. Then Sally Ann had arrived, and she was so clever, reading at five. He'd brought her everywhere, showing her off. Crabbit, Maeve had called her. Then Tim, followed by Maeve's death. He hadn't expected that either. After all he'd married a much younger woman. Sally Ann, child though she was, had tried to console him then, but he wouldn't let her. He shut his children out. It had been wrong, but he couldn't help it. He was too old. Had not the nuns thought him Sally Ann's grandfather? They were right. He was old. 'You are old Father William.'

At Glasnevin a small group had assembled at the graveside with a priest. It was sunny but there was a slight wind. It caught a woman's hat, and Richard's white hair as he stood with one hand over his face. The priest held his prayerbook as its pages blew. The men who brought the coffin were lowering it into the earth. But the grave wasn't big enough, and it got stuck, lurching to one side.

Richard laughed. 'She was always awkward.'

There was an embarassed ripple of not-exactly laughter.

The men huffed and puffed, trying to get the coffin in again. Finally they gave up, leaving it standing up at one end.

'Since Almighty God has called our sister, Sally Ann, from this life to Himself, we commit her body to the earth from which it was made,' the priest droned on.

Rita was at the back of the mourners, watching Dr Fitzpatrick. He looked so lonely standing here. What could you say to console him? In a way he reminded her of her own father. She had made her peace with him at last. It was one thing she was grateful for and it had come about because of the trouble she'd got into with the order. To her amazement he'd taken her side, advising her to leave. 'Bad cess to them, child.'

Rita smiled at the memory; his reaction had been so unexpected.

The priest scattered dust on the coffin. 'Dust you are, and unto dust you shall return ...'

The people bowed their heads.

'Let us pray for our sister to our Lord Jesus Christ, who said "I am the Resurrection and the Life, the man who believes in me will live even if he dies ..."'

Afterwards Rita went back through labyrinthine convent corridors to her own room. Her shoes squeaked eerily on the waxed floors. Ghosts seemed to follow her. Thousands of children had walked these corridors. And where were they now? Names came into her head, names she couldn't put a face on, faces without names. It was like that at the funeral. She'd recognised one or two, but couldn't put a name to them until they'd introduced themselves. It was amazing how you forgot.

She reached her room and sat weakly on her narrow and neatly-made bed. Then got up and poured a brandy into a tooth mug from the bottle in her cupboard. A cousin had brought it from America, and now it was coming in handy. She needed a drink, she needed something. The funeral had been heartbreaking. The poor husband. She had shaken hands with him, mentioning that she had taught Sally Ann. He'd been interested in this, grasping at any detail about her. But then someone else had come up and Rita had offered her sympathy to the father and brother. The brother was a nice young man. She could see Sally Ann in him. Suddenly she'd come to life again as a schoolgirl, untidy, skirt too short, wild hair and short-sighted eyes. The girl was blind as a bat and always losing her glasses. Or breaking them. It was maddening, and now what did it all mean?

'I am the Resurrection and the Life.'

Because of that promise she had stayed in a church she often had no time for. A church which was bogged down by rules. It was Maggy May who taught her how to love. The old nun had been the first to comfort her, after the demotion and disgrace. She had remained loyal when the others had shunned her. If only she had her now, but her friend was gone. One night the old nun had knocked on Rita's door for a chat. Later, when Rita had indicated that it was time to go, the old nun had begged to stay the night. 'I'm frightened,' she had said. Against all rules, Rita had let her sleep in an armchair in her cell. In the middle of the night she awoke to find the old woman dead. Her heart had stopped.

Rita finished her brandy and went to her desk. She had work to do. It had always helped her in the past and it would now.

AFTERWORD

In my youth, the 1950s and 1960s, there were hardly any visible Irish women writers. Edna O'Brien was denounced from the altar and, although I had read Mary Lavin she wasn't widely known. I remember telling a famous sculptor I wanted to write and he suggested stories for children, I might be suitable for that. Women didn't raise their heads above the parapet then. They became secretaries or worked in banks or shops. There were a few 'lady' doctors, but not many. There was no free secondary education, so most children left school at fourteen and few did the Leaving. Society was divided into rich and poor, but even the middle classes were oppressed, especially women. Only two women in my class at school graduated from university. Most female graduates became teachers. I did an arts degree and taught for three years in Irish and English schools. But I had always wanted to write and the bug wouldn't go away. So I tried my hand at journalism, writing book reviews and working part-time in art galleries.

Everyone was poor then and lived in the family home or in grotty bedsits. There were no jobs, so emigration was on the menu. In 1975 I went to Delaware, USA – which I had only heard of because of the famous song – initially to work part-time at Proscenium Press, a small publishing company. It was owned by Robert Hogan, an academic and playwright, who encouraged me to write and eventually became my husband. At first I had no green card, so could not get a real job, but I no longer had excuses to delay writing. In Delaware I started *Mothers*, my first novel, finishing it in 1978, but had no luck finding a publisher. The manuscript was rejected several times and stayed on top of a chest of drawers.

In those years I came home in the summer to see my family. One sunny afternoon I was having a coffee in Bewley's when two women at the same table started talking about a nun caught shoplifting. They were naturally shocked by this incident, which would still be shocking today. But to me the incident was an example of oppression. Nuns were just like other women. They wanted things in the same way but had to wear horrible clothes. I had been to two boarding schools, so knew this. The incident also struck me as an example of change in Irish society. Vatican II had taken place by then but thanks to the grim archbishop of Dublin, John Charles McQuaid, had hardly touched us. Now cracks were beginning to emerge. Nuns, previously cloistered, went shopping. The Catholic Church was starting to lose its hold.

Young people today are shocked by conditions in Ireland's past. Anyone who didn't conform to society's norm was shunned. Nothing was ever talked about. Women were embarrassed by their bodies. There was no contraception, even for married people. Children were abused by priests and beaten in reform schools. The treatment of unmarried women and girls in Magdalene laundries and mother and baby homes is now being acknowledged. In 1984, there had been the infamous Kerry

Babies case when a young woman was accused of killing her newborn and of the alleged murder of another newborn baby. Then the X Case in 1992, when a fourteen-year-old girl who was raped was prevented from having an abortion in England. People wanted change and this case, along with Savita Halappanavar's death in 2012 from sepsis while pregnant, paved the way for the right to abortion in Ireland. But pregnant women were not the only victims. Homosexuality was not decriminalised until 1993, but this led to the passing of a referendum in 2015 making us the most liberal country in the world for same sex marriage. Things do change.

My novel, *Mothers*, tells the story of three generations of women who had children out of wedlock. It has comic scenes and concludes with a glimmer of hope. Inspired by the nun's shoplifting, I wanted to write a short story dramatizing further change in Irish society. But how was I to do it? I had to think of a structure. Then a friend suggested comparing an older and younger nun. Two characters walked into my head. Rita, the young reverend mother of a Dublin boarding school was just back from America and thought herself modern and highly intelligent. But she was rigid in outlook, while the older nun, a simpler countrywoman who had experienced love in her youth, was the real Christian. While rescuing the older nun from an unsympathetic shop manager, Rita learnt something about herself. In 1978, Arlen House announced a new competition for debut short fiction by Irish women, funded by Maxwell House. By a stroke of luck, this story, originally called 'Underwear', was a winner in the first competition. It was published in Arlen House's bestselling anthology, *The Wall Reader and Other Stories* in 1979, which became a number 1 bestseller. Here, the updated version of this story is entitled 'Rita'.

Catherine Rose, founder of Arlen House, asked if I had any more stories. I had none, so she asked to see my novel *Mothers*. To my delight she accepted it, and published it in 1982. My second novel, *Confessions of a Prodigal Daughter*, a co-publication with Arlen House and Marion Boyars, is about the mother-daughter relationship and mental health, also a stigma at the time. Although reviewed by the *New York Times*, it was hardly noticed in Ireland. Next, I was commissioned by an English publisher, the feminist imprint Pandora Press, to write a biography of Katherine O'Shea Parnell, condescendingly known as *Kitty* O'Shea in Ireland. I had studied history in college so enjoyed researching. But I was hooked on fiction and wanted to write a novel about Ireland of that time with a broad canvas which would express the complexity of life and with more than one protagonist. So I put Sally Ann, a motherless schoolgirl, into the original story, 'Underwear'. This was the beginning of a collection of connected stories, published by the feminist Attic Press in 1990 as *The Awkward Girl*. Mainly, it followed the fortunes of Sally Ann and her search for love and identity. But other characters weave in and out of the narrative which could be classified either as a novel or a book of stories. With more than one complex female character, the title is now changed to *Awkward Women*. The stories are set in various countries, Ireland, France, America and cover different topics. All represent a phase of life and offer insights on the main players and the society they live in. Topics like suicide, college life, friendship, childbirth, holidays and buying a house are covered. Finding a home back then was just as difficult as now – so some things never change. There are comic scenes in most of the stories. Life is a mixture of laughing and crying.

Friends have asked me if the book is autobiographical. It isn't. But because a writer has only one life, there is only one story, so some events parallel Sally Ann's life. I worked in an art gallery, for instance, and used that material as a setting for Sally Ann's relationship with her father. But my father was a farmer, not an over-worked doctor like Sally Ann's. My mother didn't die young either, although my grandmother did. This tragedy caused havoc for generations of my family because of its effect on my mother and her siblings. I have mirrored this in Sally Ann's loss of her mother. There are also other American influences because, following in the footsteps of my mother and grandparents, I travelled back and forth from there to Ireland for years. The only other autobiographical similarity to Sally Ann was my happy marriage to an American, which ended in 1999 when my husband died. I am now living in Bray, which I love, and am stationary. I hope readers will enjoy *Awkward Women* and am grateful to Éilís Ní Dhuibhne for her new foreword, and to Alan Hayes, publisher of Arlen House, for re-shaping this new edition as a short fiction collection.

ABOUT THE AUTHOR

Mary Rose Callaghan was born in Ireland in 1944 and emigrated to the United States in 1975, where she lived for many years. She has written nine novels, some of which have been translated into German and Danish, and was an assistant editor of *The Dictionary of Irish Literature*. She is also a playwright and biographer, and an award-winning short story writer. Her memoir, *The Deep End*, was published in 2016 by the University of Delaware Press. She was married to Robert Hogan, a drama critic and playwright, and now lives by the sea in Bray, County Wicklow, where she teaches and writes.

BIBLIOGRAPHY
Mothers (Arlen House, 1982; Marion Boyars, 1984)
Confessions of a Prodigal Daughter (Arlen House/Boyars, 1985)
'Kitty O'Shea': The Story of Katharine Parnell (Pandora, 1989/1994)
The Awkward Girl (Attic Press, 1990)
Has Anyone Seen Heather? (Attic Press, 1990)
Emigrant Dreams (Poolbeg Press, 1996); *I Met a Man who Wasn't There* (Marion Boyars, 1996)
The Last Summer (Poolbeg Press, 1997)
Jumping the Bus Queue, editor (The Older Women's Network/Age and Opportunity, 2000)
The Visitors' Book (Brandon, 2001)
Billy, Come Home (Brandon, 2007)
A Bit of a Scandal (Brandon, 2009)
The Deep End (University of Delaware Press, 2016)